Also by Michael Schiffer:
LESSONS OF THE ROAD

Michael Schiffer

BALLPARK

SIMON AND SCHUSTER

NEW YORK

Acknowledgment is made for permission to reprint material from THE
BRONX ZOO by Sparky Lyle and Peter Golenbock. Copyright © 1979 by
Sparky Lyle and Peter Golenbock. By permission of Crown Publishers, Inc.

Published by Simon and Schuster
A Division of Gulf & Western Corporation
Simon & Schuster Building
Rockefeller Center
1230 Avenue of the Americas
New York, New York 10020

SIMON AND SCHUSTER and colophon are trademarks of Simon & Schuster
Designed by Eve Kirch
Manufactured in the United States of America

10 9 8 7 6 5 4 3 2 1

Library of Congress Cataloging in Publication Data
Schiffer, Michael.
  Ballpark.
  I. Title.
PS3569.C4877B3   813'.54   81-14625
ISBN 0-671-41796-7   AACR2

With thanks to my editors, Dan Green and John Herman; and to Paul Cirel; Steven Mann; Alex Vertikoff; Joan Raines; Robert Creamer; Brent Musberger; Paul Hagen; Anne Bernays; Jane Gross; Robinson T. Kaspar; Jason Stark; Larry Wright; Jerry Roberts; Ted Johnson; Max Belcher; Mike Farber; John Wilson; Paul Domowitch; Sarah Auchincloss; David D'Innocentis; Stephen Bennett; Lee Berger; Alex Lasker; Terrence McNally; Stanley Weinstock; Carol Tartar Nelson; Susan Victor; Michael Seifert; Judi Bloom; The Sharecroppers; Cheryl, Herbert, and Elizabeth Cutler; Ralph and Dorothy Schiffer; and Garry Maddox, of the 1980 World Champion Philadelphia Phillies.

To Morris

1976

Pardee's eyes were gray-green, filled with clouds. They watched, detached, as seagulls outside circled, laughed, and fell into the mist. Turning from the window into the darkness of his room, he was blinded, out again, under the lights—lost in the roar of sixty thousand fans—then silent, alone, listening to the waves break, leaning toward the motion of his shadow in the glass.

Stepping in, he dipped and ducked, then fired off a combination—two lefts and a right stopping just short of the reflection he kept sharp in, polished, brittle. "You really don't need this, you've had enough," he told himself, backing off, trying to resist the instinct that said he had *better* be ready—there was no reason to believe it couldn't happen again.

PART ONE

Pardee

Chapter 1

1

Pardee was big, but you'd never single him out as someone to avoid. You wouldn't pass him on the street and think, "There goes an athlete." He had a way of moving that was deliberate. He moved in a kind of slow calm.

Pulling back from the plate glass window, he crossed the darkened terminal to the airport cafe. He dropped his bags, hung up his coat, found a stool and was about to sit, when someone knocked a glass from the Formica top. In less time than it took the waitress to gasp, Pardee spotted it, caught it, went with the flow, and lifted it back to the counter, where it landed with a small splash.

The waitress put the tumbler with the dirty dishes and threw away her gum. The guy next to him, whose glass it was, couldn't help but wonder what he'd do if he had hands like that. Pardee ordered coffee and let them stare. Only one in a thousand would ever recognize him—the kind of fan who could see past the team photo that made him look bald; the type who might remember him from his minor league year in the Pacific Coast League, and would ask about some other hot prospect, who had disappeared. Darryl's answers were always the same.

"Control problems," he'd offer, if the player had been a pitcher, and let it go at that; but otherwise it was, "Couldn't hit the curve," and invariably the fan would shake his head and mutter, "Yeah, me too," or "Me neither." Beyond that Pardee couldn't be bothered. Too many reasons, he reasoned. You're better off without 'em.

This morning late in January, he was in the airport in Columbus, on his way down to Florida to get in shape for spring training. He picked up his butter knife and rotated it slowly, watching his reflection distort, then drained off his coffee and wandered back to the loading gate, looking fairly shabby for a man who'd just been signed to one of the most lucrative contracts in the history of sports.

The money, however, was secondary to Pardee, who had an agent and a lawyer to keep tabs on each other, an ample bankroll, and very little else. He didn't drive a Rolls-Royce, didn't even own a car. He fronted no pizzerias, endorsed no products, and didn't write a column for the local paper—there was no place he called home. While other players had their lives tied up with wives, women, and steady girls, Darryl made the charity stops twice a year with a group of teammates and apart from that he was on his own.

2

Spring training was a month away. The young bloods had never stopped playing. They were still down in winter leagues fighting off third strikes and chronic dysentery, but Pardee was fat. The long contract hassle had cost him his edge; he'd been wined and dined nearly to ruin.

He walked across the blacktop, breath misting in the cold, climbed the gangplank, rapped the fuselage twice before stepping in, then sidled down the aisle to his window seat in front of the wing. He was in nonsmoking, riding coach. Flying was luxury enough. It went against his nature to say first class.

Staring through the layers of the weathered plastic window, he kept his eyes on the wintry blue scrub brush along the edge of the airfield, until they were up and over it, heading west, then banking south. The city was quickly left behind, as they passed over the open heartland of Ohio, but no matter where they flew, as long as there were houses, he was sure to spot one of those perfect little diamonds, set into the corners of the schoolyards and developments. It was like that everywhere, all over the States, and just the sight of them gave Pardee a thrill. He fell out with a smile, leaning into the vibrating airplane wall, dozing on and off for about two and a half hours, until the bell rang, the seat-belt lights came on, and the captain announced the descent toward Miami.

Darryl had no great love for flying, but he hated coming down. There was a moment in every flight when the plane cut back into a glide, his ears popped, the floor dropped, and right then and there, he settled his scores, said all his prayers, and got ready to die.

The clouds were a sea of cotton beneath them, soft, bright, and inviting—then they plunged in, the cabin shook, and Pardee's stomach hit the back of his brain. He held onto the sides of his seat, sweating from his temples, until the mist thinned and he spotted the land, rising up under them. The wheels bounced and began to roll at something like a human speed, they seemed to go faster in the loud rush of the reverse thrusters, then slowed; and Pardee let go, turning to smile weakly at the guy beside him. It was like this almost every time he flew . . . fifty road trips a year.

Chapter 2

1

The airport in Miami was steamed up like a laundromat. The women were tanned, showing lots of flesh. Darryl had a carry-on suitcase and a garment bag; he traveled light and hated to wait. He moved through the corridors to the loading zone, where he waved to the dispatcher, for a limousine south.

"Tideview," he said.

"*Sí, señor.*" The uniformed Cuban put his fingers in his mouth and whistled to a blue Dodge van that cut across the traffic to stop by the curb. Pardee slung his things into the luggage pen, climbed in the side, then sat back in air-conditioned comfort for the thirty-minute ride to his destination—one more small town about to be absorbed into the outward sprawl of metropolitan Miami—on a strip of reclaimed coastal wasteland about halfway to the Keys.

The team had rooms at a convention-center hotel, but Darryl found a place of his own at a quiet private motel a quarter mile from the field. The lady at the front desk loved ballplayers, she had made it a passion in her prime, so she gave him a deal on an extended stay. He signed the register, walked upstairs, and found the customary two double beds, knotty-pine bureau, and closet with hangers attached. There was a nightstand, a lamp on a desk, an old color TV, and a bathroom with the shower head set right at the level of Pardee's neck.

He took out his glove, put it on the dresser, slipped into sweats, and hit the street, keeping his eyes on the ground as he ran, until he caught the smile of the woman by the drugstore. Down in Florida, where seasons mean nothing, ballplayers are watched like birds, and that smile said she had him pegged, as if she were thinking, "Ah, my first one of the year."

He ran through the first pangs of short wind, the residue of cigarettes and occasional pot. He could call it quits and no one would notice, but he pushed on until he relaxed—kicked in, glazed over, and saw even less of the town through which he ran, only the vague shape of his feet flapping forward, and the motion of his cheeks, bobbing under his eyes.

Now he could run forever, as if his life depended on it, as it had back in Nam one day, when Pardee wandered into the wrong neighborhood and had to beat it out over a trail he'd never seen, trying to shake a handful of local boys with Russian guns. Two things saved him then, as they would now—legs and wind. He dropped his easy, gliding gait and started barrel-assing down the street, turning heads and leaving them wondering, "What the hell is wrong with him?"

Nothing was wrong, he was just getting ready. Let the little slants make their move, let some hotshot rookie challenge for third . . . he'd send them back to Hanoi, down to Pawtucket, one by one. He shot a glance at the traffic cop at the corner of Market and Main, waving him home, and strained even harder down the last long stretch, back to his hotel.

A bus coated him with its dismal gray roar as he slowed up the tar incline, easing to a walk. Darryl's head throbbed and his heart was pounding. He was pushing thirty, and a half-step was gone. "If I were there today," he thought, "I might not make it. Great way to start a season. . . ." He unlocked his door and fell onto his bed. "What's past is past, baseball is baseball, and this is your room," he told himself. One thing at a time, and never for very long—that was his rule.

2

The first time anyone heard of Pardee was when they flew him in from Camp Zama, Japan, with about thirty other wounded and recuperating soldiers, who landed at Fort Sam Houston, in Texas, where the Army had set up a meeting with reporters. Most of the men made the usual comments about being glad to be home, but when the cameras turned in Darryl's direction, all he said as he squinted into the lights was, "I wanna get better an' play ball."

It made quite a story, especially when they found out that he *could* play ball. Unable to say no after an impressive workout in Winterhaven the next spring, he agreed to sign on with five different teams, whose representatives appeared at the same time the next morning, contracts in hand. When each refused to relinquish his rights, the dispute went up to the Commissioner of Baseball, who gave Darryl a dressing-down, then pulled the name of the Chicago White Sox out of a hat.

After a summer in Triple A with Edmonton in '69, Pardee exploded into the Big Leagues like the seasoned veteran he was. People were soon claiming he was worth two places in the standings to a ballclub—half for what he did by himself, and half for the way he could motivate. You just couldn't dog it with him on the bench. He'd been through hell, but he still ran out his ground balls. Six years later he was averaging .331 with thirty-four home runs, 106 RBIs, thirty-one stolen bases, and twenty more put-outs and assists than his closest competition at third; and now all he needed was a World Series Ring, to take with him into the Hall of Fame.

His first real chance to win that ring was to come with a brand-new franchise to be located in the American League East, the brainstorm of a fast-food magnate named Phil Raneer, who was betting an estimated four hundred million dollars, "two bucks for every man, woman, and child in the country," that folks would pile into their cars and drive as long as it took, to see Major League baseball played in what the ads were calling:

THE MOST PERFECT BASEBALL SETTING EVER CREATED
THE STADIUM AT AMERICA'S NEWEST SMALL TOWN
BALLPARK, OHIO

The plan called for campgrounds and parking lots to form a buffer zone between Ballpark and the rest of the state, inside of which a fleet of nonpolluting minibuses would circulate freely, to transport people (for a fee) to any of the many attractions Ballpark's architects were providing, including hotels, motels, inns, and chaperoned dormitories; bars, nightclubs, and movie theaters; bowling alleys, swimming pools, bridle paths, and batting cages; tennis courts, a driving range, two championship golf courses, and a lake stocked with trout; the largest amusement park anywhere north of Disney; bike rentals, a roller rink, go-carts, and penny arcades; a climatized mall with 110 stores; and finally, for those times when the pursuit of pleasure had led ineluctably to hunger, more than fifty-five fast-food franchises to be scattered on street corners throughout.

There would be apartment complexes and condominiums for ballplayers and support personnel, and three-story townhouses for corporations and baseball nuts, who could afford the rooftop decks overlooking the real attraction of Ballpark, the beautiful sunken stadium, with its red-brick and stone facade, 39,999 seats, no obstructions, real grass, and, as its owner liked to boast, "the clean skies of America's past."

Normally a new franchise would flounder for years, using castoffs from the other clubs, but in 1975 the Supreme Court ruled that the reserve clause, which had allowed a team to renew a player's contract *in perpetuity,* with or without his consent, was suddenly void. For the first time players could play out their options and sell their talents to the highest bidder, and for one year only, fittingly enough the Bicentennial Year of 1976, the baseball world returned to a free market economy, and teams could sign as many "free agents" as they wished.

The owners were now their own worst enemies, driving up prices beyond the point of reason, but their response was augured by the prophet of laissez-faire capitalism, Adam Smith, who wrote in his *Inquiry into the Nature and Causes of the Wealth of Nations,* published in 1776, exactly two hundred years before:

> The exorbitant rewards of players, opera-singers, etc., are founded upon two principles: the rarity and beauty of their talents, and the discredit of employing them in this manner. It seems absurd that we should despise their persons and yet reward their talents with the most profuse liberality. While we do the one, however, we must of necessity do the other.

Thus despised, and laughing all the way to the bank, players jumped rosters right and left, the rich got rich, the poor (especially the poor fan) got poorer, and baseball, that once classical, pastoral game, entered the late seventies. As the season approached, no one was sure just who would wind up where, so Pardee held out as long as he could, then late in December informed his agent that all things being equal, his best shot at that World Series Ring would seem to lie with the new Ballpark franchise, on the strength of its signings to date.

His agent spent the next week spreading rumors that Darryl was leaning toward New York, then tugged at the line of Ballpark President Phil Raneer, who had let it be known that he wanted Pardee in the worst way—which is precisely how he got him. Bidding the last hundred thousand per annum against himself, Raneer agreed to a package worth two-point-five million dollars over five seasons.

The news broke at a press conference, with Pardee unnoticed and uncomfortable in the back, his hands in his pockets, one shoulder against the wall, when the inimitable Fast Phil, with his slicked-back, dyed-black hair and carnival barker's grin, fielded a question about rain-outs and launched into his spiel:

"You know what we did in the Army when it rained?" He paused. "We let it rain! This is baseball, remember? Good old-fashioned baseball . . . you don't play in the rain. Clouds open up, we'll cover the field an' wait. Gotta have *some* rain, it makes the grass grow."

Raneer went on, "We'll be playin' on real grass, y'know . . . not the kind you smoke, an' none a' that damned Astroturf, or whatever the hell they call it." He laughed. "We can't wait to see the good folks from Cincinnati, Pittsburgh, St. Looey, Philly . . . *anywhere,* in fact, that they've laid a carpet, like a cloud, over our national pastime—the green pastures of baseball . . . *gone!* It's a damned disgrace!

"We take our baseball serious in Ballpark, an' we take it straight. We're lookin' forward to our first season, an' now that we've signed Mr. Pardee over there . . ." Raneer grinned as the writers' heads swiveled, "I'd say we're mighty glad to have him . . . an' with his, an' the Good Lord's help, we expect a *very* fine year. Come on up an' stand here, son . . . let 'em take a look at ya. . . ."

Chapter 3

All through February Pardee ran, shagged flies, and battled Iron Mike, the automatic pitching machine. He didn't like the cages, they made him uptight, but more than that he liked to watch the balls in flight, to step back and watch them land, so he was more than willing to pay a high school kid to chase down the drives he sprayed to all three fields.

With trainer Artie Stutz feeding the balls into the apparatus, he took two sessions a day for four weeks, building up to two hours at a crack. Very few men can hold a bat up, let alone swing it, for two hours of solid hitting, but Pardee didn't know when to quit. He didn't know how to quit. He kept on each day until his hands were numb.

Nights passed slowly. Darryl watched TV, took in an occasional movie, and daydreamed about women, although he lacked the will to go out and find one. In his relatively brief Big League career, Pardee had scored many more times on the field than off, although he was a streak hitter and owned a small corner of the town of Chicago. Just the mention of the word "Chicago" could get his blood boiling, but in Tideview he didn't have a glimmer of a flame, so he spent his time waiting for the last week in February, when camp would open.

Before long his teammates began to drift in, and Tideview came to life. The players had all hit the jackpot with Raneer, and were determined not to be embarrassed by it. A ground ball would roll through a pair of legs, someone would yell, "Hey, millionaire!" and nine men would look up. There was something ridiculous about the notion, and they knew it.

February 22, the first day of training: the freshly painted locker room was sparkling clean, with cases of candy and bubblegum and pouches of tobacco lined up on the shelves. Along with the aroma of uncured enamel, and the smell of coffee, brewing in an urn, there was a strain of mild hysteria in the air, as the players oiled and pounded their gloves, feeling the tension and quietly jiving, awaiting the arrival of silver-haired, barrel-shaped manager Fritz Hart, the Kraut.

Hart's father had pitched for the late Joe McCarthy, who made young Fritz into a Yankee mascot. After a brief career as a utility infielder, he took a coaching job with the Cleveland chain, then twelve years later got the big club, which he managed to one World Championship and two divisional titles, before a new owner started dictating trades, at which point he quit, to sign on with Ballpark.

Raneer knew talent when he bought it, and was an expert when it came to delegating responsibility, so he agreed to give up complete control over matters pertaining to the playing field. Hart installed his own general manager and pirated a first-rate coaching staff, and was ready to stake his reputation, his imminent retirement, and his legend on the results. Given that he cared more about his legend than Fast Phil cared about cash, it would be fair to state that no one had more on the line this first day of baseball, 1976, than Fritz the Kraut. He walked into the locker room at ten o'clock sharp, surveyed his troops, and began:

"Gentlemen,"—someone. laughed—"there's a lotta high-priced talent here. Fact is, we got more good ballplayers than we got positions . . . so some a' you gonna wind up on the bench.

"Now, I happen to believe that the bench is important. I always say it's the backbone of a ballclub, but if it ain't exactly your idea a' paradise, you got six weeks to show me somethin' . . . an' that goes for all a' ya. I'll sit anybody, I don't care what he's makin' . . . it's not *my* money." He scratched himself.

"My name is Fritz Hart. They call me the Kraut. I don't like it, but I'm used to it, just like you'll get used to me. The man with the big ears over there is your pitchin' coach, Charley Wedmar. If you're a pitcher, you'll answer to him. Next we got your battin' instructor, Ray Gowdy; your bullpen coach, Russell James; first base, Willie Wagner . . . Willie . . ."—Wagner grinned and bowed—"and third base, Lacy Stokey." Stokey was a pitcher in the old Negro leagues, who never played a day of Major League ball, but retired to coach semipro in Cleveland. Hart met Stokey around the community, picked his brains whenever he could, then to Cleveland's delight and the Park League's loss, hired him on as his first lieutenant in 1971. A brown oyster of Stokey's Mail Pouch dribbled from his thick lips into a square box, filled with sand, on the floor.

"Get to know your coaches, boys. If you have any questions, or get confused, call time out, step outta the box. Nobody misses a signal on my ballclub, an' nobody *farts* without a green light"—somebody broke wind—". . . unless he's like Hunsicker back there, with two strikes against him to begin with." Hunsicker beamed. The Kraut had picked him out.

"This is a new team. It's a new *era*, they tell me, so let's get it straight." Hart paused. He spoke slowly. "I only got two rules. Be on time . . . at all times, you got that, *at all times* . . . and don't drink after midnight in the hotel bar.

"That's not hard; I keep it simple, see, 'cause the only thing I really care about is winnin'. Now, there are those who say that winnin' ain't everything, and while there's much to be said for that notion, if you happen to be some kinda asshole, or jerk . . ."—he looked around—"and you win . . . you at least have some consolation.

"So go ahead, be yourself, I don't care what you wear, how long your hair is, how long your cocks are, or how many times a night you use 'em—I am not your mother. It's a long season, an' we all have to live together—God help us—so try to keep this in mind . . . I can be a great guy. I'll laugh my way right to the World Series, nice an' loose . . . but if we're behind, at any point, in any game . . . *we do not fuck around.* Is that clear? Campbell? *Zarino?* Good. Take the field, warm up . . . and get your minds on baseball."

Having dropped his voice to a near whisper, he cut loose his Bilko-at-the-motor-pool call, ending in the kind of *hut-hut-hut* that drives camels into a trot under the desert heat. Metal spikes scattered and clattered out of the locker room into the sunshine, as the players hit the turf and thundered past first, coasting out to right, to start the year, like every other year, with a lap.

They took the turn in a long line and stretched it down the fence, crowding up in left center, as the men in the rear cut across the grass, to meet the leaders on the warning track under the 375 mark. Elbows flew, one man fell, and what started as an easy lap was suddenly a race. By the time they reached the bullpen in left, they had pretty much sorted out into three groups:

All by himself, dead last, was Laurence "Puck" Bernard, a former minor league hockey goalie from Quebec. Doubts as to whether the veteran catcher's knees had healed after surgery were now answered. Puck's knees might have healed, but they weren't any better.

Thirty men laughed and swore in front of him, trying to keep from getting spiked in the confusion, while leading the charge down the line, *mano a mano,* were left and center fielders Jesus Martinez and Simon Alvarez, Mambo and Samba, each thinking only of his precious reputation as "World's Fastest Latin Out-fielder," until Pardee pulled up behind them, pumping and snorting like a bull.

The Latin speedsters were reduced to a pair of hard-luck cartoon matadors, as they crossed the plate and hit the grand-stand wall; then Pardee veered left, past a battery of cameras in the first base dugout, and over to third; where he barely had time to catch his breath before Gowdy met him with his first ground ball.

Ray's three-hoppers were precise and mechanical. He could hit a target better with his bat than with his arm—which had posed something of a problem for him back in the days when he played left field. He stroked a few to short, turned to second, then to first, gradually lengthening out on the stick, and began to blister screaming shots that dared the players to stand their ground and prove that they belonged. He held the ball for Darryl to see, then drove it on the short hop, right at his feet; but somehow the third baseman backhanded the blast and came up smoothly, to uncork a throw that popped the mitt at first with the sound of fine champagne in a hotel suite.

Outfielders were loping under fungoes, making their catches and gunning them back, the pitchers were loosening up cautiously in right, then when the whole thing was in gear, and balls were flying everywhere, the Kraut himself stepped out of the dugout and took the bat from Gowdy to assume command. "All right, get two!" the cry rang out, and Pardee grinned under the brim of his hat. It was official. Another season had begun. He passed the rest of the afternoon in a contented sweat.

Chapter 4

1

The Fourth Estate. The term came into use around the French Revolution, when society was divided into rigid classes—the nobility, clergy, and commons—and somebody noticed that outside these classes, or estates, with rights beyond their status, mobility beyond their means, and the responsibility of keeping tabs on each class for the benefit of the other two, stood the journalists (in the words of Edmund Burke, "more important than them all"), raking up muck, poking their noses into the perfumed underwear of the court, and, through it all, selling papers.

Equally devoted to those aims is the modern press, including the Baseball Writers' Association of America. Pursuing their deadlines, and a dependable weekly salary, the poor bastards who work the morning tabloids have to file one story by ten-thirty P.M. for the bulldog (predawn) edition, another an hour later, then a final, after a quick trip to the locker room for quotes, by twelve-fifteen. They start writing from the very first pitch, hanging dummy leads on running accounts, missing half the action of the game before them (they look up from their copy shouting, "What happened?" as the crowd goes wild—

"Will somebody *please* tell me what happened?''); yet despite the constant pressure there are those who contend that day in and day out, the sports page contains the best, the most poetic, and easily the most imaginative writing in the daily rag, because sports fans don't expect thoughtful analyses, they want flagrant flights of fancy, the fancier the better. They want their metaphors full-bodied and mixed, in paragraphs that go down like Piña Coladas.

By the last week in February, five men were assigned to the Ballpark beat: Randy Hathaway, of the *Cincinnati Enquirer;* Paul Franken, of the *Pittsburgh Press;* Phil Rich, of the *Youngstown Vindicator;* Chuck Loud, of the *Louisville Times;* and Marc Rubin, of the *Columbus Dispatch.* They were joined this first morning by half a dozen other correspondents, in town to check out the new franchise, and were situated down at the picnic benches, just beyond the first base stands, shedding their shirts and anointing with suntan lotion some of the worst bodies ever to hit the South.

"Hey, Frankie . . . how's it goin'?'' said Hathaway, tugging on a Tab.

"Good, Randy, how 'bout you? What you got?''

"Me? I'm just wakin' up . . . but maybe I'll do a little 'human interest' thing on 'Harry Crandall, *comma,* veteran free agent from the Texas Rangers, *comma,* who is due to break out of his ten-year slump, *dot, dot, dot* . . .' '' Hathaway made a face and turned up to the stands, where a handful of kids were diving for foul balls. Several busloads of retirees were ensconced beneath their golf umbrellas, while a woman with dark hair, in sunglasses, sat alone in the top row, jotting down notes.

Underneath the concrete risers, from the press lounge where the hot dogs and cold cuts were waiting, Ballpark's new traveling secretary and all-purpose media flack, Howie Needleman, emerged, wiping mustard from his fingers, on his way to the tables where the writers were lounging. "How's it goin'?'' said Needleman, stepping up to block the sun from Hathaway's eyes.

"Needleboy, my man . . . where the hell are those rosters you promised?"

"What're you talkin' about? I typed up a list."

"Indeed you did, but what's-her-name, Debby over there, said the Xerox broke."

Howie scowled. He couldn't understand it. He had worked for Raneer in New York, then wangled a transfer when he picked up a franchise, and now that his dream of making the Big Leagues had come true, he had thought he was ready. He had all the answers, all the stats, all the inside dope; Needleman was a dangerous man, a fan run amuck.

"Whaddya wanna know? That's Bernard behind the plate, Hamilton at first, an' right behind him, Goldhammer—great copy, went to Stanford, speaks four languages."

"I hope English is one of 'em."

"Listen, he hit for the circuit last year, called up his mother, an' all she could say was, 'You coulda been a doctor, Ira, you coulda been a doctor!' "

"Funny, Howie, you make that up?"

"That's Hunsicker walkin' over this way, hit .314 in Houston last year, an' the black dude behind him is Cleighton R. Foster . . . right-handed reliever . . . and a real prick."

"He speaks highly a' you, too. What about the rotation?"

"Fritz is goin' with four men. Danny Leary, from Baltimore; Cal Dellums, who just found God . . ."

"Oh, no . . ."

"Don't worry, he'll tell you all about it. Then the Junkman, Phillips; and our ace, Frank Fuller, known as the Brush Man— not because he throws at people, which he does, but for this funny habit of visiting married ladies in the middle of the morning. Led the league last year in strikeouts, wins, and blow jobs." The writers groaned—it was going to be a long season.

"You think I'm kiddin'? An' speakin' a' blow jobs, this is ridiculous. I'm goin' downtown an' Xerox the thing myself. Now don't go complainin' behind my back, or cryin' that you don't have nothin' to write about. You need a story? Call me up. I'll give ya three . . . catch ya later."

2

Half an hour before practice ended, two vans with microwave transmitters pulled into the parking lot, and the scribes grumbled, "Here come the talking dogs"—resentful of the kind of TV people who show up late, grab enough for thirty seconds of air time, and then have the gall to call themselves reporters. Camera crews from two local stations took long shots of practice, then cornered a few stars for a few brief words before installing themselves at the entrance to the locker room. Several writers trying to squeeze through got jostled, one guy got jammed with the edge of a lens, and a scuffle broke out as they jockeyed for position.

Pardee, trotting in, took a look at the commotion, and all the shotgun mikes pointed at him, and shied away, feeling queasy. He just wanted to be left alone, to play ball and live out his father's dream.

Tom Pardee fought the Second World War in the Pacific. He was a pretty fair first baseman when he left, who might have played for years in the minor leagues, but he tore the rotator cuff of his left shoulder in an assault on an atoll in the Marshall Islands, and couldn't throw worth a lick when he got back, so he wound up working as a security guard in the local Coca-Cola bottling plant.

He raised his son when his wife passed on, then died before Darryl got back from *his* war, so that now all Pardee had for family was the memory of standing at the high school backstop, watching ballgames with his dad from the time he was three. Once a year it would hit him hard, and when spring would roll in, baseballs and flowers would jump into his eyes like tears. It was happening now, as the newsmen closed in, crowding around and firing their questions.

"Howdy, Darryl . . ."

"Hi, Pardee, what's with your hitting?"

"Hitting?" He turned to his locker.

"Yeah, you know . . . the bat . . . the ball . . ." The writers laughed. "You didn't take your cuts today . . . anything wrong?"

"Well, I feel a little weird, sir. . . ." They all looked up. What kind of word was that for a ballplayer to use? Might as well say *deviant*. "I'm a little over-hit."

"What?"

"From here on I bunt."

"Bunt?" The newsmen fed him one-word interrogatives, as if it were a drill.

"Yessir. I'll get in shape beatin' 'em out . . . save my hittin' for the season."

They checked again to see if he was kidding. Pardee had been known to crack a joke or two, and they were usually like this, wry and easy to miss. "Have you told Hart?"

"Not yet."

"Don't worry, *we'll tell him*." They broke off, laughing, to run to Fritz's office, but as soon as he found out what was so funny, he turned them around, saying:

"Would you fellas please excuse me for a moment? *Pardeeee!*" It was his calling-a-player-to-his-office call. No matter how far away from it you were, if it was meant for you, *you heard it*.

The writers filed into the hall, as Darryl hustled past and the door slammed shut. "How come," Fritz wanted to know, "I get all my news secondhand . . . from *reporters?*" He pronounced the word as if it were a disease.

"Just thought of it, sir . . . look at this." He unfolded a set of raw blisters from his long bouts with Iron Mike, and the Kraut grunted. Why should he worry? His best player had bleeding palms and would be bunting for the next few weeks. No cause for alarm. . . .

"All right, Pardee, but next time, you tell me first."

"Yessir."

"Nice workout. Show Stutz those hands."

"I already did."

"What'd he say?"

"He said I was stupid."

Hart waved him out of the office, into the circle of scribes. "What happened? What he say?" Darryl kept silent.

"Stutz!" Fritz's call rang out again, and the Ballpark trainer appeared on the run.

"Coming!"

"What's going on?" The reporters didn't know whom to ask.

"Nothin'," said Pardee.

"Stutz, goddammit, what the hell is goin' on?" Hart's door closed again. The writers were tempted to listen at the keyhole, but they had to live through a whole year with him too, so they moved on, and in a few minutes were kneeling like acolytes as Gowdy recited the baseball catechism:

"What kind of race do you expect?"

"Tough. Real tough. We could finish first, or we could finish fourth." Gowdy frowned. This was serious stuff.

"Who scares you?"

"Boston, New York, Cleveland, Baltimore . . . Toro—"

"But that's everybody!"

"We'll take 'em one at a time."

The writers were getting edgy. It was only the first day of spring training, but with all the TV lights and people pushing, it felt as if a pennant had been clinched, and many of them had this deep gut feeling they were missing something. Voices from the back grew increasingly shrill as the players rinsed off and started clamoring for towels, the whole thing built to a nervous peak; then she walked in, removed her shades, took a look around, and piped up:

"Hi, boys . . . Pauline Reese, *Lifetimes Magazine* . . . mind if I come in?"

"Hell, no!" and a stream of oaths came cascading over the water's roar.

"Might as well get used to me . . . the Supreme Court says we shower together. *How about that?*" She said it just the way Mel Allen, the old voice of the Yankees, used to, and they liked it. They *loved* it. Choruses of "There is nothing like a dame," from the back, where Hamilton, Goldhammer, and Bernard pressed in naked, soaking everyone in front.

She was what they meant when they said Big League, dressed in duds with designer labels, sewn where you could read them. Pardee, for his part, didn't mind her being there, but the perfume wasn't fair. He ducked into a stall and peered out over the edge, as she strolled along, saying, "I'm here to work . . . the same as you . . . any objections?"

"Yer goddamn right," grumbled Lacy Stokey, but Hunsicker came mincing forward, gushing:

"Oh, my, no . . . I just *adore* lady reporters. . . ."

"Back in your box," she warned him.

"Your place or mine?"

Martinez slid behind and started waving his hips, raving about her enchiladas, until she answered him in Spanish and sent *him* packing; then Campbell, the backup catcher, dropped his towel and boasted, "You can write a *column* on how lucky my wife is."

"All right, fellas, fine . . . I'm impressed. No kidding, I am really impressed. You're beautiful. Unbelievable. Any more problems before I take off?"

"Yeah." It was Hunsicker again. "How do you spell *vagina?*"

"Same as you, Dutch . . . only I don't have to look it up."

"Whoo-ee's" swirled, as she spun and took off up the ramp, to where the *Lifetimes* staffer was waiting for his cover shot: *Women in the Locker Room,* with Pauline Reese trailed by twenty hounds.

Flash! and just like that all the writers and TV lights were gone and everything got quiet. Pardee poked his head out of the can and crossed the floor into the shower. His body was tight; the hot water caught him just in time. He steamed awhile, then hit the cold and took it to the limit—gave his heart a shock just to see what it could take, dropped two time zones and let it pour down on him in a mountain stream. Twenty minutes later he toweled off and left, the last man out.

Chapter 5

Long after the crowd of kids had gone, he strolled through the gate to his rented car, to drive across the causeway to the Tideview Hotel, a falling relic of a genteel resort, left over from the days when the town still catered to the rich. Service had been poor lately, and the food was disappointing, but he could count on its being calm, with white linen, palms outside the windows, and a sea breeze instead of air conditioning. It was the kind of place where he could eat in peace, because no one was waiting for his table.

Darryl finished dinner and was sipping a beer when a waiter appeared and handed him a note. He followed the man's glance over to the corner, dropped his napkin on the plate, and got up to cross the room. This wasn't the first time it had happened, just the first time in a long time.

A woman sat with her back to him. He reached her table, placed his hands on a chair, leaned over, and was about to speak, when, "Sit down," she said, "I'll buy you a drink."

"I won't talk baseball," he told her, straightening up.

"Sit down, Pardee. This is a bar, right? I know the rules."

He sat down quickly. "What's the matter?" she teased him. "Don't you trust me?"

"You *are* a reporter."

"Well, I'm flattered . . . but I'm off duty, what's the big deal? If this is going to be a . . ."

"OK."

"Good," said Pauline. "What'll it be?"

"Heineken." He waited for her to order, then, "Rough time today?"

"About what I expected. I've been in locker rooms before, I spent a season with the Nets, although I must say . . . basketball players are a little bit cooler." He shrugged. "They're a little less . . . publicly obscene."

"Do my friends embarrass you?"

"Sometimes. Do they embarrass *you?*"

He laughed. "Sometimes." He looked down at her hands, her lacquered fingers, her lack of rings. "Tell me. Do you find yourself, uh . . . checkin' 'em out?"

"How about you? Wanna compare notes? Are you the one who's been sneaking looks?"

"I try not to."

"Well, same here. I've got better things to do."

"That don't mean I don't see things," he said.

"Jesus, I see things, all right? I've got eyes. Are you going to keep this up? What's so great about ballplayers, anyway? You've got big arms and thick butts. If I wanted to gawk, Pardee, I'd go to the ballet . . . or a tennis match."

"Is that so?"

"You brought it up. Look, I am tired of the subject. I went through the same dumb questions all afternoon."

"Now you know how it feels."

She lifted her coffee in a silent *touché*. The last light of day was glowing in the clouds, yet somehow the sea seemed brighter than the sky. Pauline sat silently, drinking it in, until Pardee, drumming a fork on the tabletop, said, "Sorry you had such a hard time today, but maybe you were askin' for it."

"I just wanted to get it over with." She swung around to face him.

"Look," he said, "If you wanna go unnoticed, why come on so strong?"

"Unnoticed? Do you think I can go *unnoticed* in there? I know what I'm doing. I want them to know that they can fool around . . . that I'm not out to cramp their style. We'll see who can take a joke, Pardee. I'll bust their balls."

"Yeah, well . . . I figured you for a ballbuster."

"Only when I'm joking."

"And when you're not?" He didn't intend it, but it came out as a dare, and Pauline took him up on it—staring into his eyes until neither of them could pull back. She grinned, glowed, and seemed to grow larger, threatening to envelope him in a halo of ethereal dark hair. Pardee weakened. In a last-ditch effort to maintain control, he demanded, "What the hell is goin' on?"

"Can't you tell?" She smiled. Pauline had been watching him for years; it was part of her job, and she was a pro. She kept a book on players the way pitchers keep a book on batters—charting their flaws and tendencies—but the page on Pardee was blank, like his eyes, the eyes of Greek statues in museums, empty, wide, implying a terrible force, all-knowing, all-nothing.

At some point she realized that he simply had it for her, and since that time she'd had it in for him, nurturing a crush, a secret little fantasy kept separate from her work. Now that she had him before her, however, she was beginning to see that those eyes weren't blank, they were afraid. Pardee afraid? She almost had to laugh.

"Darryl," she said, "I want you to know something. I am not in the habit of picking up ballplayers . . . but when I saw you here tonight . . . I thought we could introduce ourselves."

Pardee looked up slowly. Pauline was apologetic. Neither one knew why. "Fine with me," he said, extending his hand, "Darryl Pardee, third base, from Crawbanks, Louisiana." He gave her the same tight-lipped, self-conscious smile that he always gave the cameras for the folks back home, who hadn't had a star like him since Billy Cannon, LSU, and the Chinese Bandits. They shook.

"Pauline Reese. Manhattan, Smith College, Class of '69."

"Rah, rah. Got any brothers?"

"Two. Both older. How about you?"

"Thought so. Me? No, nothin'." He looked down again as she reached for her purse.

"Listen," she said, "let's get out of here. Wait a few minutes, then walk out alone."

"Got you." Pardee could take orders. He could take them from a man, he could take them from a woman. He knew how much time was lost explaining things. He watched her out the door, walked back to his table, settled up and left a tip; then stopped by the front desk, took two mints and a handful of toothpicks to use instead of smokes, and was last seen down by the curb, climbing into *her* rented car, on his way, her way.

Chapter 6

A staff writer for the past six months, Pauline was on assignment for *Lifetimes Magazine,* an old news weekly fighting for survival against the new *People*-genre publications, by stepping up its emphasis on style and sports. Her locker room entry made the news that night, and with the wisecracks bleeped out, the whole thing seemed even funnier than it was. She stayed up through the weather report, and nothing is more boring than the weather in Florida, then flicked off the tube and settled in beside Pardee, who was already asleep.

He was gone without a trace when she woke the next morning, so she showered, dressed, and ate breakfast alone, before heading down to Phil Raneer's first Florida press conference—nothing anyone hadn't seen at a numbing succession of Super Bowls, just the same thirty (count 'em) beautiful naked girls, draped in fragments of the American flag, and "Take Me Out to the Ballgame," instead of "Semper Fidelis," by the marching band in back.

Raneer introduced his front office staff, his PR men, Needleman, and the ten junior partners he had taken into Ballpark, franchisors in their own right, representing the collective indigestion of roadside America in the form of pizza, root beer, roast beef and soft ice cream, fried chicken and fish, donuts, tacos, and countless incarnations of the hot dog.

No one listened to his opening remarks, they were too busy grabbing up the food and drinks, hollering "More leg kicks!" between mouthfuls. The boys were in good spirits, and Raneer was pleased. He went on, ". . . so you see, we didn't call you down to make you work for a livin' . . . Lord knows you work hard enough. We're jus' givin' you a feel . . ."—he paused— "for the kinda personal treatment you can expect, 'long as we get what we need from *you*.

"Now, I am not tellin' you what to write. I know that your friendship is not for sale—even I don't have that kinda money —we jus' wanna play ball. We're not askin' for favors, we're handin' 'em out! Once we start winnin', you'll all jump on the bandwagon, so what I'm sayin' is, 'Jump on now! Get a good seat, you'll like the view.' "

Raneer raised his eyebrows and hoisted his drink, toasting the panorama of sleek, well-oiled limbs. A number of writers started to laugh, but those closest to her turned to Pauline. Raneer took another sip and said, "Any questions?" but when she raised her hand, he called on someone else, who asked if he planned to have any input into his team.

"Input?" he answered. "Yeah, I'm puttin' in the money, I'm puttin' in the stands. As for runnin' this team, I'm puttin' in Mr. Hart, an' keepin' outta his hair. I have total confidence in the man." Behind him, Fritz was shifting in his seat. He hated ceremonial functions and detested being put on display.

Raneer ignored the upraised arms and continued, "Oh, yeah, almost forgot . . . listen up. We do have one surprise for you today, somethin' for right up top page one, Sports . . . an' that is that we here at Ballpark have found us a name. We looked long an' hard for somethin' to call ourselves . . . the Ballpark Broncos . . . the Ballpark Buzzards . . ." He got his laugh. "But while we were searchin', we got to sayin', 'Damn boys . . . we got to find us a name for this here ballclub.' Then I pointed that out to Gene Royster, the singin' cowboy an' roast beef honcho over there, an' he liked it, so I said, 'That's it! That's what we'll call it!' '' A drum roll. "I give you *the Ballclub,* gentlemen . . . from Ballpark, Ohio."

The band struck up as nine blondes on stacked heels paraded out in shirttops bearing the monogram *Ballclub* in a dark-blue Dodger script that could almost pass for *Brooklyn* at a distance. The writers nearly choked. They could swallow quite a lot on a bellyful of drinks, but naming a team the Ballclub? Raneer was asking for it. He got it.

The Kraut kicked over a folding chair, as the ladies rotated, showing off their numbers; then Fritz split and the writers charged, as Raneer hollered that the other teams would have enough trouble beating his Ballclub (henceforth capitalized— highly capitalized) without worrying about what he called it.

Spotting Pauline in the center of the crowd, he gave her a big smile and said, "Yes, dear . . . I forgot your name . . ."

"Pauline Reese, *Lifetimes Magazine* . . . and I'm less concerned with *your* name than with the number of free agents that you've—"

"Young lady, before you go on . . . we have a Commissioner, Mr. O'Neill, with what they call 'extraordinary powers' —that means he's like God—to veto any transaction 'not in the best interests of baseball.' Now if he has no objections, then—"

"People say that you're buying a pennant, and that money is ruining the national game."

"Honey," he said, smiling, "money can't ruin the national game . . . it *is* the national game! You show me a man who isn't buyin' a pennant, an' I'll show you a guy who doesn't want one. You think they're *givin'* it away? Maybe you are, but they're not." Pauline blinked, as if she'd been slapped. "This is high stakes we're talkin' about. I'm not worried about a little bitty pennant . . . I'm lookin' to buy a damned *dynasty!*"

Needleman jumped up, shouting, "Thank you, Mr. President," and hustled Raneer from the podium; Fast Phil's laugh echoed all the way out the door, as the writers went racing for the telephones provided; and by the time the working press got done, his simple statement of fact had been blown up into the hottest controversy to hit baseball since the Black Sox scandal of 1919. The only difference was that there were no little newsboys with tears in their eyes, asking anyone to "Say it ain't so."

Chapter 7

1

Pardee had to agree with Raneer, it didn't matter what you called it, baseball was still baseball. Kids were still out in backyards all summer long, playing all nine positions on their favorite teams, broadcasting the play-by-play and tipping their hats to the crowd's roar.

He closed his eyes and saw the all-time greats, playing out their days on Elysian Fields, then falling out in the clouds, cooling in the shade of grandstands where archangels sipped elixir and cheered. He pictured Walter Johnson, from a faded old-time photo, in a duel against Lou Gehrig, with his powers restored; and could see old Tom in a folding chair, watching from his spot behind the golden backstop, joining in a battle charge led by Gabriel on a ram's horn. Pardee could see it, he just hoped that there'd be green up there—that was another place he agreed with Raneer; a ballfield had to be real.

Green. That's all he could see as he lay on his bed, green covers, the green underbrim of his hat pulled down by fingers tugging at both sides, green, like the green spring grass beneath his window, rich and damp, crawling with so many worms the birds just *had* to sing. . . .

"Heaven must be earth," thought Pardee, "this blue sky, this uniform, and I don't care. . . ." He drifted off.

2

There was a jolt, as his chute stretched out over a dome of air. Dazed in the harness, his heart churning, there was time to think. Two worlds. That strange one far below . . . and for a few moments more, this one . . . hung like a puppet, rocking gently, wondering what would happen if he never came down, just hung here peacefully, warmed by the sun, massaged by streams of rushing wind . . . four . . . three . . .

The parachute folded over him like a dark blanket. There were voices in the hallway, footsteps on the street below. Pale forms, paisley and microbic, streamed behind his eyelids, pressed tight against an onslaught of voices and faces that screamed up, then dropped off into emptiness. Silence. The smothered odor of carpet, wood furniture, and dust.

Darryl hollered, and old Tom came in, like he used to, saying, "What is it?"

"I heard something."

His father's face clouded up, and he said, "Go on, lie down . . . it's just the TV."

But as soon as he did, he started dreaming again, and he found himself up against lanky schoolboys, who drove him from the plate, while old Tom watched, spinning curves like buzz saws, and fastballs that called his name, as he woke into the night.

Pardee . . .

3

He failed to go out for his high school team, and the coach ignored the quiet kid hanging around practice every day, until late one afternoon, when he raced after a foul, caught up with the ball in the parking lot, whirled, and in one motion fired a strike, more than two hundred feet to the bag at third.

Coach Barnes, nobody's fool, recruited him on the spot, and would have put him in center on the strength of that arm if he hadn't seen him field his first ground balls. Even then, it took many a shot hit Pardee's way before Barnes would believe it. The new kid caught the ball on the ground, at the belt, off the hip—he trapped the bad hops in his armpit—and threw so hard that the coach had to switch his shortstop to first, to keep his regular first baseman from getting killed. The kid had a cannon, but Barnes wouldn't tell him to take too much off the ball, it'd mess him up.

A lesser man might have stuck Pardee at short, because the throws are longer there, but the baseball-wise teacher of history realized he was third base, born and bred. It did not surprise him to find out later that the lad was Tom Pardee's.

Darryl was pro material from his very first day on his high school squad. That's the way it often is with pros; they seem to spring up full-grown, surrounded by boys. His father stopped over to have a talk with the coach, who called Darryl in after practice one day to try to convince him that despite what happened at night, it wasn't really the pitching that was bothering him—he could *cream* the pitching—what bothered him was thinking about it, blowing it up and making it worse than it was, which he encouraged him not to do.

Darryl learned, starting way back then, to put everything out of his mind until he dressed for a game, when rivulets of sweat would trickle down his arms, to drip into pools on the locker room floor. Through all his years of competition, it never got any better, but no one would have guessed, to watch him play, what went on in his mind from the time he entered the gym until the time he had his feet on the grass.

4

Four years of stardom in the Intercounty High School League, and Pardee was well known to the bird dogs, that mixed breed of paid, semipaid, and volunteer scouts assigned to the Deep South. Every so often the scouts agree, and when they do they're just as likely to be wrong as right. They liked Pardee, but for some reason the consensus was that he'd find his limit around Double A ball, so they offered him no more than a thousand-dollar bonus, and a minimal salary in the minor leagues.

His dad was for it, that was all he'd ever wanted, but Pardee defied him and signed up with the Army, hurting the old man, who always felt that the Army had ruined him. They were bitter at the end, and a sullen handshake at the door of the bus was the last they ever saw of each other. Darryl nearly cried as he rolled down the road, but the fact was he had thought it through. He knew he'd be drinking nothing but jerkwater if he signed onto some farm circuit, and after eighteen years in Crawbanks, Louisiana, he knew all about the taste.

Crawbanks was flat, dead flat, with rice and sugar cane growing in the fields beside the elevated roads that ran through the marshes. While other boys had paper routes, Pardee pirogued through the swamps, culling Spanish moss to ship up north for General Motors (he always thought it was a person) to stuff inside the upholstery of his cars. By the time he left high school, the cypress and tupelo were all cut down, and water hyacinths, originally imported to beautify the region, choked everything, like Cajun kudzu. The cattle were Charolais, fat and indolent, like the people themselves, thick-limbed and stout. Everything down there felt heavy. The gravity really weighed on you.

Darryl could easily have swung a deferment, but there was a world out there, not to mention a war, and the word going around Louisiana in '65 was that we were just about ready to kick some ass in Vietnam, all we needed were a few good men, and he figured he was one of them.

People who have never set foot in a boondock often mourn the passing of the minor leagues, and wonder where the players will come from soon, but Pardee came up with one alternative to life in the American bush . . . he fought a war. Darryl's answer to the decline and fall of the minor leagues was and is the Army. The real draft. In the Army a kid can make a mistake without a rabid sports public following every move. He can get killed if he wants to, but he doesn't have to read about it in the papers.

Assigned to Pleiku, he lost his cherry, got the clap, then volunteered for action to clean up his act. They put him on patrol with the infantry, and in less than a week he had bagged his first slant—the guy never saw it coming, went down like a deer, as sweet as you like. Pardee jumped and hollered, so they threw him on the ground, shouting, "What the hell you doin'?" He still thought it was a game. He was out to skin it and hang it out to season. "Waste not what you kill," his daddy had taught him, but the new word coming down was . . .

"Waste 'em. Waste the little s.o.b.'s. We call that superior firepower, son . . . nice goin'."

The same old hand and eye thing that attracted the scouts to his bayou high school made him a crack shot. It wasn't even aim; he would pick up his rifle like an easy ground ball and just fire—and went way over the limit that first season, because the ground rules were different in Vietnam, where ties were *not* awarded to the runner.

5

The phone rang and Pardee caught it on the second ring, saying, "Hello? Hold on. Yeah?" Then he sat up in the darkness, rubbing his eyes until the insides glowed, black and incandescent.

"Get ready," said the voice. "I'll be there in five minutes."

He walked into the bathroom, ran the cold water, dipped his

face and went reaching for a towel, then returned to the bedroom to slip into loafers, wondering what she would look like. Her face seemed to have changed a hundred times the night before, leaving him no idea who she really was.

All he knew was that she kept her word, and was right on time, driving up the alley in her Mustang convertible. Darryl climbed in and was settling down when she popped the clutch and burned out into traffic, setting her jaw with the look of a woman who liked to drive hard, and leave them shaking their fists in the rearview. He shut his eyes, forcing himself to trust her.

"How was practice?"

"Not bad."

"You look terrible." She laughed.

"What's so funny? I fell asleep." He cupped his hand into the onrushing wind, as strands of hair escaped her barrette and whipped across her face. She pulled them from her mouth, tried to tuck them away, then turned her attention to the road ahead. The bright lights dimmed, and the night grew quiet.

"Big news," said Pauline, "your team has a name."

"I heard."

"What do you think?"

"What do *you* think?" said Pardee.

"I think it's bullshit," she answered. "I can't believe they're letting him do it. He must *want* us to attack him . . . probably figures it'll help sell tickets."

"Well?"

"I suppose it will. Does it bother you?"

"Couldn't care less. I'll let you people worry about it. My job is third base."

"It's not that simple."

"Oh, yes it is . . . nothin' simpler in the world." She hit the brakes and wheeled around. "Where we goin'?" he asked.

"I've got some Scotch up in my room. I think it would be better if we weren't seen together . . . no public displays of affection, OK?"

"I ain't advertisin'."

"Good."

"I got my own self to look out for."

"I know. That's why it might work."

"You know why I think it'll work?" Pardee slid his hand up her skirt, and felt her soft thigh, warm against the vinyl. She crossed town and went down the ramp, into the parking lot under her hotel; then ushered him upstairs, where they both undressed.

They said Pardee had fast hands, but he took his time, tracing the lines of a body finer than an athlete's, more responsive. Pauline was his opposite. She didn't move by reflex, but by feeling. She thought only of his hands, as her skin came alive, and he touched her in small involuntary places that took her breath away.

"You're beautiful," he said, watching her smile, as she lay with her eyes closed, grateful that there was nothing more he had to do for a while. She wasn't ready for his shoulders and hips. It had been too long since she'd been with a man, and she was a bit sore, and a little bit scared.

Darryl knew that by now. He was beginning to see through her hard talk and bravado. "Damn . . ." he sighed, feeling her tremor, as she arched her hips and turned to embrace him; but Pauline stopped short, as she had the night before, when her fingers encountered the raised flesh of his scars. Pardee was sewn like a two-dollar baseball, puckered up and stitched from the middle of his back, around his right side, to a point just under the muscle of his breast. He felt her shock, her fear, and finally her acceptance, as he moved above, and she took him in.

He lay still at first, lost in the wonder of it, waiting for the rhythm of their bodies to merge, then, propped on his elbows, taking his weight, he began to move. Left. Left again. Right.

"All right," she whispered, pulling him closer, knitting her hands behind his neck, "all right . . ."

Chapter 8

The press corps came out gunning for Raneer, but like the cosmic charlatan he was, some kind of jujitsu medicine man, he turned their venom into snake oil and sold it to the fans. Fast Phil was a merchandising genius. He once made a series of funny commercials claiming that his Philburger at thirty-five cents was the same as his hamburger at four bits, and that only an idiot would order the latter, and wound up doubling his hamburger sales, because nobody wanted to believe him. He gave out buttons saying, "I'm a Hamburger Jerk," with every ten sandwiches at the inflated price. The buttons cost two cents each.

"You have to admire a guy like that"—that's what they said as they lined up for lunch, because a guy like Raneer justified people's faith in America. "If a second-rater like Fast Phil can make it," they figured, "why not me?" Listening to the cash registers whirring away, they kicked themselves for not having snapped up the franchises that were going for peanuts only ten years back.

Raneer opened Ticketron outlets at selected Philburgers and gave out soft drinks with purchases of grandstand seats. He would gladly have given the tickets away, but he knew if people bought them, they were more likely to show up, and all he had to do was entice them in, and the profits would take care of themselves. Concession income around the league averaged about two-fifty a head, but he was counting on ten times that amount, even with his Kids Free in the Motels ("if they don't wanna fuck, fuck 'em") Policy.

He'd be hitting them up for three meals a day, lodging and sideshows, countless amusements, and acres of consumer goods. When Mom tired of baseball, she could dump the kids on Dad and shop. New sneaks, a summer dress, a few souvenirs for the folks back home—it would all add up. Hamburgers would be small potatoes after Ballpark took off, but Raneer had yet to see a dime, so he kept himself busy staying in the news, and Pauline had no trouble arranging for an interview, which resulted in the following:

QUOTATIONS OF CHAIRMAN PHIL
by Pauline Reese

TIDEVIEW, Florida, March 9—I was looking forward to talking to Phil Raneer, the president of Ballpark and Philburgers Inc., but as I found out quickly enough this morning, one doesn't talk with a man like that, one listens. I opened my notepad, saying, "Well, Mr. Raneer . . ." when he cut me off—

"Oh, you can call me Phil, or you can call me Fast" —he laughed—"but you don't have to call me *Mr. Raneer.* What's in a name? Like the poet says, any team smells like a rose if it wins . . . winners smell the roses, an' all the rest smells like *bleep!*" And he didn't say burgers.

I asked him what he thought of the charge that his money upset the league's competitive balance—a question that turned out to be my last.

"Horse*bleep!*" he hollered, "I didn't start it. Who signed Evans an' that Candy Bar *bleep*hole? The *bleepin'* Yankees, that's who! They even bought Babe Ruth!

"We've always had money . . . money won't ruin

it . . . if baseball has a problem, which I believe it does . . . it's designated hitters, carpets on the base-paths, an' computer scoreboards tellin' people when to cheer, when to clap, an' when to blow their *bleepin'* noses!

"When I was a kid, we went to LaGrave Field, the Fort Worth Cats, Brooklyn, Double A . . . when the wind was right you got this wunnerful smell from the stockyards. The point is, we'd stomp our feet an' yell like hell till we had us a cheer took over the whole damn ballpark. *We* did it! Little peanuts 'bout that high . . . didn't need no scoreboard spellin' *Charge!* like it was a goddamn football game. These kids today think it's all a damn television. They're waitin' to change the damn channel!

"Now, my notion a' baseball is nine innings, pure, with no additives." (Unlike his food, I failed to point out.) "My philosophy is: We got one thing an' one thing only once you pass them turnstiles . . . *base-ball!* Face it, that's all we got in common.

"We got red an' green lights for the balls an' strikes, an' a midget out there to post the scores by hand, an' that's all I need . . . 'cause I got me the best manager in the game today, an' the best damn Ballclub money can buy . . . so I'm jus' gonna sit out all summer in Ballpark an' relax, with no IBM computer, no instant replay, nothin' but what God gave us as our birthright —baseballs sewn in Haiti . . . an' His own green grass!"

"Cute," said Pardee, dropping the magazine and rolling over to face her as she let down her hair. "He's a foul old bird, but he sure knows how to talk."

"I cannot *stand* guys like that," she said into the mirror. "He says all the right things, for all the wrong reasons. Phil Raneer cares as much about 'the purity of baseball' as I do about . . ." She let it drop.

"Why not say so?"

"I did what I could. You have to draw your own conclusions." Pauline bent over and brushed everything forward, then flipped it back like someone in a shampoo commercial. It never failed to amaze Pardee, who had grown up without a woman in the house, how the ladies always did things the way they were supposed to. He wondered if they went to school, or had minor leagues of their own to learn moves like that, then sank back onto the mattress, slowly replaying the sight of her hair, falling about her shoulders like a mantle of rain.

Chapter 9

The East Coast circuit took her from Tideview to Miami (the Orioles), Fort Lauderdale (the Yankees), Pompano Beach (the Rangers), West Palm Beach (the Braves), and up to Vero Beach, the country-club winter home of the Dodgers. Except for Vero, every camp was within easy striking distance of Tideview, so although it was the last thing either of them had anticipated, Pauline and Darryl saw each other nearly every other night for the next five weeks.

She would never have let it stretch on as it did, had she not known that the regular season would keep them apart. There was a built-in safety valve to this affair that let her ignore the usual signals. Pardee, on the other hand, was used to seeing as much as he could of a woman for as long as possible, before the bus would pull out and he'd have to move on, so he pushed ahead without really thinking, pursuing her with a directness she found hard to deflect. "Will you see me tonight?" he would ask.

"I'm not sure."

"Why not?"

"I'm not sure why not. Look, Darryl, I'm . . ."

"What else you gonna do? Work?"

"Of course I'm going to work. I have to file by eight."

"Well?" he would say.

"Well . . . all right, but you'd better make it nine."

"Fine. Nine it is."

"Can I go now?" she'd sigh, giving in again, wondering why

she had let him get so close that the pressure was on her to come up with some excuse. The problem, she decided, was Tideview. It was so damn dull down there that she would have been spiting herself to refuse him. Outside of wanting to see her, however, he made few demands, and did nothing to which she could really object. She certainly couldn't fault the way he made love to her. Pauline had never felt so thoroughly (physically) loved in her life.

April 1. A holiday of sorts. Pauline's instructions were to return to New York, to lend a hand with the season's preview. The players were already slacking off, saying that they wanted to start playing for keeps, but Pardee, who had a different notion of playing for keeps, was as happy playing baseball in Florida as anywhere, so he was a little down as he carried her suitcases over to her car in the underground lot. She pulled him to the corner, right beside the dumpster, where they squeezed hands, trying to think of something to say.

"Goodbye, kid. . . ." She tossed her head with a quizzical look, as if to say, "What are *you* gonna make of it?"

"So long. . . ."

"There's a three-game series in the city on the fourteenth," she said brightly.

"I know. Look me up if you need some quotes." Pardee's eyes softened like one of those dumb old Charolais. They kissed, then they held each other at arms' length, and finally let go and went their ways.

Darryl walked back to his small hotel, as Pauline took the highway toward the airport, along with carloads of kids who were driving up north to resume their studies after the Easter break. The young girls were staring out dreamily, dangling their painted toenails from the back-seat windows, and one look had Pauline wondering, "Have they been loved? Did they take a chance and find some guy, or waste their time hanging out with a pack of dopey girl friends?" She was one of the lucky ones. Her spring fling was all she could have asked for, but she was glad it was over, and delighted to be heading home.

Chapter 10

Hart managed the training camp brilliantly. He broke them in slowly, downplaying the pressure, but put everyone on notice by sticking Hunsicker with the B team, warning him that if his fielding didn't improve, he would wind up as the designated hitter. The Dutch Man, a right-handed slugger with his own dreams of the Hall of Fame, despised the very concept of DH. Vowing to earn that spot in right, he drove himself like a madman, setting a standard that made mere hard work look like loafing.

Over at second, little Bobby Leopold, Hart's sleeper, picked up on waivers from Oakland, was holding off the challenge of Roland Howard, a nineteen-year-old kid with nearly awesome potential, but a need for one or two years of seasoning. Howard was a superb natural athlete who could have played point guard at UCLA, but chose baseball instead.

"Smart lad," thought the Kraut, watching as Leopold dove into the hole and threw from his back to nab the phantom man at first. "Incredible . . . now, *that* was a Major League play . . . as good as the kid is, he'd never have made it. . . .'' Fritz, who had a special place in his heart for guys playing on guts, made the cut right on the spot. Leopold would play second, as long as he lasted, and Howard would head to Downingtown to pay some dues. "Have to put a few obstacles in his way," he decided, " 'cause when he does get up, he'll make it look so damned easy, it'll be ridiculous!"

The last few days had been heartbreaking. A kid would pitch his ass off, give up a couple of bloop hits, get yanked, and walk off the playing field, into the dugout, right into the minor leagues. The only part of baseball that Hart disliked, the hard cuts were over now, so he made up a lineup to see how it sounded:

—Leading off would be Martinez, caramel-hued with a gold front tooth, the man who said, "Batting is like making love . . . I like it to last," to Goldhammer, who translated, after fouling off fourteen against a kid from Notre Dame.

—Second would be Alvarez, café au lait (Fritz thought in flavors, rather than race), a hit-and-run artist, unselfish and smart, who protected the plate with a unique defensive stance he acquired playing cricket in the Bahamas.

—Number three, Pardee, and after him,

—Hunsicker, a nappy blond, weighing in at two-ten. It could have been the other way around, but then Pardee would have been running up Dutch's heels all season. "If he can catch Martinez 'n' Alvarez," mused the Kraut, "he can keep 'em."

—Fifth would be Hamilton, a righthander, platooning with Goldhammer,

—And sixth would be Bernard. Old Puck was painful to watch, he ran for comfort, not for speed, but his lifetime average of .265 shot up to .310 with men on base.

—Seventh, the shortstop, was the feisty Paul Hogan. "Good little hitter," the Kraut conceded grudgingly, "if he'd only stop goin' for the walls. Some guys never get over bein' small. If he'd just forget his occasional power, his average would climb about twenty points. *Make contact,* I tell him, but does he listen? Nooo . . . too damned stubborn. Make a great manager someday. Where was I?"

—Eighth, the DH, was the only weak link. Collins and Patterson were singles hitters, when Hart wanted power; while Johnny Robinson could put the ball in orbit, then strike out his next eight times at bat.

—That left only Leopold, bittersweet chocolate, who would bunt and chip and bloop you to death. With the bases full and a game on the line, he would lean right in and take a fastball in the ear. Fritz just flat out loved the guy. He shook his head. He had to laugh.

Five weeks ago he had stormed off the stage at the sight of those uniforms, and now he was lying awake at night, wondering when he'd actually get to say to them, "Gentlemen . . . we *are* the Ballclub!" He could see the statue in Cooperstown, *Fritz Hart Holding His Hat,* like Connie Mack with his scorecard, waving at the outfielders, or shielding the sun from his eyes.

Looking around, he decided his team was not only potentially one of the best, but easily the strangest he'd ever seen. Danny Leary was a pothead. The boys called him Tiny Tim. The catch was that he'd been doing it for years, and Fritz knew better than to tamper with success. Martinez 'n' Alvarez sounded like a goddamn tango team, Goldhammer kept bothering Bernard with his French, and even Pardee dipped now and again into that awful Cajun patois . . . but after that it just got worse.

Hart's first base coach, Willie "Wa-Wa" Wagner, stuttered. He could bark out "Back!" when a pitcher made his move, and had the hand signals down cold, but ask his name and he'd go "W-w-w . . ." until somebody slapped him on the back. He made a mint on a credit card ad that faded out with him stammering, as his name was stamped in plastic. Clay Foster and Junk Phillips, meanwhile, spoke an inner-city street dialect that even Stokey couldn't follow; Fritz himself had a German lisp, with an Irish lilt that came from his mother ("Bless her soul . . ."); and Mike Lopez, his number-two reliever, spoke a combination Puerto Rican/Philadelphiaese that was the worst-sounding trash Hart had *ever* heard.

Fuller was a fucking sex maniac, the backup catcher, Campbell, was queer—this team was something new, they were all foreigners or weirdos, there were more Americans on some pro soccer squads. Not one of them was what Fritz called a "regular ballplayer," except perhaps for Hunsicker, which made him invaluable.

The Kraut surveyed the Phillies' camp in Clearwater, where the twelfth game would begin in an hour. A small group of writers talking salaries and egos sat in one corner of the stands, wringing their hands, while the rest were gaping at the Ballpark pitching staff, working out with the minor-league catchers under Wedmar's supervision along the first base line.

Hart listened to the salvos through the clean dry air. He heard the sound of cannonballs being fired at a head of state, his boat, battering the decks, the docks, everything in sight. Fritz smiled; the old Prussian in him stirred. "Artillery on the mound, plenty of ammo at the plate, and a goddamn barbed-wire defense in the field. Now, *that*'s how to start a campaign! Lookit Pardee, he's got a trench around third . . . he's a Major League ballgame all by himself. A guy like that comes down the pike maybe once every fifty years at most . . . you figure Honus Wagner could stand next to him at short, an' I got him, *he's all mine!*" The Kraut danced a jig.

His Ballclub's record stood at 3–8, but so far he hadn't done a thing to help them win. He had stayed with pitchers who were getting shellacked, taken a good long look at the rookies, and kept Hunsicker, going crazy, on the sidelines. Hart knew his trick would put the Dutch Man in his pocket. Come opening day he'd have him running through walls.

Frank Fuller was blazing fast, mean as a snake; Martinez was the All-Star left fielder, period; and as for Pardee, the longer Fritz watched, the better he played. His hands flashed in the familiar scoop that signaled the start of another DP, 5-4-3. "Look at him out there," thought the Kraut. "The man's a pro . . . solid . . . steady as a rock."

PART TWO

The Regular Season

OFFICIAL 1976 BALLPARK SCHEDULE

APRIL

S	M	T	W	TH	F	S
				1	2	3
4	5	6	7 DET	8 DET	9 DET	10 CHI
11 CHI	12 CHI	13	14 NY	15 NY	16 NY	17 BAL
18 BAL *	19	20 OAK	21 OAK	22 OAK	23 TEX	24 TEX
25 TEX *	26	27 CLE	28 CLE	29 TOR	30 TOR	

MAY

S	M	T	W	TH	F	S
						1 TOR
2 PHO *	3 PHO	4 PHO	5	6 BOS	7 BOS	8 BOS
9 MIN *	10 MIN	11 MIN	12 CLE	13 CLE	14 CLE	15 KC
16 KC	17 KC	18	19 PHO	20 PHO	21 PHO	22 CAL
23 CAL	24	25 OAK	26 OAK	27 OAK	28 SEA	29 SEA
30 SEA	31					

JUNE

S	M	T	W	TH	F	S
		1 MIL	2 MIL	3 MIL	4 KC	5 KC
6 DET *	7 DET	8 DET	9	10 MIL	11 MIL	12 MIL
13 PHO	14 PHO	15 TEX	16 TEX	17	18 SEA	19 SEA
20 SEA *	21 CAL **	22 CAL	23	24 DET	25 DET	26 TOR
27 TOR	28 TOR	29	30 CLE			

JULY

S	M	T	W	TH	F	S
				1 CLE	2 CLE	3 NY
4 NY *	5 NY	6	7 All-Star	8	9 BAL	10 BAL
11 BAL *	12 BOS	13 BOS	14 BOS	15 BAL	16 BAL	17 BAL
18 OAK *	19 OAK	20 OAK	21 BOS	22 BOS	23	24 MIN
25 MIN	26 MIN	27 CAL	28 CAL	29 CHI	30 CHI	31 CHI

AUGUST

S	M	T	W	TH	F	S
1 KC *	2 KC	3 KC	4	5 MIN	6 MIN	7 SEA
8 SEA *	9 SEA	10 TEX	11 TEX	12 TEX	13 KC	14 KC
15 KC	16	17 OAK	18 OAK	19 SEA	20 SEA	21 CAL
22 CAL	23 CAL	24	25 PHO	26 PHO	27 TEX	28 TEX
29 TEX *	30 NY	31 NY				

SEPTEMBER

S	M	T	W	TH	F	S
			1 TOR	2 TOR	3 CHI	4 CHI
5 DET *	6 DET *	7 DET	8	9 MIL	10 MIL	11 MIN
12 MIN	13 CHI	14 CHI	15 CHI	16	17 TOR	18 TOR
19 TOR *	20 MIL	21 MIL	22 MIL	23	24 CLE	25 CLE
26 CLE	27 BAL	28 BAL	29 BAL	30		

OCTOBER

S	M	T	W	TH	F	S
					1 BOS	2 BOS
3 BOS	4 NY	5 NY	6 NY			

☐ Home Games   ▨ Away Games
Home Starting Times: *Day Games . . . 2 P.M.
Night Games . . . 7:30 P.M.
**Twi-Night DH . . . 5:30 P.M.

Chapter 1

Detroit, April 7. It was no kind of night for baseball, that freeze-ass Wednesday in Tiger Stadium, with six thousand masochists shivering in the stands, but play they did, and it looked, to everyone's horror, as if it might go into extra innings, when Pardee caught a slider on the thin part of his bat and muscled it down the line to left. There was nothing pure about the stroke, he didn't get all of it, or even most of it, but somehow his chip shot carried just over the wall.

His hands stung around the bases, and burned as he blew on them, back in the clubhouse. "Good feeling?" he was asked.

"No way," he said. "It hurts."

The next night he went two-for-three, then two-for-two, with another homer and two walks. Darryl tore up whatever Detroit threw at him, then moved to Chicago and did the same. His hitting was contagious, and the Ballclub got out of the gate fast. They took two from the Tigers, three from the White Sox, then finally hit New York and dropped three to the Yanks.

Four of Fritz's starters were from the National League and had never played in Yankee Stadium before, so it was hardly surprising that they choked. There's a little bit of Yankee in every player who ever pulled on a stirruped sock. Cooperstown's the shrine, but New York is the altar of the baseball gods, the place they go when they're out for blood; and the Yankees, self-anointed high priests of the ritual, were already in late-season form. They liked the cold. It reminded them of October.

Hart did his best to take the poundings philosophically. April is the cruelest month, after all, a good time to get philosophical, and as good a time as any to get outclassed. His team had been acting cocky. If they thought it was going to be easy, then the Yanks had done them a favor, and if New York wanted to coast from now until the fall, that was OK with Fritz too.

Chapter 2

When Pauline found herself thinking back, she had to admit that Pardee had been amazing, but she'd always figured that he would be. He was a world class athlete, a pro, and if the sex was good—fine. She kept telling herself that's all it was.

When the Ballclub hit New York, she took him home to make love again, but although she tried to remain aloof this time, she quickly lost her detachment. Pauline had had sex before, she could lose its scent in an afternoon, or wash it off in the shower; but whatever this feeling was, it lingered. It crept up and made her skin glow at odd moments, like the last inning of the third game, when she stood up, stretching. Pauline stretched languorously, like a cat. She made quite an impression on the press box regulars, who exchanged glances, muttering, "Geez, gimme a break."

Women writers were one thing, they had their rights, but when they lost it like that in reveries—giving off auras that spread through the smoke, however thick—they were a menace. If she'd kept it up, she'd have had them howling.

One night together brought the whole thing back, with even more force now that she knew it had survived. Like it or not, her emotions were coming into play. She couldn't go through it and remain untouched.

She looked for signs that it was happening to him, but Pardee never said a word. Feelings never escaped his lips, only his eyes, which would call out to her every so often, without his even being aware of it. Darryl would go on as if nothing were wrong, but one flash of that sadness of his, striking home, could take her down for hours. If she asked what the matter was, he would shrug it off, but Pauline couldn't. The whole thing was upsetting her. Her estrogen got all out of whack.

She stopped in the locker room after the last game to pick up quotes for a profile on Goldhammer, the closest thing to a Big League intellectual since the late Moe Berg. Berg, a journeyman catcher from the slums of Newark, a student-athlete at Princeton, and later a coach for the Boston Red Sox; hobnobbed with Roosevelt, spied on Japan during a 1938 All-Star tour; donned worker's clothes during World War II, to walk into Germany seeking atomic secrets; and at one point was just a password away from assassinating Werner Heisenberg, whose uncertainty principle is still a metaphor for the age.

Goldhammer wasn't half the linguist Berg was, and he lacked his nerve, but he could outhit him any day of the week. He worked in a think tank during the off-season, and had scenarios for everything, from the End of the World to Goldhammer as Series Hero.

Pauline got him alone by his locker, to ask what it was like, being a Jew in the Big Leagues. "The Big Leagues are fine," said Goldhammer. "It's the minors where you have to watch it. Montgomery . . . Charlotte . . . fuck Charlotte," he told her, "and Jacksonville can kiss my ass." She looked up. "Go ahead, print it."

"Thanks," she said, "I will," then she moved on to ask Bernard about his knee.

"My knee?" he said, handing over a soft plastic tube filled with a clear yellowish liquid. "Here. Zey take zees out of him . . . two time zees winter." Pauline gagged and nearly dropped it.

"Sorry I asked." She handed it back.

"Not so good, eh? But now is better. *Ça va,* you know? Is OK . . . no pain." She knew he was lying, but she wrote it all down, then hurried into the manager's office, where Fritz was holding court, a beer in one hand, a cigarette in the other. He paused when she entered, to nod in recognition, so she nodded back and found a place against the wall, where she did her best to listen as the Kraut talked baseball, although her mind was on Pardee. Suddenly everything connected with the game, from the smell of tobacco and leather to the sound of laughter in a tiled room, had become an erotic signal for her; and the fact that he was back in the shower somewhere was distracting her beyond belief.

Chapter 3

Ballpark was located off U.S. 70; on the border of Bloom and Greenfield townships, Fairfield County; at the junction of Coonpath and Carroll Southern roads; about equidistant from Lithopolis and Lancaster; on an old spur of the Chesapeake and Ohio Railroad; north of where the Penn Central came up from Cincinnati, and the hills of south Ohio rolled down to West Virginia.

Situated on ten thousand acres of once-prime farmland, the site had a number of advantages. First, it was cheap. Second, it was less than thirty minutes from Columbus, whose Triple A team, the Clippers, had actually outdrawn the Oakland A's one year, with ten fewer games.

Raneer was forced to compensate the Yankees for moving the Clippers to Indiana, but he felt that it was worth it. Not only could Columbus almost support a team by itself, it was within a day's drive of a giant circle that took in the better part of twenty-one states, and was the locus of a proposed convention center that would draw in people from all over the country.

Lancaster, where he set up his temporary headquarters, was a quiet little town, the home of Anchor Hocking, the glass people. Raneer took over a lovely old house beside the Sherman mansion, above the Hocking River, then tore down the walls and gutted the place, to create office space for the dozens of contractors who would be handling Ballpark's construction.

He liked the way it looked that October morning in '74 when he climbed the hill at Beck's Nob to look out over the county, and he liked the way it felt among the God-fearing hard-working people of the region, but most of all, he liked the way it sounded. Ballpark, Ohio. Once he had said it, he couldn't get it out of his mind.

His first choice would have been a football team, but he said he couldn't bear the thought of competing with the Cowboys. If Fast Phil could have wound up in the owner's box in Irving, barking orders into a headset, crying, "You heard me, go for it! Get that left-footed Mexican outta there, an' run the goddamn ball!" it would have made his life; but denied that dream, he settled for baseball, since he didn't really care much where he played it.

He had planned to buy an existing franchise, but when that fell through, he convinced the Commissioner that he had so much to offer the game, including huge sums of cash for any of the owners whose toes he might wind up stepping on, that they ought to just make up a new one for him. After scouring the nation for a site, he opted for Ohio, and set out to construct his town with a zeal that would have shamed the Pharaohs. Like the Pharaohs, however, Raneer had labor problems. Major contracts had to be negotiated, and there were wildcat strikes when management proved recalcitrant, so they weren't quite ready for the season's opener, despite the fact that crews had been working around the clock for weeks, collecting time-and-a-half overtime and double time on Sundays.

With the cold weather continuing through April, hardhats almost outnumbered the fans for the first home stand, and Raneer was incensed. "Goddamn unions!" he cried. "A pack a' fuckin' thieves."

Phil was a bit behind the times when it came to labor relations. He was from Texas, and still thought unions were for busting . . . like horses, or heads. The workers flashed the peace sign, as he led a press tour under the scaffolding of the giant Ballpark Roller Coaster, a tubular steel loop-the-loop that would be far and away the largest in the world, if it ever got done.

Raneer scowled and gave them the finger. He had always gotten around the union problem by hiring teen-age girls. He gave them orange-and-white skirts and cute little argyle knee socks, which gave his burger joints the look of a Catholic school at recess, which was just the way he liked it.

"Unions," he snarled, to the writers who trailed him, "are bringin' this country down. Look at those assholes. You know what they're makin'? You call that work? Cost us four thousand jobs down in Fort Worth . . . closed down the stockyards, but what'd they care?"

By losing his sense of humor, he was blowing his cover as a good ol' boy, and exposing the robber baron lurking in his heart. Fast Phil, it seemed, was all for the working man, as long as he was working for somebody else.

The whole thing might have blown over if it hadn't been for the weather. Late-spring snowstorms kept the crowds under eight thousand for the first two home defeats against Baltimore, and attendance was equally poor for two out of three losses to Oakland, and a one-and-two series with Texas. By the end of the home stand, the Ballclub was 8–9, in fourth place, and Raneer, who really did think it would be easy after all the money he had spent, was looking for someone to blame. He called a press conference to shoot off his mouth, criticized his players for not really trying, then took off in a private jet to an outpost in Bermuda, to wait out the cold and think things through.

His Ballclub, however, was scheduled for Cleveland, and Cleveland is a steel town, and the people up there, fed up with Raneer's attitude, showed up en masse to harass his team through two more losses, which dropped them down to sixth.

Hart, surprisingly, took it in stride. When asked about Raneer, he said he knew what he was in for when he signed the dotted line. "As long as he keeps his hands off my team, he can say what he likes, you boys can write what you like, and the fans can yell what they like. It's all part of the game." Fritz excused himself to move through the clubhouse, slapping butts and encouraging his troops, but none of them had played together before, so there were no past loyalties to draw on; and when the team facade got stripped away, reporters in the room had a field day gathering quotes.

Among the few who stayed quiet through it all was Pardee. He wasn't the type to piss and moan, or go slinging his helmet, or denting the water cooler with his bat, he just kept to himself, blending in, making an occasional wisecrack that seemed all the funnier because it came from him.

The fact was that there was little in the game to upset him after what he'd been through before. He was in a different space from the men around him, and although some of them may have sensed that, no one made an issue of it. Most of his teammates had never done anything but play ball anyway, and wouldn't have been able to relate if they'd tried. They never asked about the war, or brought it up in passing; they figured it was better off forgotten. Even the press corps had let it drop, mentioning his background only when it dovetailed into some convenient, and often specious, hyperbole, and Pardee slipped into the relative obscurity (for a player of his stature) in which he felt most comfortable. He acquired a reputation for being rotten copy, and wore it like a mask.

Chapter 4

1

Thursday, May 14. The call came in to *Lifetimes* at ten. Pauline, who had spent the last hour drinking coffee and reading the paper, had just slipped a clean sheet into the typewriter when she grabbed the receiver, answering, "Yeah?"

"Pauline Reese? Mr. Bob Sylvester calling. One moment, please."

She took another sip and made a face. The coffee was cold, and the half-and-half had formed a little film along the top. "Miss Reese?" said a man's voice.

"Yes?"

"This is Bob Sylvester, NBC."

"Good morning, Mr. Sylvester, NBC, what can I do for you?"

"Are you free for lunch? I'd rather not talk about it over the phone."

"I think so." She knew perfectly well that she was.

"Good. Why don't we meet at the Four Seasons? Is that all right?"

"Fine with me."

"Good. Is one o'clock all right? I have a late meeting."

"Fine. I'm off to a slow start myself."

"Terrific. See you then." Click.

Pauline hung up and took another sip, forgetting how horrible the last one had been. "That certainly was efficient," she thought. "Bob Sylvester? Never heard of him." She had, however, heard of the Four Seasons and NBC, and hoped it was understood that lunch was on him.

Shrugging and turning back to her desk, Pauline put the phone call out of her mind. She was working on an update of Dominic Nucera's battle with the A's, the one in which the veteran outfielder claimed that he hated Oakland, couldn't stand their owner, and wanted to be back with his family in Chicago.

The problem was that when Pauline had stopped in Florida this past spring, she had heard through the grapevine that that wasn't the case at all. It seems old Dom had gotten involved in a kinky little triangle involving a woman and her daughter. When Mrs. Nucera got wind of the action, she let her hubby know that he could get his ass traded back to the Loop, where it would wind up in a sling, or find himself missing one wife, two kids, and half his earnings for the rest of his life.

The only trouble with that story was that Pauline couldn't write it. She had heard it in confidence, and owed it to her source to keep it quiet. She would have dropped the whole thing, but when Nucera became a Cubbie, she'd been ordered to write a feature that she knew was a pack of lies. That in itself was nothing new, her files were filled with untold tales, but this one was a shame, it was *so* choice.

Three hours later, the article was done. She checked her watch, yanked her copy from the rollers, and dropped it on the desk of her senior editor, Frank Sullivan; then rode down on the elevator, to catch a cab that got her to the restaurant just ten minutes late.

2

Pushing through the glass doors, she walked by the cloakroom to the stairway on her left, then climbed past the landing to the top, where she took a moment to catch her breath. The far wall was gray glass, striated and polarized, to let in an even light that would remain the same no matter what the weather outside. It was all very quiet, elegant, and airy. The gray light kept the place on an even keel.

Searching the room, she suddenly realized that she had no idea what this Sylvester fellow looked like. The voice had not suggested a face. She was about to approach the maître d' when he stepped up to her and said, "Miss Reese?"

"Yes."

"Mr. Sylvester is expecting you. Would you care to follow me?"

"Of course."

Heads turned when she crossed the room, but heads will turn almost anywhere. They'll turn when you pass through a Greyhound bus station at two in the morning, no matter what you look like, but the difference is that when you look like Pauline, they'll take a longer time turning back, and sometimes they'll whisper, and then other heads will turn in such a way that you know that what was said was, "Don't be too obvious, now . . . but over there—quick!"

At any rate, heads turned as she crossed the room, to a table located on the ground floor, back wall, center, where a young man rose to greet her.

"Pauline," he said, "I'm Bob Sylvester, NBC." There it was again, the corporate logo.

"Hi, Bob." She shook his hand.

"Please, sit down."

The maître d' helped her into a chair, then a waiter arrived to inquire about cocktails. Pauline looked at Sylvester's glass and said, "White wine." He smiled. She put up her guard.

He was not only young, but a little too good-looking, of a type that generally left her cold. He looked like one of those preppy guys who get recruited off their college campuses to pose in sweaters for the *Esquire* Fall Fashion Previews. Sylvester was no Ivy Leaguer, however, but a kid from the Midwest who'd been moved up from assistant program director of a small station in St. Louis to be aide-de-camp to Bernie Kleinfeldt, who had just deposed his own boss as head of NBC. Kleinfeldt had met him on a trip into the hinterlands, and was so impressed with his energy and judgment, not to mention the fact that at his tender age he presented no threat, that he made him a Baby Mogul, to help keep an eye on the old Young Turks.

"Baby Bob," they called him at first (the female executives and secretaries swooned), but now, after a year in office, he was "Hey, Bob, baby . . ." a force of his own, not too well known (this was before the *Newsweek* spread), but increasingly powerful. He was looking Pauline over in a way that let her know that he wasn't embarrassed to be caught doing it.

"Well," he said, "how's the newspaper business?"

"Fine, I guess. I work for a magazine."

"Right." He smiled and sipped his wine, and Pauline felt a twinge of resentment. When the waiter came with the menus, he said, "Alexis, I'm going to London in a few weeks . . . do you think Tom might suggest some restaurants?"

"Certainly, sir, I'll ask."

"Thank you." The waiter took off, as Pauline checked the fare, the rack of lamb, the lemon sole, the veal, and something called Graavlax.

"How are things at NBC?" she asked, just to be civil.

"Fine, Pauline, that's just what I wanted to talk about. I saw you on television last week . . ."

"You saw me? Impossible."

"Now, don't argue with me. I said I saw you, right? And I called you up today . . ."

"Yeah . . ."

"And I'm buying you lunch . . ."

"I'm glad to hear it."

"So then don't argue." The waiter returned to take their orders, and Pauline took the Graavlax. She would find out soon enough. "Now then," he said, "think hard. You were on television recently . . . and I've got the tapes to prove it. It was the first day of spring training, and you were—"

"Oh, God . . ."

"You were making something of a spectacle of yourself in a room full of naked men. Am I right?"

"Was that on up here?"

"It was brought to my attention."

"Is that why you called?"

"I *loved* it," he gushed, then the maître d' came up behind him, and he got terribly annoyed, saying, "What is it?"

"Alexis asked me to . . ."

"Oh, Tom, excuse me." He took a sheet of paper and looked it over quickly. Typewritten on five lines, it contained the names of the five finest eating establishments in England. "Excellent, thank you, that's just what I wanted."

"They are not in any order . . . you may choose from them equally, and please, mention my name."

"Wonderful. I'll tell you how they were." Tom bowed discreetly and withdrew from the table, as Sylvester smiled, but Pauline found his forbearance disgusting. He folded the list and put it in his pocket. "Where was I? Right . . . I saw you down in that locker room the other day . . ."

"Two months ago."

"And thought you were great. Fabulous. Now, baseball is dying, Pauline. Attendance is up, but ratings are down, and we've got to find a way to make Monday night work, since we're stuck with a two-year contract. I'm sure you've seen football on CBS, with three men and a woman? Well, I'd like a woman on baseball, too, only one who knows her stuff, and isn't just window dressing. What do you think?"

"Sounds fine. It's about time. Do I understand that you're considering me?"

"Not only that . . . I want you."

Poor choice of words. Pauline frowned. "I'm a writer," she said.

"Look, Pauline, you've been around, you have the respect of your peers, you know your sports and the players respond to you. What more could we ask? Broadcasters are writers, in a sense . . . they have to put features together, speak in whole sentences, think on their feet. Being able to write is no handicap."

"But—"

"Let me finish. Your voice is excellent, I've been checking it out, which is why I wanted to meet you . . . and you're certainly attractive enough, so . . ."

"Wait a minute. Slow down. How old are you?"

"Twenty-six."

"Well, listen, kiddo . . . I'm not sure you're on the level—"

"Take my word."

"—but I already have a job, and I've worked hard for it."

"You can keep it."

"Oh, yeah?"

"We only need you on Mondays, Pauline, and your work is due on Sunday night, right?"

"I still have to be there Monday morning."

"Most of the time, that won't even matter. You can get to Boston in an hour . . . but if you have to leave early, we'll work something out."

"You don't know my boss."

"Yes I do."

"What does that mean?"

"It means we'll fly you around, foot your bills, and send you to big games every week. It won't cost the magazine a penny, and it'll be worth millions to them in free publicity—we'll bill you as *Lifetimes'* Pauline Reese. Do you really think they'll mind?"

"You've already talked to them, haven't you? Before you talked to me."

"It doesn't matter, Pauline. Now, I've made you an offer."

"You have?"

"The job is yours if you want it. Do you have an agent?"

"A *what?*"

"You do have a lawyer, don't you? We're prepared to offer two thousand a game—that's standard—but if you wind up full-time, you'll make a lot more."

"Well, that's good."

Pauline tried to laugh it off, but Sylvester wasn't smiling. The money was real, and the offer was firm. Suddenly she was nervous. "I'll have to think it over."

"Naturally. But the season is already under way, so I'll need your answer within a week. OK?"

"Fine, Bob. And thanks . . . I'm overwhelmed."

"Well, I hope so."

Sylvester grinned, as the waiter served their meals, and Pauline shoveled up a forkful of Graavlax, which was some kind of salmon, marinated and broiled. Just her luck, it wasn't to her taste, but Sylvester was buying, and he'd found her price.

3

When she got home from work, she made it a point to turn on the tube and check out the talent. That had always been one of her favorite jokes, that they called the on-the-air newspeople *talent,* like a bunch of cheap hookers in a small town, by an Army base.

And now she was one of them. Not yet, of course, she didn't want to seem too eager, but despite the fact that it made her uneasy, all she could muster was a token defense. "First of all," she told herself, "you don't like TV, so obviously the whole thing comes down to money." Pauline liked to think that there was more to her career. She had set out to prove that a woman could write sports, but even when she succeeded, they said it came too easy—that because women sportswriters were suddenly in demand, she'd been able to skip up from a small paper on Long Island to a big-city spot on the staff of *Life-times*.

Her first job there was as a lowly reporter, something of a misnomer, for a reporter's task was to highlight with a yellow marker all the facts in the articles submitted by the writers, then get on the phone and check them out. Occasionally she'd feed in a fact of her own and get patted on the head, and although sufficient pats were cause for advancement, usually it took a year and a half, whereas Pauline became a writer in a record four months. She was good, of course, as were most of her fellow trainees, but the magazine wanted that female by-line.

It was hardly time to be moving on, she was still busting her buns to justify her luck, but . . . "Two thousand a night," she thought. Her colleagues might resent her, but if she turned it down, they would never speak to her again.

Her senior editor, Frank Sullivan, made it easy when she talked to him that afternoon. "As long as we get your material on time," he said, "I can't see a problem. If you miss a few Mondays it's no big deal, I'll assign the rewrites, or do 'em myself. I might do damage to some of your pretty little sentences, Pauline, but the fact is, they've been putting the squeeze on lately. The cost of paper's going up . . . production . . . and travel . . . we can't do things the way we used to—send out two writers with a whole team of photographers.

"I guess that's a bit before your time, but the point is, with the network paying *your* way, I can send somebody somewhere else. Our coverage will improve, and having you on TV has got to help sales—so basically we think it's a fine idea . . . and I think you'd be nuts to even consider saying no."

Pauline sat through the evening news, waiting for the sports, which opened with a clip on Phil Raneer, detailing more of his union-baiting, followed by an action close-up of Pardee, doubling to right. "Ain't that nice?" thought Pauline, smiling. "And Monday Night Baseball will cross his path maybe four, five times in the course of the year. I'll do it!" she decided, as if that were the reason. "Who wouldn't? And why the hell not?"

Flicking off the picture, which imploded into the void, she paused a moment to adjust her hair, in the dull reflection of the inert green glass. "Be careful now . . ." she warned herself, but it was too late. It had already begun.

4

30 Rockefeller Plaza, New York City. Ten minutes after walking in, she had a headache. Pauline was used to the clatter of the newsroom, but this was like a newsroom to the tenth power. AP, UPI, Reuters, and the local services occupied one corner, unattended, while a staff of thirty was scattered under klieg lights, for the newsroom was part of the set, and the cameras were on for one of those midmorning newsbreaks, the kind that give you a heart attack when they break in suddenly, as if it were the end of the world.

"Details at noon," said the anchor, smiling.

"Hold it . . . that's it," ordered the floor director, a black man in headphones, and the announcer's smile dissolved into a twitch. Pauline, although watching, had been warned not to stare. You were supposed to pretend you were working, or chatting casually, to make it look the way a newsroom was supposed to, and in this case actually did. Illusion blurring into reality.

There was a small TV on every desk, and most of them were on, tuned either to the game show that had resumed now that the newsbreak was over or to tape segments being edited in adjacent rooms. Digital readouts on the six-inch screens kept everyone aware of the passage of time, while high on the back wall, six color consoles were permanently tuned to the major local stations, so they could keep abreast of the competition. There was a crazed, insect intensity to the place, and a waxen pallor to the skin of some of these people that said that they had been in the racket too long.

Pauline was greeted by Bob Sylvester, who took her to the executive vice-president in charge of network sports, who led her in to the news director, who gave her to the executive producer, who dumped her on a writer for the fifty-cent tour. He took her around step by step, pointing out the typewriters with their half-inch letters, which made their copy look like captions to a child's coloring book. This was *not,* he assured her, a commentary on the mental age of the average viewer, but a means of producing a script large enough to be reflected upon the two-way glass hung directly in front of the cameras, so the newscasters could read their lines while looking into the lenses and the eyes of the home audience. Their last stop was over by the editing rooms, where reporters were sitting in and dictating their cuts to union technicians, who were the only ones allowed to actually touch the tapes shot earlier that day, on location, in the field.

Pauline had started out editing film at the age of twenty-three, fresh from Smith, when she fell in with a producer who did syndicated specials on over-the-hill sports legends. At the end of eight months she had had it with both him and the job, but the lore she picked up during that period had proved invaluable.

Scratch a male sportswriter and you'll probably find a guy who at one point figured that sports were what he liked most in the world, and were the only thing he really knew anything about, but he couldn't play them too well, so writing about them had to be the perfect way to make a living. Most of them outgrow that stage, but the original fallacy may inform their work, whereas women writers have a tendency to imply that the games they are covering are *not* the most important or fascinating things in the world, which is precisely what your sports fan does not want to hear. He already knows that, doesn't need to be told, and especially doesn't want another woman to remind him.

Pauline, however, through hard work and dedication, had lost just enough perspective to do the job right. A history major with a minor in English, she didn't start out with the games in her blood, but had cultivated the habit line score by line score for the past six years, so that by now she could nearly match the most obnoxious know-it-all twelve-year-old in the world, who everyone knows is the most feared fan of all.

This TV business was fairly straightforward, but the thing that kept Pauline from taking it too lightly was the way she felt after her two-hour tour. That headache of hers had climbed up her neck, and was twisting her forehead into a scowl. "These people are nuts," she thought. "They're media junkies. Their electronic threshold is so high that they can walk around in the midst of all this chaos and ignore it." She assumed that she would reach that state herself after a while, but the question remained—did she want to?

Chapter 5

1

There was no more war in Vietnam (go tell that to the Cambodians), and no reason yet to jump on the Iranians, so for a short time prior to the Bicentennial, popular resentment was focused on Raneer. It was nothing very serious, just something to do. A little beer, a lot of noise, and a rich man's team in a tailspin were all that were needed for the crowds to go home satisfied; and the Ballclub was suddenly the best draw in the game.

By the second week of a disastrous month of June they were dead last, 23–34, with a won-lost percentage of .402, two months in and ten games back; then they hit the road and dropped three to Milwaukee, two straight to Phoenix (the other new franchise), and a two-game miniseries to Texas.

Returning to Ballpark, they got a lukewarm reception from their carpetbagging fans, gave up trying to please anyone, finally got loose, and went out and bombed the Seattle Mariners 11–1, behind a four-hit performance by Fuller. More than a win, it was the end of a drought, and when they hit the clubhouse, they were ready to raise hell. Collins and Hunsicker grabbed the trainer, Artie Stutz, to give him what is known in certain circles as a "whirly," holding him upside down in a toilet bowl, then flushing it. Goldhammer and Leopold got into a vicious towel fight, raising welts on each other's flesh, then someone pushed Foster into Fuller, and the two men squared off in the center of the room.

The whole team gathered to cheer them on, as they sparred awhile, flicking their lefts, stopping just short of each other's faces. No one gave Fuller a chance at first, Foster was stronger and equally mean, but the tall skinny white man forced his way in, blocking, faking, and taking control. Finally defeated, and forced off balance, Foster lost his footing and slipped to the floor, where he stayed, out of breath, by the bench beside Pardee.

"That's it," he said. "I've had it."

"Come on, nigger," said Fuller, with a laugh. It was the familiar "nigger," the locker room "nigger," but the mood changed abruptly; and sensing it, Fuller got even more truculent. He was still pumped up from the game. "Get up," he said, "I ain't done with you yet," leaving the black man with two choices.

He could charge Fuller and tackle him, bang his head against a locker and beat the living shit out of him—risking, of course, the same thing in return—or shrug off the insult and defuse the situation, by turning to Pardee and saying, "How 'bout it?" shaking his head. "You gonna let him get away with that?" The message was obvious: Police your own.

Pardee wanted no part of it. He looked down, trying to ignore the whole thing, until the rest of his teammates started calling his name, before rushing in, grabbing him, and pushing him out to the center of the floor.

"Forget it, guys, I'm . . ."

"Bullshit!"

"Chickenshit!"

He tried to back away, as Fuller, still laughing, walked over and looked down from his full six feet four, saying, "Too small —throw him back."

"Bullshit, Fuller, he'll eat you up."

"How much?" came another voice.

"Twenty!"

"Fifty!" and they crowded in again.

"Ladeez an' gennlemen . . ." chimed Goldhammer, in a perfect nasal East Coast twang, "Tonight's main event is this heavyweight contest between the Champeen, from Piscataway, New Joisey . . . Frank 'The Brush Man' Fuller . . ."—boos . . . Fuller raised his fists and bowed—". . . and the challenger, from Dipshit, Louisiana . . . Darryl Pardee! Pardee. You boys know the rules of the—"

"Cram it, Goldhammer."

"Ding!" He pulled the cord and the shouts grew loud, as Darryl stood with his palms up, protesting. Fuller flicked a left that landed by his ear . . . and another . . . then finally, looking as though it was the last thing he wanted to do, Pardee raised his hands to defend himself.

Fuller was a pretty fair boxer, he had proved that with Foster. As a high school kid he had specialized in picking fights with football jocks and punching out their lights. He circled quickly, right to left, jabbing and feinting, as Pardee waited, moving just enough to keep his man before him. He did not like what was going on. Suddenly it was clear just how much he didn't like it.

Fuller led with his left again, trying to take advantage of his reach, but before he got his arm extended, Darryl met him with a chopping right that would have taken off his head. Pardee pursued, as Fuller panicked, backpedaling and flinching, completely overwhelmed, until he lashed out with an awkward overhand slap that struck Pardee across the eye.

"Whoa, hold it." Darryl dropped his hands, as Fuller hurried over, saying,

"Jesus, I'm sorry."

"Bullshit, Fuller," came a voice from the back.

"Forget it, Frank, you had to," said Pardee—and that put a chill in the Brush Man's heart.

"You sure you're OK?"

"It's nothin' . . . I was askin' for it."

Although something inside him felt good about that punch, Fuller knew that if the fight had been for real, he wouldn't even have been standing at that point. He immediately put some distance between them, as the rest of the men drifted off to the showers, relieved that the whole thing had gone no further. Darryl would wind up with a little shiner, but he could take it, and as for Fuller, he was damned lucky. Now that they'd seen what Pardee could do, not one of them would ever think of messing with him again.

2

The Ballclub split even through the rest of June, and returned home in fifth for the Fourth of July, to witness a monstrous fireworks display staged by Raneer to cap off a weekend of festivities, during which he dedicated the last of Ballpark's buildings, and made his peace with the labor movement by inviting a committee of union stewards to throw out the game balls.

The crowds were immense. Raneer had cost himself some income with the opposition he'd engendered early in the spring, but memories were mercifully short, and the lure of Ballpark was simply too great for people to bother holding a grudge.

All in all, the Bicentennial couldn't have been in better hands. Raneer provided flower-bedecked floats, marching bands, and a circus parade with elephants; and he rode atop the biggest one, in jangles and spurs, like a dimestore maharajah. Fast Phil was in heaven; he took America's birthday and made it his own.

The Ballclub came on to win three out of five, but it didn't seem to make much difference to the fans. No one had any real stake in this team, so the people could satisfy their deepest urges by rooting for the underdog, riding with the front-runner, or switching horses in midstream, as often as they liked. Everyone was a winner in Ballpark, Ohio, and if he wasn't, he had only himself to blame.

Chapter 6

1

July 7. Flying to Chicago for the All-Star game, Pauline banged out her thirty-ninth baseball story of the season, her obligatory number on fan violence:

> . . . it has gotten out of hand. Last week alone, Cleveland fans waylaid umpire Leon Schroeder after a game; New Yorkers crippled a Boston youth by throwing him down a flight of stairs; and Houston fans livened things up by attacking a group of Chicanos on a Job Corps outing.
>
> The owners won't even consider banning beer, but until they do, it might be wise to label those tickets: "Warning: Attendance at a Major League Ballgame May Be Hazardous to Your Health"; although we don't need a Surgeon General to tell us—the handwriting is on the wall. Either someone does something to clean up this disgraceful, widespread hooliganism, or somewhere, one of these days, someone is going to get killed.

She closed up her portable, thinking back to the Fourth, when the city got crazy. They were dropping their fireworks from apartment buildings, and throwing them, lit, into moving cabs. People didn't seem to care anymore, and the ballparks were just as bad as anyplace else. Pauline couldn't speak for everyone, but she had had enough. She landed in Chicago and rode down to the Hilton, where she sent in her copy through a telephone transmitter in the press room. It was a decent morning's work, but equally important, it had kept her mind off what was really making her nervous, her network debut.

They had decided to save her for the All-Star game, to break her in when the greatest number of people would be watching, and for several weeks had been touting a surprise. Pauline had tried to laugh off the hype, but she could feel herself tightening. When she met the production crew upon arrival, they gave her the thumbs-up sign, as if she were some kind of Allied hero, flying off to war.

She took half an hour to freshen up in her room, then they trotted her out for cocktails with the board-level executives of twenty major network sponsors, some of whom were celebrities in their own right, because of a new trend in advertising that had the bosses speaking for themselves. "I'm just a working stiff like you," they would imply, "so what if I make four hundred fifty grand a year?" Pauline wound up talking sports with them, and found herself laughing at remarks that in another context she would surely have found obnoxious. On her way to the ladies' room, after two hours of chit-chat and one too many gin and tonics, she bumped into Pardee, who was back from his workout.

"Sorry, Darryl, I have to . . . wait. . . ." She bolted through the door, leaving him standing there, rocking back and forth with a grim little smile. He had been looking for her all over the hotel. Pardee wasn't used to working so hard to see anybody.

Pauline walked out in a few minutes, with her makeup restored, feeling refreshed. "Hi, Darryl. Come on over here, I've only got a minute."

"Sorry to bother you."

"That's not what I meant. I wasn't allowed to tell anyone,

but I'm doing some TV now . . . handling the color for tomorrow's game.''

"Well, put in a good word for me.''

"I'd better not tell them what I really know . . . you'll have ten thousand women after you.''

"I'm only interested in one. At a time, that is. Say, I'm all done, so why don't we have dinner, take in a movie, and . . .''

"I was afraid this would happen. Darryl, I can't. I've got a meeting with the producers, then a taping that'll go on late.''

"Well, if you got work . . .''

"I'm so frustrated I could scream. And I'm so tired of talking about myself that . . . did I say that already?''

"Not to me.''

"I've been talking for so long I don't know *what* I'm saying.''

"Uh-huh.''

"I'm sorry, Darryl, believe me. Part of the reason I took this job was I thought I'd see you.''

"Well, here I am.''

"Don't remind me. Listen, it won't be so bad after tonight. They're making this into such a huge big deal, I can't believe it.'' She looked down the hall. "I have to get back, and soften up those business types, so they can hit them up for millions of bucks. Don't worry, the schedule worked out perfectly, I'll be in Ballpark all weekend, then in Boston Monday night. It'll be just like old times. All right?''

"I guess.''

"I know. I'm sorry, but I've got to run.'' She snuck a look and kissed him on the cheek, saying, "See you later,'' then took off down the hall in that unique, amazing, and ungainly gait that women achieve in high heels and tight skirts, their legs crossing as they go.

"Goddamn . . .'' said Pardee, watching as she pushed through the door into the conference room. "Shit.''

2

Engulfed by reporters down in the lobby, Darryl kept his answers simple. When asked if he liked something, his new team, for example, he said he liked it fine. As for the All-Star game, and the fact that the National League had beaten the American League nine years running: "Don't bother me at all," he told them. "It's an honor to be chosen, but one game never proved much about anything."

Excusing himself, he checked in at the desk, received his schedule for the morning's practice, then headed out the door. He had been hoping to see Pauline, but the one thing he was counting on was not being alone, so he raised his hand and flagged a cab to ride over to the lakeside suite of his old friend Lanette Kane.

Six feet tall and blond, with racehorse shanks and uptown thighs, Lanette was a secretary in the White Sox front office. The only woman in his life before he met Pauline, she had an open-door policy for Darryl, and more than once had thrown some sucker out—handed him his hat—when Pardee's plans had changed and he'd strolled up unannounced. Lanette had made it clear that he was welcome at her place anytime, and he took her at her word. She wasn't one to fake it; she didn't have to. If Lanette didn't want a man around, she disposed of him, but for some odd reason she felt comfortable with Darryl, he never crowded her, so he could come in and talk, come in and sleep, anything he wanted.

Darryl could content himself for hours, listening to her go on about this or that, watching as she held her long legs, curled up on the sofa. They got along so well, in fact, that they were both surprised that they hadn't ruined it by trying to take it further. Although he knew she had other lovers, coming into town as he did, for just a few nights whenever the schedule dictated, he was in no position to complain. He was simply grateful for her company and companionship, which were more than he had ever expected from a woman. He paid the cabbie, walked up, rang the buzzer, and rode up in the elevator to step into her arms, open and outstretched, as if she'd been waiting for him all along.

"You in?" he asked.

"What kind of question is that?"

They kissed in the hallway, their bodies flowing in all directions, then Lanette broke off when her phone began to ring, and Darryl followed her into the living room, to wait for fifteen minutes, until she finally came back to take him down with a technique that kept getting better as the years, and the night, wore on.

After a while, she led him to her room, drew the curtain, and put on the stereo. Time slowed. Cars rushed by outside. A mote floated in a shaft of light. The first song ended with a standard blues riff, descending to a scratch of vacant vinyl; then a harmonica blew the first notes of the next tune, with a sound between a moan and a gurgle, cuckoos and mourning doves. He slipped inside her with a liquid thrill, her brass bed vibrating like a reed.

They called out for dinner.

Much later, in early-morning light, he arose from the forest of arms and legs, the storm-blown, angular cascade. Outside, the birds were soggy. Dark smells issued from the damps. He kissed her, drew a frown, then stumbled over to kill the stereo, which had been revolving a stack of records, whose claim to Long Play had been laid to waste beside their lovemaking.

Lanette lay in a stupor, and Darryl let her sleep. He stole out the front door to walk back to his hotel, through streets still glistening from the predawn shower. Back in his room, he showered and changed, then went down to the coffee shop to eat and relax, before hopping a cab that took him to the stadium, where he slipped into something *really* comfortable—cool, baggy American League polyester—to warm up.

The Comiskey Park grounds crew wheeled out the batting

cage, as the field filled up with players and press. Limbering up with two bats, one in each hand, circumscribing large arcs around his shoulders and behind his back, Darryl watched a cadre of TV people, in the center of whom he found Pauline. The whole group moved from third to first, behind the backstop; but although, or precisely because, she said nothing, Pardee knew. She knew. "Radar," he thought, shaking his head, as he stepped in to take his swings. "How do they do it?"

Fortunately, he felt too good to let it bother him. His whole body was singing. A cluster of players were ragging him from behind, cracking jokes about "raising Kane," but he tuned them out to go to work on the ball. You only got ten swings on your first go-round, and he liked to make them count.

Chapter 7

1

Two nights after the All-Star game, Fritz confronted his fourth-place team to let them know that the honeymoon was over. "I've had it," said the Kraut. "Either you turn this thing around, or I am gonna make you so goddamn miserable, that . . . fuck it," he said, slamming out the door. "Just try me."

Team meetings are often a joke, but willing to do anything to pacify the Kraut, the men put aside their collective cool, put their hands in a circle, and took off with a hard-on and a high school rah-rah after the Orioles. With the score tied at zero in the bottom of the sixth, Fritz lit out, fuming, after a called third strike, went cheek to jowl with the home plate ump, ignored his warnings and got the heave-ho; then galvanized his dugout by going berserk, kicking dirt on the batboy and his on-deck batter, Collins, as Wedmar and Stokey hauled him from the field.

The Kraut just wanted his boys to know that the old man had it in him, and apparently the spectre of him waiting in his office was even more effective than him standing there, glowering; for the Ballclub hit for five in the bottom of the seventh, then rode in on Dellums' commanding three-hitter for a 7–0 win that would set the tone for the next eighty-odd games.

Afterward, Pauline bypassed Pardee to join the crowd at Dellums' locker. The North Dakota cowboy's Adam's apple bobbed up and down like a twig on a trout stream as he recounted his gem. "The fastball was *movin'*, I'll tell ya . . . didn't even need the slider . . . sometimes it dipped, sometimes it took off . . ." His hand veered right. "Ol' Puck did a *job* tonight . . . *heckuva* job."

Dellums' eyes filled with the Holy Light. "Don't even know what it was I was doin'. It's just like in basketball . . . as soon as it leaves your hand, that's it. You shoot . . . but it's the *Lord* who puts it in the hole." Praise be . . . the writers rejoiced. Dellums' leap, or rather jump shot, of faith had a mortal lock on four lines in the morning papers.

Bernard stopped singing and stepped out of the shower, jumping on each leg to clear his ears, his big balls slapping up against his thighs, as he tried to explain how he and Dellums had been in what he called "the Zone." "Ah, *oui* . . ." he said, drying off, "nights like zees, everysing is right. Ten strikeouts, yes? But five times I say bad pitch . . . bad pitch . . . an' he give me, an' zey swing, eh? Too much. Nobody hits tonight . . . very sharp . . . ah, *oui* . . ."

The big trapper faded out, his eyes glazed at the memory of those last two strikes, tearing off the corners of the plate, then he pulled on his clothes and hurried out the door, his mind set on the local fur trade. One by one the players left, and gradually the scene shifted to Pardee. Darryl had had a brilliant All-Star game, with two triples and a sensational throw to second on a sacrifice bunt, but the A.L. had managed to lose again, to make it an even decade without a win.

"How 'bout it, Pardee," said Loud, of Louisville. "You think you shculd have been MVP?"

"Doesn't really matter. Who got it?"

"Who was it? Griffin? What about the pressure? Are you getting tight?"

"Of course ya feel pressure . . . who'd pay money if there weren't any pressure? Pressure's good, it keeps ya awake. Our only problem was scorin' enough runs . . . but I can't worry, I'd rather win tonight."

"One more thing . . . what about the boos?" They had loved him in Chicago for six solid years, but now the crowd was hostile. The writers were silent, as Pardee thought it over.

"I guess I've got it comin', I ran out on 'em." He paused, then tried to shrug it off. "But basically, you always boo your opponents. Little kids love to boo. I know I did." Before long the quality of his answers declined, the writers dispersed, and Darryl dressed slowly, one sock at a time, sitting and staring at the next article of clothing as if it had to speak before he'd put it on. Pauline waited in the training room, then walked in and sat down beside him on the bench. "Well, Pee Wee," he said, looking over, "how'd it go?"

"How'd what go?"

"Chicago." Pardee laughed at his feeble joke, tied his laces, and started for the door.

"Don't talk to me about Chicago," said Pauline. "I don't have to ask how you did."

"Did what?" He pushed through into the night.

"I went down to your room, Darryl. I got done earlier than I thought, and went down at ten, then at eleven, and just because I'm a glutton for punishment, a few times more before I gave up at two. I couldn't sleep . . . you know what I mean?"

"I guess so."

"Well?"

"Well, what?" said Pardee. "She's an old friend."

"I don't care how old she is, Darryl."

"Fine."

They walked on, saying nothing, then, "Look," said Pardee, "you said you were busy. I knew her a long time before I ever knew you . . . and am I to understand that you're just sittin' home at night, back in New York?"

"As a matter of fact . . ."

"Not on my account, I hope."

"Look, Darryl, I wasn't in New York." And he wasn't into

arguing. If she wanted to stay angry, that was her prerogative. They continued on, until Pauline said, "I'm sorry I mentioned it. I hope you enjoyed yourself."

"I did," he answered, shaking his head, "but I can't understand it . . . I missed ya the whole time."

"Maybe you were looking in the wrong place." Pauline smiled briefly, then took his arm, trying to ignore the thought of his making love to another woman. They walked up the stairway into his suite, decorated in early-sixties office furniture, with a skinny-armed wooden couch with soft foam cushions, and several chairs supplied by the management. She dropped her purse, sat, and started chewing on her thumb. "I need a story," she said.

"What about the three-hitter? Not good enough?"

"I don't care about the game, Darryl. I need an angle, something to justify all this running around."

"Campbell's in love with Radivin . . . they can't take their eyes off each other out in the bullpen."

"You think that's funny?"

"I'm sorry I said it. C'mere. We'll talk about somethin' else."

Pauline crossed the room to join him on the sofa, trying to decide if he was good-looking or not. His features were regular, but his skin was rough and weathered. It was a face one had to see past, or get close to, to appreciate. Darryl slipped his hands beneath her arms, pressing his wrists against her breasts, but Pauline pulled back, saying, "Who was it?"

"Will you forget that?"

"Tell me, Darryl . . . I want to know. Does *she* know about *me?*" When he didn't answer, she started to leave.

"All right," he said, "it was Lanette Kane. You satisfied?"

"Was she better than me?" Pauline was standing in the center of the floor.

"Aw, look, Pauline . . ."

"No, you look, Darryl. I'll see you tomorrow."

Quickly she spun and went out the door, before she could tell if he made a move to stop her. Pauline had heard about the great Lanette, and now she felt like a country girl who has just discovered her sweetheart's initials carved with another's on a big oak tree. DP and LK, the sap was still running. *Dplk,* like a penny dropping into water. It was infantile to run out this way, but she knew what she was doing. She wanted to hurt Pardee, so she did so the only way she knew how—by making a fool of herself.

2

Pauline apologized at the ballpark the next morning, but Darryl acted as if nothing had happened. He'd seen all kinds of aberrant behavior, he made allowances for everyone. She wandered down the baseline during batting practice, to where Howie Needleman was leaning against the fence. "What's up?"

"Hiya, Pauline."

"How's it going?"

"Going? It goes." They turned to watch Goldhammer, stroking out line drives like topspin forehands.

"Ever play any ball yourself?"

"Sure," said Needleman. "I was in the Phillies chain. Actually, I was that round rubber thing at the bottom of the sink." He looked over, then back at the field. "You think I wouldn't rather be out there? Step in an' take battin' practice? You might laugh, Pauline, but I could hit BP as well as a lot of 'em."

Pauline checked him out. Needleman's body was nothing special, six one and a touch soft, but sometimes these guys could surprise you. He went on, "Now, that's just BP I'm talkin' about . . . 'cause I take one look at that other shit, an' forget it. Ever stand close when they're warmin' up? That's a stupid question."

"Not too close, Howie . . . I don't want any part of it."

"Hardest thing you can do, hit a baseball. You take golf, tennis . . . ya never miss. People forget why they quit. It's too damned hard, Pauline. Nobody *ever* quit baseball hittin' .453— go ask. They won't let 'em." A long silence as they watched some more. "That's why I'm here, an' they're all out there."

He pointed to the absence of fans in the stands. " 'Cause I'll tell ya . . . as much as I hate these guys sometimes, an' a lot of 'em are first-class jerks, I admire their guts. You won't catch me doin' it.''

Goldhammer was replaced by Bernard, who fouled the first pitch off his foot, and was utterly comical stamping out the pain. Pauline calculated that with the ball coming in at seventy-five miles an hour, and leaving the bat about twice as fast, it had to be doing a cool one-fifty when it crushed an instep, or landed on a toe. She tried to recall how many times she had seen someone take a shot like that and wind up getting a hit. Not often. Hardly ever in fact, which made a strong impression on her, which only proved how much she had to learn.

3

She spent the night with Darryl, trying to make amends. Pauline was acutely aware of his qualities as a lover, and if she wasn't too keen on sharing him, she had to admit there was enough to go around.

For all his power, however, he never acted as if he had something to prove. Pauline herself was the one who was pressing, competing with other women in her mind, trying to figure out what might make one woman a better lover than another. She knew that was a particularly male way of looking at it, but something about him was keeping her off balance—something was missing.

At first she assumed it was something in herself, that she wasn't doing, or wasn't doing right; for it certainly wasn't his passion that was lacking. Darryl made love singlemindedly, totally, as if it were the only thing going on in the world. He made love to her the way she had always wanted to be made love to, and though he frightened her at first, little by little she had learned to trust him, until she could abandon herself to him.

It was dawning on her, however, that apart from lovemaking, he initiated nothing, and never volunteered any personal information. Pauline was suddenly aware that she knew no more about him than she had back in March, although she did know quite a bit more about herself—more, in fact, than she might have wished. That meant her relationship with him was almost narcissistic, not that she was so preoccupied with herself, but because he had never been real to her, but was a reflection of the way she felt loving him, and watching from afar.

Their last night in Ballpark, he stepped out for a stroll, leaving Pauline in a shallow sleep from which she arose immediately, sensing him gone. She thought of putting on her clothes to follow, but the lights outside had a ghoulish air, and although it was warm, the air conditioning made the night seem uninviting, so she flicked on the TV, flicked it off, then slipped into his shirt to wander about the room, poking into drawers. She knew she had no business doing this, but prying was second nature to Pauline, and she was only looking to distract herself.

Slung over a chair in front of his desk was a lightweight sports coat, made of a synthetic fiber she would make it her business to cure him of, if she stuck around long enough. Flipping the lapel and feeling the material, she noticed a letter in the inside pocket, and as soon as Pauline saw the writing, she was certain it came from Lanette. The only thing that almost stopped her was her fear that the details might prove too intimate. She felt an intense, defeated, yet utterly sexual excitement, as she forced herself to get it over with, to withdraw the note from its hand-lettered envelope, and read:

> Dear American League All-Star:
> Practice for the morning of July the 7th is scheduled to begin at 10:15. It is suggested that . . .

She crumpled the paper, stashed it in the trash can, slipped from his shirt, and turned off the light. This thing with Lanette was driving her crazy. The sheets were cold, so she curled up tight, huddling from the chill, until Pardee came back about thirty minutes later, kissed her shoulder, and promptly fell asleep.

Chapter 8

1

Pauline had made a tactical error, booking her flight to Boston through NBC, which put her in first class. A mechanical problem just before takeoff gave her time to drop in on the rest of the writers, back in coach, but she sensed the resentment. These guys wrote every bit as well, but she was the one who'd had all the breaks. She could hang in all she wanted, but was not now, and never had been, one of the boys.

Part of the problem was that she was so good-looking that she couldn't help but put them off. Her smile just about paralyzed them, so they had to fight back by cracking jokes, which she picked up behind her on her way back to her seat. Trying to forget it, once the plane was airborne, she wound up in an excruciatingly dull conversation with a businessman who had seen her on the All-Star broadcast, then retreated into sleep as the plane swung east through Pennsylvania, and north across the Catskills to Massachusetts.

The delay in Columbus had set them back into rush hour, and the Callahan Tunnel, between Logan Airport and Boston proper, was filled with fumes that seeped through cooling systems, giving the air inside the buses a nauseating tang. Half an

hour later, through the dense city traffic, they pulled within
sight of Fenway Park, the opposite of those modern multipur-
pose stadiums, that dwarf the human scale, and take all the
wonder out of a pop fly, or even a Major League home run.

Fenway dwarfed nothing. Its old-fashioned light standards
just managed to poke their heads above the warehouse architecture of Kenmore Square, where it nestled. With the Big Green
Wall they called the Monster in left, more angles and corners
than pocket pool, and its much-maligned home run porch in
right, Fenway had character. It had real grass, real spit, and
wooden seats; and was a last hop on the whistlestop of Eastern
baseball, a throwback to the glory days of Ebbets Field, the
Polo Grounds, and Connie Mack Stadium (the old Shibe Park),
a place where a whole sports-crazy town lived and died with its
team.

Lately, however, a bad crowd was taking over, and as the
Ballpark buses neared the visitors' gate, they got showered with
rocks and bottles. Goldhammer, who had grown up on bedtime
stories of Nazi Germany the way other kids heard Winnie-the-
Pooh, jumped to his feet, screaming, "Cocksuckers! Morons!"
The Hammer had a way of taking these things personally. He
couldn't understand why everyone else was so calm.

"Siddown," yelled Hart.

Goldhammer dodged, as his window shattered. "Are you
nuts?"

"Goldhammer, sit!"

"Fuck you, Hart. I ain't no dog. This ain't no . . . I'm sitting,
boss. Hey, Alvarez, am I sitting?"

"Yo no comprendo."

"Repeat after me. I am sitting. Good. I am *standing . . .
whoa!"* Another rock struck the bus, and Goldhammer bounded
into the aisle.

"You're fined, Goldhammer, that's what you are. How do
you say *that* in Spanish?"

"But . . ." He sat.

"Fifty. Do I hear a hundred?"

Goldhammer slumped, hiding his grin. He knew that one tooth would cost him. Hart waited for the motor to shut off, as the heckling outside grew louder. "I want you outta here two at a time. Keep your bags in your outside hands, don't look left, an' don't look right, you got that? Goldhammer, keep yer mouth shut."

Hunsicker and Fuller lowered their shoulders and led their teammates onto the street. The crowd pressed in, but nothing happened, and inside the park it was quiet. Unaware of it at the time, the Ballclub had just crossed the tail end of an anti-busing demonstration, cruising the streets while waiting for the game. The summer before, a gang of white youths had beaten a black attorney on the steps of City Hall, using an American flag as a weapon. For two years there had been pitched battles over a tiny patch of beach, by a polluted inlet off the Boston Bay; and just two nights before this game, a black gang had murdered a machinist, driving home through Roxbury.

The whole town was divided into armed camps—Southie, the North End, Franklin Park, and Dorchester. No one knew what to do about it, and both sides felt that no one really cared, so they were taking matters into their own hands these days, and the situation was in danger of degenerating into the kind of endemic violence that plagued Northern Ireland.

Things had been particularly dangerous in Fenway, ever since a bloody brawl with the Yanks, four weeks back. The New York centerfielder, a black man, had sucker-punched the Boston shortstop, and local talk-show radio hosts were still playing it up and inflaming passions.

Fritz had no idea how bad it was when he sent out his pitchers to get in some running. They lined up in deep center, to take turns throwing passes and sprinting under the baseballs; then just as they were getting winded from the first few turns (nobody ever said a ballplayer had to be in *great* shape), lefty Dan Radivin caught a blow on the head.

Spun around, he fell to his knees, and reached for his temple, where he felt something wet, which he assumed was blood;

until he spotted two paper cups, compacted around a ball of ice, glistening on the grass. He started up after a group of fans, laughing and pointing at him, thirty rows back, until Zarino interceded and steered him out to left, where it would have taken a rifle to reach them.

Tension increased as the game approached, and even Hunsicker, who prided himself on giving autographs, was afraid to go near the rail. Over at third, a cluster of freaks were passing a joint and riding Pardee, but longhairs never bothered him. They never bothered anyone but themselves. He scooped and threw to Leopold, who relayed the ball to Hamilton, who brought it in to Bernard. Once more around the infield, and the Red Sox took over, the base paths were dragged, the lines were limed, and Fenway Park was full.

Sanchez took the mound for Boston, and retired the side as the home crowd cheered; but when Phillips left the dugout, the fans jumped all over him, and even though he'd heard it all his life, the Junkman let it get to him. Pumped up, he threw nothing but fastballs, walked two men and came in fat, and gave up a towering home run to rookie sensation Charlie Robb.

Bernard came over between innings to chew him out for shaking him off, Phillips told him, "Mind your own fuckin' business," and the two of them got into a heated argument over whose "fuckin' business" it was to call a ballgame, and had to be pulled apart. Lacy Stokey took Phillips firmly by the arm, to pull him aside for a little chat, but their voices quickly shot up an octave and a half, until all that could be heard was:

"Don't you loud-talk me!"

"Don't tell *me* what ta . . ."

"You wanna loud-talk, go back to your *mama!*" Then Stokey's voice descended to a reassuring murmur, and . . .

"I *know* . . ." said Phillips. "Uh-huh . . ." And finally, *"That's cool . . ."* and they did the secret handshake with a quarter twist, degree of difficulty two-point-five, and came back to the game.

Reassured, the Junkman set the Sox down through the third;

then Sanchez sailed a fastball over Leopold's head; the fans, who had been looking for a target, began to holler, and all kinds of hell broke out in right. A melee commenced when a young punk doused the row in front of him with beer, then decked the first guy who turned around to complain. When the victim's friends began to protest, the first guy's buddies came wading in, and the fight spread from row to row, until the cops had to seal off the entire section and let it die down of its own accord. People lit bonfires out in the bleachers, there were two more major brawls in left—a lot of shit hit the baseball fans over the next four innings, during which time, almost forgotten, the Ballclub cut Boston's lead to 3–2.

When his team came in for the top of the ninth, Hart yanked Bernard for the power-hitting Robinson. J.R. took his time, swinging his bats and calling for the pine tar; then stepped into the batter's box, but raised his hand and backed right out, claiming there was something in his eye. He took off his batting glove, fiddled around, then climbed back in, nodding that he was ready; then Sanchez stepped off the mound himself, establishing his own rhythm before returning, only to have Robinson call time again; at which point umpire Tony Farese—milking the moment for all it was worth—walked out in front of the plate, put his hands on his hips for the crowd to see, and waited for a nod from both men that they were ready to proceed.

The crowd roared, but the laughter died when Robinson met the first pitch and lined it into right; then Sanchez, seething, decided to dust off Leopold again, only this time Bobby was looking for the curve, so he held his ground until it was too late, and the pitch caught him flat on the helmet, with a loud plastic pop that sent him sprawling in the dirt.

He lay on the ground for a minute and a half, scaring his teammates to death; then got up slowly, saying he was fine, insisting on running for himself. The next batter, Collins, dropped a sacrifice bunt, to move the men along to second and third, then Martinez hit a chopper that dribbled into left, for a two-run single and a 4–3 lead.

Leopold crossed the plate with a smile, and went to slap hands with the on-deck batter, Alvarez, but a fan came out of nowhere and got there first, to blindside Bobby with a roundhouse right. It was absolutely sickening—the grin stayed on his face as he fell to his knees, then passed out cold.

Hunsicker rushed out and started whaling the fan, until the cops pulled him off, to finish the job themselves; then they carted off Leopold and completed the inning, with Alvarez fouling out and Pardee popping up.

Poor Boston was having a rough year. Not only did they have racial unrest, and their perennial problem with the Yankees, now they had a new nemesis in this Ballclub, which threatened their traditional stranglehold on second place. Hart yanked Phillips after the delay and brought on Radivin, who got his revenge for that ice bomb by blanking the Sox for his eleventh save.

A win was a win was a win, but with Hunsicker bandaging his knuckles, and Leopold, who had never regained consciousness, on his way to the hospital, the clubhouse was silent after the game. The press wanted reactions to the incident, a few reckless quotes to stir things up even more, but no one on the Ballclub said a word.

2

Pauline wrapped up her second network broadcast, but instead of escaping in the NBC limousine, she went down for comments to the Boston clubhouse. "What do you make of it?" she said to Boston's manager, Don Moran.

"Nothin' new. We been losin' a lotta close ones lately."

"Not the game. I'm talking about the fans."

"Nothin' new there, either. I remember"—she started to write—"one time, way back in the thirties, when a guy jumped Bill Klem. 'Course he creamed the little fucker. . . ."

"What about those brawls, out in the bleachers?"

"So what? Lookit England . . . what about South America?

'Fifty Killed at Soccer Game' . . . you read that all the time. It ain't so bad here. It comes an' goes.''

"Not so good, either, is it?"

"I wouldn't say that."

"What would you say?"

"I already said it." Moran took off, and the interview was over. Pauline had tried to put words in his mouth, and he knew it, so he split. She asked a few more questions, then walked out to find a cab, but was surrounded by a pack of teen-agers with megaphones, who screamed into her ears, while a city cop less than ten feet away did nothing.

A bit unnerved, she made it to her room, only to find Pardee, sparring in her mirror. "Look at you!" He turned. "The Great American Male!" she sneered, throwing her handbag onto a chair. All she wanted was a little peace, and now she had to deal with him—shadow boxing, for God's sake—looking so thick and stupid at that moment she wished he would dry up and disappear. "Wasn't that bad enough out there? You still have to go beating people up?"

"I'm not lookin' to go beat up anybody, but there's a lotta maniacs out there. What happened to Leopold ain't happenin' to me."

"How is he?"

"Stutz said he had a concussion."

"Beautiful. You know what concussion *means*, Pardee? It means he got hit in the head."

"Well, now they're sure." He feinted in the mirror.

"Do you mind? How'd you get in here?"

"How do you think?"

"Well, next time . . . ask."

"Ask what?"

"Maybe I need some time by myself. Maybe I want to come home and not find a goddamn war going on."

"Pardon me."

"Look, Darryl, I'm not in a very good mood. Suppose you just sleep in your room tonight . . . I'd like to be alone."

"Fine." He started for the door.

"I'll be leaving for New York tomorrow . . ." Her voice softened.

"Here's your key." He threw it just a bit too hard and struck her in the chest. The door would have slammed, but it was on one of those hydraulic hinges that let it close slowly, with a wheeze. Pauline sat on the edge of the bed, fingering the plastic, thinking, "What the hell is the matter with you? Why take it out on him?" Then, "Who cares? I don't have to answer for it, this is my room, my key . . . my life!"

Chapter 9

Lifetimes hit the newsstands Thursday with her article on fan violence, running side by side with a commentary on her network debut, which ended:

> Pauline Reese knows her sports, that much is clear from her work as a reporter, but as low person on the NBC totem pole, she may never get to prove it. They should either encourage her to open up, and hang herself if need be, or get her out of the booth, because the last thing we need is one more token anything . . . whether black, white, or woman.

"That's not fair!" she stormed up, waving Jack Smith's column in his face. "How can you write that?"

"What am I supposed to do? Lay off because you work here? You're acting like some idiot ballplayer who gets all pissed off because you write about a bad game. You weren't too hot, Pauline . . . OK? You wanna be a star? You'll have to learn to take it."

"I don't want to be anything," she said. "Forget it." She retreated to her office, a small square cubicle cluttered with mail, books sent her way in hopes of being mentioned, and notes piled up or pinned to the walls—the average spillover of a working writer—and put a sheet of paper into her machine, but was too angry to concentrate. "What does it matter what they write?" she thought. "Nobody reads that shit anyway." Missing out entirely on the irony of that notion, she went down to the street-level cafe, where she calmed down over a glass of iced tea.

"Take it easy," she told herself. "It wasn't so bad. Smith put the blame on NBC. It wasn't their fault, of course, but . . ." She chewed her ice cubes. Pauline wasn't used to being exposed like that. She liked to pile up her prose until she got it right, and could defend it, but a live mike was entirely different. Once the words came out, you couldn't haul them back. Intimidated by her lack of control, she had tried to play it cautious, thinking that her comments were terse and clipped, while in reality, they were tepid. If she was going to do color commentary, she realized, she would have to start being colorful.

Back upstairs, she stopped in to apologize. "I'll tell you, Pauline," said Smith, "that's a rough job. I can understand your being nervous. Those two guys have been in baseball all their lives . . . what the hell are you going to tell them that they don't already know? You can hear it in their voices."

"They were perfectly nice to me, Jack."

"Maybe. I only know what it sounded like . . . a little condescending."

"What would you do?"

"You want my honest opinion? Take the money and run. And don't pay attention to people like me. Go in there and have some fun. It's just a stinkin' ballgame, Pauline."

"You're right there."

"Of course I'm right. And don't compete. No one wants to hear a broad talk sports. Just keep it light and keep it rolling. Get in, get out . . . shock 'em a few times, and make 'em wonder what you'll say next. That's what I'd do."

"Never thought of it that way."

"I know. And you're not going to, right? Well, you asked me and I told you. No hard feelings?"

"Thanks, Jack. It could have been worse."

"You're darned right." He laughed. "Just kidding, Pauline. Remember now, this is show business. Break a leg."

"Yeah, you too." She rolled her eyes and walked back to her desk. What Smith said made sense. It might set the women's movement back twenty years, but there was no point fighting it. "At any rate," she thought, "I'd better get over my hangups on the subject, because if I'm upset by his little review, the network boys'll be stampeding."

Chapter 10

Now that they were playing the way they were supposed to, every old complaint about the way they'd been put together, every lament about Big Money in Sports, every emotional, yellow-journalistic trick ever used to hype a story was hauled out and set in print.

The results were predictable. There were death threats as the Ballclub hit Baltimore, and even though security was doubled for the first game, no one believed a few more cops around the infield would deter some psychopath in the upper deck. Laughing fans chanted, "Kill him . . . kill him . . ." every time Hunsicker, the target of those threats, took his place in right. Dutch said it didn't bother him, but he wore a plastic helmet, and kept glancing behind him, as if a big X were painted on his back.

Pardee was trotting in at the end of the third when for no apparent reason he stopped in his tracks. He called to trainer Artie Stutz, who came out running with a loud "What the fuck?" that carried into the seats.

"It's my leg."

"I can see that. Just wait . . . Leary! Hunsicker! Get over here!"

"What do you think it is?" said Pardee. "Cramps?"

"I assume it ain't no hamstring, 'cause you are not lyin' on the ground, screamin' wit' pain. You do feel pain, Pardee?"

"Yessir."

"That's nice. Come on, you two . . . carry him inside."

The men made a throne and Pardee hopped on, wincing as he held himself off their shoulders in a sort of modified iron cross. Leaving the field, they were met with boos, from a group of six men, five rows back.

"Fans," said Leary, shaking his head.

"Who, them? said Stutz. "They're not fans. Ten bucks says they got money on the game . . . obviously on us."

"How can you bet baseball?" asked Hunsicker. "Where's the percentage?"

"The precentage is wit' the bookies, dummy. Here. Put him here."

They started for the door, as Darryl mumbled, "Thanks," and the short, hirsute, billiard-bald trainer slapped him on the back, and said, "Drop your pants an' lie down, son . . . time for Golden Hands Stutz." Pardee obeyed. "Ever feel golden hands? They're cold, they're hard, an' they weigh a ton. Ask Midas. The king . . . not the muffler people."

"Ouch."

"Hurt?"

"You're killin' me."

Stutz dumped some wintergreen onto his palms, then rubbed it into Pardee's thigh. His hands blurred as he punched and pulled, up and down from the buttock to the knee. "Whattya think? Am I hired?" He stepped back to catch his breath.

"I'm goin' back."

"The hell you are," said Stutz, pushing him flat. "You go out now, you'll be out for a month. Lie down. Look at that thing." He bounced his finger on Pardee's thigh, then walked over to turn on the water leading into the whirlpool. Ten more minutes on the massive muscle, braided like steel cable, and he gave up, saying, "Shit. I can't do nothin'. Get in the tub, make it as hot as you can. I'll be back."

"Thanks, Artie . . . give me a hand." Darryl hobbled over to the horizontal bar, to pull himself up into the stainless-steel crucible. He entered slowly, glancing at the thermometer, which said 108 degrees, then the water started boiling, and Pardee freaked. Stutz had hit the switch. The motors gave off a high-pitched hum.

Listening to the roar, Darryl went under, into the sound of muffled turbines. When he rose, the dial said 114 degrees and rising, but Stutz had said, "Make it as hot as you can," and it didn't say Danger for another six degrees, so Pardee pulled himself up to a ledge, where only his legs were immersed, as the heat increased, taking his mind off his troubles.

These last few weeks, he had felt his body aging. He still had the speed, but now when he put out something extra, he paid the price. His knees were sore almost every third day, and little muscle pulls around the hips and groin slowed him off the field. He could run, but he couldn't walk. He'd had to duck so many pitches this past week, there was an imprint of his back pocket fossilized in the lime of Fenway Park.

The crowd's yowls pounded in his ears. A concrete throb split his head, and the loud hum continued. Darryl was just beginning to find out the meaning of the word *professional*. It meant you had to go out and play, when play was the last thing that entered into it. It meant you had to sacrifice your body, and not give a shit if you could run at all in ten years. Pardee had no sympathy for people who complained about playing hurt. His boyhood idol, Mickey Mantle, spent most of his career with his legs taped ankle to hip. When asked years later if he played any tennis, Mantle replied, "Tennis? If I could play tennis, I'd still be playing baseball."

The hot water was making him drowsy, when Stutz returned to cut the switch and chase him out. Trainers don't like it when people fall asleep on them. The last guy who fell asleep on Artie was a prizefighter who never woke up. That taught him a lesson —and now he was passing on some of his hard-earned wisdom.

"You're gettin' old, Pardee. You're gettin' like me. Ya think I didn't have a body like a Greek god? They used ta fall down on their *knees* for me, but then I got old . . . an' now look at me. Gettin' old, that's all. Go home, an' get some rest. Yer off tomorrow . . . I'm puttin' you on report.''

"But . . ."

"Get out. I got all them other prima donnas due here any second. I want you in that whirlpool at least three times tomorrow, twenty minutes at a shot. And you're not playin' . . . you got that?''

"Yeah, Artie, but . . ."

"Don't butt me, you goat, get goin'. Little bit a' rest, you'll be as good as new.''

Darryl lay awake most of the night, with an intense throbbing in his legs, hips, and head. He called room service for aspirin, which did nothing; then at three A.M. walked down the hall to bang on Danny Leary's door. Leary was bitching when he opened it, but one look at Pardee and he got real quiet, real fast.

"Can't sleep."

"The leg?''

He nodded. "You got somethin' I could take?''

"Are you kidding? I got Darvon, codeine, Percodan, Valium . . ."

"Stutz says I'm off tomorrow. Give me somethin' that works.''

Tiny Tim went back to fumble in his satchel. "Here. One a' these'll do ya.''

Pardee grunted and returned to his room. He looked down at the three pills Leary had given him, and swallowed two. The sleep they induced was deep and troubled, drugged and unnatural. His mind shrunk to a tiny dot in the corner of the room. The visions of his dream grew more and more disturbing, until he found himself watching Pauline, her face suffused with pleasure, being stroked by hands that were not his own.

PART THREE

The Truth, Not the Whole Truth, But Something Like the Truth

Chapter 1

1

After Boston, the crash. Poor Pauline was lonely. It was like being thirsty in the middle of the sea, ironic, but thirsty nonetheless. Her job, which kept her busy all weekend, isolated her enough to begin with, but combine it with a sports beat that had her working night games, and her social life was a shambles. The one thing she had going was her affair with Pardee, and that only upset her. She kept wondering what made her stay with it, and the answers she came up with bothered her. Her life was hard enough when she kept it running smoothly, but seeing him, and then leaving, kept plunging her into depression. She realized that she had sent him away in Boston, just to establish some measure of control. "You're leaving tomorrow, so get him out now," her heart was crying as he slammed out the door. "I can't stand it. I'd rather be alone."

Pauline wondered if this was her fate, the price she had to pay if she wanted to make it, and once again she retreated into work. Down at the office on Thursday, July 22, a copy boy stopped by her desk with a clipping:

> BALLPARK, Ohio, July 21—Seven members of
> his front office staff were fired by Ballpark President

Phil Raneer today, in what sources described as "an angry fit." A spokesman for Mr. Raneer had no comment.

She dialed Ohio. "Hello, Howie? This is Pauline Reese."

"Hiya, Pauline . . . what can I do ya for?"

"Nothing, just talk. I'm looking for a 'reliable source.' "

Needleman laughed. Talk was not nothing. In his line of work, talk was everything. Just talk? Talk was Howie's whole ballgame. "You got it," he said. "Talk . . . ask."

"What's with Raneer?"

"You tell me."

"It says here he had a violent, no, an 'angry fit.' "

"Right. Angry, but not violent. More like a temper tantrum, from what I hear. Took all his toys an' went home."

"Why?"

"How do you figure a guy like that? We take three straight from Oakland, big crowds, no problems . . . then he walks in late last night an' fires half the office."

"There must have been a reason."

"Tell that to them. You know how hard those people work? For what? Sixteen grand, an' the honor a' bein' in the Big Leagues?" He coughed. "I'm tellin' ya . . . if I had any brains I'd take off, too. If I was here yesterday, I'd be gone already. The guy says one thing one minute, another the next . . . you do what he tells you, then he blames you for it."

"That bad?"

"You cannot believe the aggravation."

"Was he always like this?"

"He was nuts, but not like this. It's goin' to his head."

"I just wanted to see if the report was true."

"It's true all right, but don't use my name."

"Of course not. Like I said . . . 'a reliable source.' "

"Better not, he might wise up. How about 'an informed source'? That could be anybody."

"All right, then . . . 'an informed source.' I appreciate your talking to me."

"I'll make a note a' that." Needleman was the favor man, the tit-for-tat man, the *quid pro quo* pro. Pauline had never hit him up, but now that she had, he was ready with the tat.

"One more time . . . do you have any idea what's bugging him?"

"When you're that rich, you don't need a reason. Raneer is Raneer, that's all I know."

"How's Hart?"

"Fritz? Fritz is fine. Anything but baseball and he'd be dangerous."

"And Pardee?" She did her best to sound casual.

"Lousy. Just ain't hittin'. Hurt his leg back in Baltimore, but who knows? He'll snap out of it. I ain't worried about *him.*"

"What does worry you?"

"You got a week? My PR man got hit in that purge, we got three days in Minnesota, then right back here, then two weeks on the road out west. Wanna come along? I'll teach ya the ropes."

"You'll be all right. Especially in Minnesota."

"Whatta you know about Minnesota?"

"My lips are sealed. Thanks for the information. Knock yourself out."

"You too, doll. Talk to ya later." He hung up, and Pauline tapped her pencil, devising a headline . . . *Raneer on Rampage: One More Egomaniac in the Big Leagues.* Firing an office staff that way was the moral equivalent of beating your wife. It happened when you could no longer stand the looks in their eyes, as if they could see right through you. One thing for certain, if Needleman didn't know what the problem was, no one would, at least no one she knew, so she had to move on to something else.

She thought about calling Pardee to apologize, but Needleman had said that he wasn't hitting, and he was hard enough to talk to when he was in a good mood; so she placed a call to Raneer's office, to see if she could get through. A secretary took her name, then said he wasn't in, but ten minutes later her phone lit up and Pauline answered, "Hello?"

"Pauline Reese? This is Phil Raneer. They said you called."

"Why, yes . . ."

"Somethin' the matter? What's the story?"

"That's what I wanted to know. What happened with your people out there?"

"What people?"

"The ones you fired."

"Weren't workin' out. Simple as that. Sometimes you just have to shake things up."

"Did anybody do anything in particular?"

"I'm not gonna go bad-mouth 'em after I fired 'em . . . let's just say we had a difference of opinion."

"You and seven people?"

"Seven people . . . seven hundred . . . don't matter to me, this ain't no vote. I'm runnin' a business here. You try an' run one, you'll fire people too. Anything else?"

"I don't know. How are things out there otherwise? Happy with your team?"

"What are they, in third?"

"They've been playing good ball."

"Good ain't good enough. I'm payin' 'em to win."

"You're a tough man to please."

"That depends. Some things I'm real easy. Anything else?"

"I guess not . . . but thanks for calling."

"You bet. Anytime."

Pauline sat and stared out the window, irritated with herself for not having pushed him. She was so surprised to hear from the guy that she never quite got her questions together. Her only solace came from the fact that she knew he would never have admitted being wrong. She worked through the afternoon, seeking meaningful statistics in a week's worth of box scores, and was sitting back with the *Sporting News* just before quitting time when the phone rang again.

"Pauline Reese?" asked a woman's voice.

"Yes."

"Mr. Sylvester calling. One moment please." Pauline hadn't

heard from Sylvester in a while, but she had a hunch what this call would be about, so she sat up quickly and ran through her arguments.

"First of all," she would tell him, "Cosell got bad reviews, but he always got good ratings. The bottom line was viewers, and the Nielsens were up (not much, of course, but a point was still a point). Second of all," she would explain, "some of the criticism is probably justified . . . and here's what I propose . . . " which is where he came on, saying:

"Hi, Pauline. Am I interrupting?"

"Not really. I was just about to leave."

"Good. There's something I have to—"

"Listen, Bob . . ." But she lost her nerve and said, "Never mind . . . go ahead."

"I've been thinking, Pauline, that asking you to break in with your comments is putting everyone in a funny position. It's almost as if you're trying to force yourself on the situation. Not that it's *your* fault, but that's the way it works."

"So?" The ax flashed at the top of its arc.

"So what I'm thinking is . . . what if we reversed things and let you take care of the play-by-play? Then they could interrupt *you* with *their* comments. See what I mean?"

"Not really."

"I don't want to sound patronizing, but it's all a matter of the proper roles. You represent the women out there, whose knowledge may be vague . . . and they represent all the guys in the audience, who think they know everything. You stick to details, describing what you see . . . and they supply the expertise. What do you think?"

"I don't know."

"I know what you're thinking."

"You do?"

"You think I'm giving up on you. Well, believe me, I'm sure you could become a perfectly competent 'color person'—that sounds like you're black—and so what? If we do what *I'm* suggesting, we'll be doing something that's never been done—

taking the most basic part of the broadcast and making it all brand-new. And your salary'll go up a thousand a week.''

She took the phone away and looked at it, then, "Well . . . if you put it that way . . .''

Sylvester laughed. "You writers are great, you're all alike. You talk about 'journalistic integrity,' but dangle a dollar bill out there, and . . . you like the idea, Pauline?'' He paused. "I had a feeling you would.''

2

Her debut came on Monday, July 26, during an otherwise per-fectly boring game between the Dodgers and Mets. The first time she found herself intoning, "Here comes the windup . . . the pitch . . .'' she got a strange case of *déjà vu,* and it turned out she was a natural. She knew when to keep silent, to let the moment speak for itself, and parceled out questions adeptly, with an innocence that kept her partners, Lee Letts and Dick Donovan, fully engaged.

That Pauline did a good job, however, was beside the point. Like Dr. Johnson's talking dog, it wasn't what she said or how she said it that mattered, but the mere fact that she was saying it at all. The phone lines were jammed at NBC, with violent opinions about equally divided, and the controversy that had always served Monday Night Football was now a part of base-ball too. Sylvester was exultant.

He invited the whole crew out for drinks, then Pauline re-turned in a cab to her apartment, but was too keyed up to sleep. The liquor in her bloodstream, combined with the cigarettes she had smoked out of sheer extravagance, had her heart thumping. The apartment was stuffy and much too still, and slowly that letdown she'd been fighting since Boston came creeping up again.

She looked down on the cabs and cars that cruised their way uptown on Third, wishing that they would go away and leave her in peace—just her and her apartment building, out on some desert island. "Stupid," she thought, turning on the air conditioner, to drown out the sounds. "Now what? A little music? *Eine Kleine Nachtmusik?* Keep it low, now . . . wouldn't want to bother the neighbors . . ."

She made a face and flipped on the radio, spun it through an ocean of bad rock-and-roll, then settled on static and turned it off. There was a car crash several blocks away, and sirens came whining down the street. Several floors above, those neighbors of hers were fighting.

"I don't care!" he shouted.

"Of course you don't, that's just the point!"

Pauline sat on the edge of her sofa, staring across the half-dark living room, as patterns of the street reflections crawled across the walls. "Big star," she said out loud. "Big deal."

Chapter 2

Right when they needed it, Hogan got hot. Hit three homers in five games, and the Kraut thought, "Oh, no, here he goes," fully expecting him to start flailing away, shooting for the walls on every pitch, but the amazing thing is that he *stayed* hot, and the Ballclub managed to get by Minnesota, on his next two homers and a game-winning double.

"See that?" he said, after crossing the plate. "Encourage your power to hit away. Never give up your power, Fritz . . . I been tellin' ya all along. Maybe *you* shoulda tried it. It sure could'na hurt *your* career."

He doubled over, in hysterics, as the Kraut thought, "Keep laughin', ya little prick . . . I love it when they laugh," and he made it his business to be *right there*, every time that Hogan connected.

"See that, Fritz?" Hart would shake his head. "Ya see that? An' I ain't even swingin' hard."

"Like hell," thought the Kraut, "but enjoy it while you can. I sure am. Keep talkin', ya little asshole . . . just keep talkin'. . . ."

Thank God for Hogan. He wrote it on the walls. Every time the reporters asked, he said the same thing, "Thank God for

Hogan," and when they pressed him about his other players, he'd say, "What do *you* think about Hunsicker? Hunsicker's hurt. I told you that. He's got a bone bruise, it might take weeks. *Yes,* it's from the fight in Boston. He had his thumb inside his fist. How the hell do I know? Bench him? How can you bench him?"

"And Pardee?" they would ask.

"He's fine. He'll be all right." But the Kraut had his doubts. Pardee seemed distracted. Gowdy drilled him in the cage, saying, "Bat speed, bat speed . . ." but it just wasn't there. He had an eight-game average of .151, but Hart wouldn't tamper with a winning lineup, so he sent up the Dutch Man, bad digit and all, and put up with Pardee's slow rollers to the mound. A star's not hitting could so occupy an opposing pitcher that he'd let down somewhere else. He'd be making the big man look awful—it was something to tell his grandchildren—while everyone else was trashing him.

Hunsicker would eventually play out of his pain, and although Pardee was fighting himself, Hart had been around long enough to know that it happened to the best of them. Pardee was Pardee, but "a slump is a slump is a slump," and that's what Fritz recited to reporters. "You boys wanna talk about it? Go see Ray, my resident expert. I'm the home run coach."

Gowdy welcomed the writers to his corner, threw his leg on the bench, and started to expound. "It's a slump. You know what a slump is? It's like not gettin' laid. It's OK at first, but then you start to wonder . . . you get all bottled up an' somethin' goes sour. When you're hot, you're hot, there's nothin' like it, but once it stops—it's an awful feelin', an' the sad thing is, it just gets worse, an' tellin' yourself not to worry's like sayin', 'Don't be jealous'—it ain't that easy." Gowdy laughed. He brought out a corncob pipe and tamped it with his thumb.

"Now the worst kinda slump is when a guy's not gettin' laid, while his wife is." He lit the pipe and drew on it. "We had this one boy could not hit on the road. I went nuts tryin' to figure it out, till I took a look at the Mrs. You think these boys don't get to thinkin'? Half of 'em are scared ta death—they know what *they're* doin' out on the road. You take that Mrs. Gomez, travels with the Braves. Think that's *her* idea? You print that, Franklin, I'll wring your neck."

"You're supposed to warn us *before* you say it, not after."

"Try me."

"Jesus Christ, Ray, you come up with one good quote a year, and you won't even let us use it. What the hell good are you?" Gowdy took his leg down. "All right. That's enough."

"Come on, Ray, you haven't said a thing. What about Pardee?"

"You go ask him. I ain't gonna psychoanalyze the dude. Hey, Pardee! Franklin wants a word with you."

Darryl ducked into the players' lounge and shut the door, as Fritz, who had been listening, returned to his office to size up the rotation.

Dellums was throwing hard after an erratic start, and Leary looked like he might just parlay that goofy off-speed stuff of his into seventeen-eighteen wins. Pitching them back-to-back, fast-slow, or slow-fast could really screw up an opponent's timing, and the same went for Fuller and Phillips, although right now the Junkman had a spasm in his back. "Have to go with Turkel this week, an' if he don't work out, Reed."

Down in the bullpen, pitching coaches Wedmar and James were using Lopez and Zarino on a daily basis, while letting the great one, Cleighton R. Foster, stew. He branded them racists and bitched to the press, but that's the way they wanted him, well rested and ornery. Foster wouldn't admit it, but he had a way of fading late, so they used him now about once a week, and planned to crank him up in August, in time to point him at the rest of the league.

"Just stay close to New York," thought Hart, "and the arms'll win it in September." The Ballclub, meanwhile, was picking up ground at a rate of about a half game per week, so a grateful Fritz got down on his knees and prayed, "Our Father, Who art in Heaven, *hallowed* be thy name . . ." He moved his lips and said all the words—the Kraut was taking no chances.

Chapter 3

1

That conversation with Raneer kept rattling in her mind. It wasn't so unusual to get called back by anyone as publicity-hungry as he was, but the fact that she hadn't gotten anything out of him got her thinking not only of the quantity but the quality of the reportage he'd inspired, including her own interview-article in which he had talked, and she, except for a few minor parenthetical digs, had dutifully recorded.

Scheduled for a Rangers broadcast in Arlington, a half hour from his hometown of Fort Worth, she hit the files, which covered one whole wall of a large reference room, where she pushed a button and racks of stacks rotated up and out of sight, until she came to what she wanted in a pull-out drawer marked *Raneer, Phil*. Although she found volumes of clippings from *Lifetimes, Time, Newsweek, Fortune,* the *Wall Street Journal,* and the *New York Times*—*Lifetimes* priding itself on its extensive library system (this before the computer revolution that would render its wonders obsolete)—there was basically nothing but the same old hype.

Raneer was such good copy, she realized, that almost every story was composed of his quotes. "Damned smart," she had to admit, closing the box and putting it back. "He never repeats himself, gives us all something new, puts up a great big target to shoot at, but meanwhile he's laughing, off to the side." Even her cursory reading had revealed the fact that the book on Raneer had yet to be written.

2

August 2. It was summertime everywhere, but as soon as Pauline stepped out of the plane, she knew she was in Texas. An incredible heat wave was scorching the state, threatening to turn it into a brand-new dust bowl, which is why she was teamed with Gordon L. White, a staff photographer sent out to get shots of heat lines shimmering over the highways, and cattle dying slowly with their flesh baked into their bones.

White went nuts at JFK to keep his cameras from being X-rayed, and escaped arrest at the very last moment only by faking a seizure. He calmed down once past the security guards, telling Pauline he did that several times a month, to keep those "ignorant asshole searchers," as he called them, from exposing his precious film to radiation that they persisted in claiming was harmless, despite documented proof, which he carried in his wallet, to the contrary.

"Bad enough they make you sterile," griped White down the aisle of the plane, "and bad enough they hassle you over hand luggage," he added, hoisting his bag into the overhead rack in blithe defiance of federal regulations, "but they will *not* get at my images." The man didn't take pictures, he took images. He leaned back in his seat, talking with his hands, and listening with his eyes, holding forth about photographing nudes and Third World prostitutes, and drew more ears up and down the aisle of that plane than an E. F. Hutton rep at a convention of advertising firms.

White wore square, wire-rimmed glasses and a light khaki colonialist suit that would have made him look out of place anywhere. A Pulitzer Prize winner, for war photos taken at the age of twenty-one, he was now a dissolute twenty-eight, the type whose idea of heaven was three weeks in some foreign port, blasted on contraband. Unprepossessing to the point of invisibility, he had a knack for finding trouble, squeezing off his shots, then escaping while others had their cameras smashed by zealots. Pauline eyed him in the adjacent seat, wondering how he'd made enough of an impression at *Lifetimes,* where camera people queue up by the thousands, to get his chance in the first place. Obviously he knew his stuff, and was ruthless. They're shooting the President? You shoot them shooting the President. Then duck.

Met by a network limousine, which took her to the hotel, she had half an hour to shower before the evening's game. Pauline had just finished blowing dry her hair, and was applying her makeup, thicker than usual to stand up to the lights, when the NBC gofer knocked on her door.

"Miss Reese?"

"Coming."

"We're due in twenty minutes."

"Jesus Christ, I'm coming, I'm coming," she muttered, hooking her bra, then, sweetly, "Be right there." Grabbing her rosters and tucking in her shirt, she switched off the light and hit the hallway running.

The driver sped her down to the ballpark, where she threw off her fatigue and stepped into the booth. The producers filled her in on the format, then she put on her headphones and took a place before the monitors, clearing her throat. "Good evening, sports fans, this is Pauline Reese for Dick Donovan and Lee Letts, welcoming you to Monday Night Baseball for tonight's game, featuring the Texas Rangers against the Phoenix Sunbirds, *live,* from Arlington, Texas." It took her three times to get the rhythm right, then the red light went on, her director nodded, and the rest of the evening took care of itself. Afterward she chatted with the local reporters, who had hung around to meet her, then she returned to her hotel to fall asleep around one.

3

Seven-thirty A.M., Tuesday, August 3. The sun coming in from an unaccustomed angle startled her, leaving her wondering where she was. Pauline got up gingerly from the tangled sheets, showered again, and combed out her hair. She read the morning papers at breakfast, then rented a car to drive from her hotel in Arlington, a bedroom community just south of the airport, to check out the other half of that twin star of Texas known as Dallas/Fort Worth.

This was the best part of her job—to wake up, paid, in a strange location, and go out on a foray on the flimsiest of pretexts, with no locker room smells to contend with, and no one to care whether she found anything or not. She spoke a few words into her pocket recorder, played them back to make sure it was working, then held it in one hand, with her other on the wheel, as she cruised through Bedford and Euless counties, where the six-lane freeway was surrounded by plains.

Southwest on 121, the horizon was broken only by logos thrust on sticks, high above the fields, proclaiming *Gulf, Wendy's, McDonald's, Shell, Exxon, Pizza Hut, Taco Plaza,* and *Burger King*. This was the country that had spawned Phil Raneer—it was like following the Ganges back to its source.

Suddenly, in the midst of this wasteland, a skyline appeared, dead ahead, like a backdrop from a movie about Texas in the thirties. It had a curiously unconnected feeling, she found, rising as it did out of a countryside that no longer featured the vast herds and feed lots of the cattle industry from which it had grown. Dictating notes and observations all the while, she skirted the city, got off at Rosedale, and made a short loop through the south side of town, where tall trees lined the streets, old black men guarded the stoops, and most of the houses had front and back yards, no matter how many rusty iceboxes and wringer washing machines they contained.

Detouring north, she took the main drag past the modern Hilton and Convention Center, into a hodgepodge of old-time architecture, including the Blackstone and Hotel Commercial, and the Tarrant County Courthouse, 1893, a stolid brownstone with copper-roofed wings, crowned by the tower with its Lone Star and clock.

She checked out the lawyers in their gray felt hats and alligator boots, their string ties and business suits, then continued north on Business 81, under the power lines of Texas Electric, through an area filled with auto-parts stores and beer distributors, to the stockyards over on Exchange Avenue, where the town turned touristic.

Once these alleys echoed with the cries of steers, being prodded through chutes on their way to the hook. Armour and Swift ran the town back then, until patterns of distribution changed, the unions came in (when in doubt, blame the unions), and the notion of a slaughterhouse so far from its market ceased to make sense.

The only things remaining of the cattle business now were the auction rooms, rich with the good smell of sawdust and animal sweat, banked up like lecture rooms in an Eastern university; but elsewhere it was knickknacks, what-nots, and art galleries, with walls of pastel prairies and watercolor Sioux.

"Apparently he got out just in time," she said into her recorder as she waited for the light, "before the local economy crumbled. If Raneer weren't some kind of financial genius, he'd be down here still, riding in a pickup truck, leering out the window at the women in their blue jeans—Fort Worth is heaven if you like women in blue jeans—hanging out with the same old crowd. The entire downtown area," she continued, returning to the airport, through the wide-open country ranging to the east, "is all of about five streets deep. It's the kind of place where a man will whip your ass in a high school football game, and be around for the next forty years just to remind you of it." Pauline smiled. "Fort What's-it-Worth and Fast Phil . . . the two go together like burgers and buns."

Chapter 4

1

Her plan was to pitch Raneer to Sullivan, when he called her to his office on Friday, August 6, to discuss her assignments for the next few weeks; but she was sidetracked, when he handed her the mimeographed sheets containing the breakdown, department by department, of the stories projected by the editorial board.

"We've got a special issue coming, Pauline, I think it's on page five"—she thumbed through—"and there've been some changes, so you'll have to put aside whatever you've been doing and help us out. I'm going to be supervising you, for Panawicz, on a retrospective issue on Vietnam vets. Find it?"

Looking down, she saw her name under *Cover Stories: Vets,* in the subheading *Sports,* listed *Reese,* in a small square box, next to another box with the name *Pardee.* It made her very uncomfortable. "What's this about?"

"Our slant is that they've all been overlooked. We got vets sniping from bell towers, and vets running crazy in supermarkets, but nothing upbeat . . . nothing that really tells their side of the story, nothing to imply that they were there for us, whether we like it or not, whether it was wrong or right. Kind of like they died for our sins."

"And I'm supposed to do Pardee?"

"Aside from Rocky Bleier, he's the only sports guy we could think of . . . and Bleier's been getting so much ink that all we want to do is refer to him in the lead. There hasn't been much of anything on Pardee, so . . ."

"Maybe there's a reason, Frank. He doesn't like to talk about it."

"Maybe there's a *reason* he doesn't like to talk about it. I don't know, that's what *you're* going to find out."

"I'm not sure I can."

"And why not?"

"Well, for one thing, I hated that war, and I'm not about to stop hating it now, just because it's getting fashionable."

"It has nothing to do with politics, Pauline. For the most part, they were just a bunch of kids. You're not about to blame *them* for what went on."

"That's not the point."

"What is the point?"

"I just don't want the story, Frank. Can you give it to someone else?"

"No, Pauline, I can't. For one thing, *Esquire* is working on the vets, which is why we decided to push the whole thing up. You're the sports expert, you covered his team, it's your beat, it's your job. We all write stories that aren't to our taste, it's part of what we do; so I'd suggest you get your own feelings out of it, find out the facts, and write the damned thing. Is that too much to ask? I want six hundred words by the twenty-first."

"Anything else?"

"There's a rumor around that Garland is out and Norris is in down in Philly. Heard anything about that?"

"No."

"Well, now you did."

2

Pauline called the Pentagon on Monday, August 9, to find out
the procedure for researching records, and was informed that
due to the Privacy Act, she wouldn't be permitted to look up
anything without a release. "I'm a reporter," she told them.

"We're sorry, ma'am, but no one's allowed access to personal records, without permission from the person himself."

Sensing that there was no point arguing with the soft-spoken
disembodied Army voice on the other end, she went to Yankee
Stadium for her broadcast that night, then got up at nine on
Tuesday the 10th, to telephone Darryl at his hotel in Texas.
There was no answer at his room, so she left a message, and
tried again several times more before noon.

At two o'clock she met a friend to go shopping, taking advantage of the new bankroll she'd acquired; then three hours, several hundred dollars, a pair of shoes and a few silk shirts later,
Pauline escaped in a taxi uptown, where she stopped by her
favorite gourmet Italian store to pick up some pasta and pesto
sauce for dinner. She had settled in for a mindless evening,
watching TV while reading *The New Yorker,* until midnight,
when the phone rang.

"Hello?"

"It's me. I got a message you called."

"Hi, Darryl, just a minute." She took a deep breath. "So,
how are you?"

"Good, great."

"Win tonight?"

"Four to two."

"Great. Listen, I wanted to tell you, I still feel bad about that
night in Boston. I'm sorry I got angry. It wasn't you."

"Oh, no? Who was it?"

"No one. I'm sorry. Are you still mad at me?" She sat down
and kicked off her shoes.

"I'm not mad, but it sure was a waste."

"I know. I was in a bad mood."

"Well, save your moods for somebody else."

"Fair enough. What else is new?"

"Not much. I hate talkin' on this phone, though . . . it makes me feel about a thousand miles away."

"You're two thousand miles away. How's that make you feel?"

"When am I gonna see you again?"

"Anaheim on the twenty-third. Can you wait?"

"What if I can't? Listen . . . we can't fight like normal people . . . it takes too damn long to make up."

"I know. I agree with you. Listen, the reason I called was . . . they put me on this story here."

"Yeah?"

"They're doing an issue on Vietnam vets."

"And?"

"Could I ask a few questions?"

"Not really. I thought this was a personal call."

"It is, Darryl . . . but they want me to write about your experience there . . . and I was wondering . . . they want something upbeat . . . that will bring people together. Are you there?"

"I'm here."

"What do you think?"

"Something upbeat on the war?"

"If that's possible."

"No comment."

"Darryl, it's me."

"Nothin' personal, but . . ."

"Do me a favor. If you don't feel like talking, would you at least give me a release? Otherwise I can't even look things up. What do you think?"

"I think I'm gonna hang up now."

"Please, Darryl . . . this is important. Your story might help somebody else."

"Don't hype me, Pauline . . . I'm not interested."

"Darryl . . ."

"I'm sorry."

"Listen to me, Darryl . . ." But the line went dead, and when she tried to call him back, it just kept on ringing.

Chapter 5

Back at the Ballclub, August was getting old. On Sunday the 14th in Kansas City, Fritz went through seven pitchers in nine innings. The Kraut earned his reputation as a managerial whiz that day, when the temperature on the artificial surface hit 129 degrees—he used every man on the roster with the exception of Fuller, slated for the next start, and Goldhammer, who had played the entire previous game and nearly had a stroke.

The heat was no joke. Martinez and Alvarez begged to come out in the fifth, *in English* (Fritz knew it was bad, then), and Bernard had to be revived in the eighth, with a blast from one of those ethyl chloride canisters they use to freeze ankles. Nobody lost less than eight pounds in sweat, and equipment manager Billy Colangelo, who spent the afternoon hauling cold drinks from the clubhouse, lost fourteen. The final score was 9–8 in favor of the Ballclub, with twenty-two men stranded on base, and they were *stranded*.

Afterward, the Kraut sat in his office, his head wrapped in a terry-cloth turban, telling newsmen, "Had to win that one. How hot was it? Christ, a fuckin' furnace. If we'd a gone extra innings, I'd a needed Shadrach, Meshach, an' Abednego out there."

"Who?"

"Never mind," snapped the Kraut. "You shouldn't have ta play when it gets like this . . . an' that artificial crap should be outlawed!" It tore Fritz up to watch his men in that heat. It would take them days to recover.

Players were dunking their heads into the icewater buckets usually used for elbows, as Stutz fanned Bernard with a towel, and the Frenchman, splayed out naked on a bench, spread his legs and murmured endearments. Hart watched helplessly as his players showered, then dragged themselves to the buses, to ride to the airport, for the bodyracking flight to Oakland. The only live one on the whole squad, as they boarded the plane in the sweltering dusk, was the rookie, Adelaide, a utility infielder called up from Downingtown, who was riding a plane for the very first time.

"How'd you get out here?" asked Campbell.

"Took the train."

"How'd you get to camp?"

"That's my home."

"*Tideview?* You poor kid. I can't believe it. You never flew?"

"No."

"Here . . . sit by the window."

"Hands off, Campbell, I saw him first!" yelled Hunsicker.

The boys dubbed him "Sweet," put the kid behind the wing, then laughed as Adelaide started jumping against his seat belt, screaming, "Wow! This is great! I can't believe it!"

"That's it, rook," said Fuller. "Play it cool."

"We're up! We're in the air! . . . and I'm in the *Big Leagues!*"

"Jesus Christ, he's droolin' on himself. Hey, waitress! Get the child a bib."

The flight attendant stopped over to see what he wanted. "How about a whiskey sour?" he answered, thinking hard.

"A what?" said Hart. "Give him a ginger ale . . . no, wait . . . make that milk."

"But . . ." said Adelaide.

"Pipe down," said Hart.

"But . . ."

"Shuddup. Here's a postcard with a picture of an airplane. Write to your mother. Tell her not to worry. If she has any questions, she should call me up. Go ahead, write it. Then give it to me . . . I wanna make sure it gets mailed."

After a while the cabin lights dimmed, and people started nodding off to sleep, as Pardee put his forehead against the window, to look past the reflection of his face. There was a sky above and a sky below, a firmament balanced, top and bottom, its heavens mirrored in the dark lands, where small towns formed constellations, and cities exploded into galaxies. Far to the north, off to his right, the aurora borealis shimmered with a sort of neon excitation reminiscent of port towns.

At 29,000 feet over Utah, Fritz announced a practice upon arrival on the Coast. The Kraut knew a player's body, his muscles and nerves, the way some men know horses. He knew when to run them, and when to walk. He knew that sometimes the best way to cool down was to keep going. "You can lead a horse to water," he was fond of saying, "but you can't always let him drink."

Hart's team was on a tear. He would not let them let down. If they were tired, he'd have them dog-tired, so they could sleep. None of this restless nervousness for his boys. Fritz didn't bother with curfews, he just wore people out. He didn't care where a man slept; he'd had a ballplayer in Cleveland who spent the night in a gutter and hit three home runs the next day. As long as they showed up ready to play, they could sleep in a tree as far as the Kraut was concerned.

The boys griped at all the hard work, but a certain amount of griping is mandatory, it's written right into the standard contract. Take a roster of twenty-five men, have them compete for pay and glory, keep them from their wives, so they're rutting like a pack of dogs, and you'd better hope they're griping. When they stop complaining, they're ready to kill, or flip out.

Ricardo Vega, a Seattle reliever, stopped complaining one afternoon—he went into a catatonic trance. Vega held a shoe out at arm's length, for an hour and a half, after a Sunday game in Detroit. Poor Vega, a Puerto Rican journeyman, probably just got to thinking, "What's the difference if I go or stay? What if I never put this shoe down? No difference at all . . . *hmmm* . . ."

An hour and a half later they sedated him and got him down off that limb. *An hour and a half later.* If he hadn't been a ballplayer, he'd probably be in some loony bin, or out on some street corner, mumbling to himself, right now. No, Hart didn't mind the griping, it was music to his ears.

His plan was to make it easy for his boys, to reduce the amount of thinking they had to do for themselves, and most players will tell you that that's the way they like it. There's always a flake or two who wants to read books and engage in meaningful dialogues on the road, but the majority agree that there's plenty of time to think in the off-season.

Right now the idea was to be Out of Your Mind, a crystal-clear state often brought on by a mantra, some baseball mumbo-jumbo, or singleminded phrase, like "Get a hit," that drowns out every other sound in the universe. Everything narrows to the bat and the ball. Side bets are suspended and the orbs cease to rotate—until the contact, the explosion, and the setting into motion of the normal laws of cause and effect. Freeze that moment, and you'll find within it the very essence of sports, and, some would say, life itself. The cosmic connection. The Big Bang.

Pardee, when he was going good, was as close as they came to being Out of His Mind all the time. He reached that fifth plateau described by European mystics. He made Zen archery look like target practice. A hippie commune in Oregon claimed that they picked up the vibrations of Pardee's "Get a hit" every time he played the Coast. At first they thought it was interference from a CB radio, but when they found out the truth, they started buying blocks of tickets to his day games in Seattle, to sit among the empty seats behind third, meditating in blissful oblivion.

Each man, of course, had his own private litany, depending on his particular personality and position. Fuller, all business, said, "Hit the target," on every toss; while Foster snarled, "In your face," and Phillips got into a combination baseball/street jive that even *he* didn't understand.

Hogan did jungle calls out in the field, occasionally losing it in a spine-tingling Tarzan; Bernard hummed "La Marseillaise"; and Hunsicker, "The William Tell Overture," which he knew only as "The Lone Ranger Song." Pardee, meanwhile, when he wasn't at bat, sang snatches of his favorite Zydeco music, a godawful melange of Delta blues and Mexican mariachi, with its overtones of accordions and German polkas, filtered through the culture of the exiled French Acadians (the Cajuns), who gave it its name, Zydeco, from *les haricots,* which means beans, which is what those Mexicans ate. . . .

Yes, Hart had his wish, this Ballclub of his was definitely Out of Its Mind, and the result was a win streak that kept them within four of New York, who were downright psychotic. Boston was no slouch itself, and while Baltimore might be a bit too balanced ever to pose a serious threat, one never knew. Another hot spell like they'd suffered in Kansas City, and the whole league would be frothing at the mouth.

Chapter 6

1

Thursday morning, August 12. Pauline went in to Sullivan to beg off the assignment. "I tried, Frank, but they won't let me in without a release, and Pardee, as usual, is being totally uncooperative."

"Sit down. Let me make a phone call." He pointed to a chair, but instead of dialing the Pentagon, as Pauline had expected, to pull some magic contact out of a hat, Sullivan got in touch with a friend of his at a publishing house. "Hello, Dan? Frank. Not bad. I read about that deal yesterday. . . . That's a lotta money, is it any good?" He laughed. "I hope you're right. Listen, I've got a problem here. I assigned a writer to this story on a Vietnam vet, and I was wondering how to get at his personal records. . . . No. He won't sign it. How'd you get through on that My Lai thing? . . . Uh-huh. Right. Good idea. . . . Would you do that? . . . Great. . . . No, I can't make it Monday. . . . OK, fine. I'll call in the morning. Talk to you then."

Sullivan made a note on his desktop calendar, then turned to Pauline. "Just bought a book for half a million bucks. Doesn't even like it, but he's got a movie sale, Book-of-the-Month—he's going to send a messenger with a cover letter. You see, they won't let you in directly to the personal files, but they will let you research a point in Army history, so all we have to do is target Pardee's unit and you can track your way back to almost anything you want."

"What's the letter for?"

"He figured they might be less suspicious if you were an author, instead of a reporter, so he'll type up a letter on his stationery, saying you're under contract." He paused. "But I don't think I'll bother sending you, Pauline. We'll get one of our research people on it. Just get your other work done, so when they get something to you, you'll be able to pursue it."

"Fine, Frank. You want to find another writer, that's OK too."

"But you're doing such a good job, Pauline."

2

Four-thirty P.M., Friday the 13th. Pauline got a call from the researcher in St. Louis, who told her he had finished at the Army Records Depository and was sending his findings through the phone lines at that moment. She went down to the communications room, where the Rapifax transmitter drum was rotating, and waited for a technician to stop the machine and peel off the first of two sheets that were an exact, if somewhat difficult to read, replica of photostats containing the details of Darryl's enlistment.

He was in the First Cavalry, II Corps, stationed in the Central Highlands, divisional firebase, An-Khe. He fought with the third brigade, infantry, having entered as a private and emerged an E-5; and was awarded the Purple Heart (which she knew) for being wounded in action, and the Distinguished Service Cross (and here a text was supplied):

> For exemplary courage in standing off the enemy for five days without support or relief, maintaining his position against overwhelming odds, in the highest tradition of military service.

Pauline put the paper down and stared across the room. Having so vehemently opposed the war, she wasn't too hip on its medals and perks, so she called her local Army recruiter and was informed by a polite young man with a delightful Southern drawl (everyone in the Army seemed to own or affect one) that the Distinguished Service Cross just happened to be the second-highest honor that the Army could bestow. Everyone, of course, got decorated in the Army, her father had a whole boxful of medals, but this was something else. She began to wake up.

She took a second photostat, fresh off the drum, skimmed a letter describing the difficulties Darryl had experienced while recovering from his wounds, then got on the phone with the *Lifetimes* stringer in New Orleans, to ask him to see if there'd been any notice in the local press, around the time of Pardee's award.

Monday at nine she tried the Pentagon again, and armed with information this time, instead of a mere request to pry, she found that the officers were quite responsive. Referred from desk to desk, she was eventually connected with a Colonel William Allen, who said he had served with the third brigade, and was in Pleiku, the divisional headquarters, when word of Pardee's exploits came through.

"How is it possible that nobody knows about this?" asked Pauline.

"It's really quite simple, ma'am. Medals and honors are awarded in the field, and published in General Orders, but if the soldier doesn't want us to send the word out, there's no reason anyone outside his unit would know. He gets a medal, a miniature medal for his dress uniform, a tietack-type ribbon for his civilian coat, and a certificate to hang on the wall back home, but unless he displays these things himself, that information, is privileged."

"And these General Orders?"

"They're just a listing, ma'am . . . and in a few years they're such a mess that nobody ever looks at them."

"Did you happen to know Pardee yourself?"

"I can't say that I did . . . I certainly didn't know every man I commanded, but we did hear the story."

"Don't you think it's odd that no one ever wrote about it . . . after he became famous?"

"I guess I would, if I thought about it . . . but we never saw eye to eye with the press, and it's hardly my place to . . ."

"What else can you tell me?"

"Well, sometimes when a man gets decorated, his outfit gets so... recognition too . . . and in this case our brigade got a Presidential Unit Citation."

"Could you make a copy and send it up?"

"If I find it, I'll have it in your hands the next day. I'll be very pleased to have this story come out. This Pardee was a very fine soldier."

"The description I got is fairly vague. Could you give me an idea of what went on?"

Colonel Allen was happy to oblige. He detailed the general mode of engagement, how the Scouts and Cobras would raise a fight, then the ground troops would be radioed in; and he explained to Pauline how a man could get cut off, and pinned down, so that a passing helicopter would see nothing, and how if the radio got destroyed, and the enemy fire was thick enough to interdict further passes, a man might be abandoned.

Pardee was fortunate to have attracted the attention of a troop-carrying Huey flying by, which called in the full-scale invasion that was ultimately necessary to get him out. Colonel Allen described his stand as nothing short of miraculous, then went on to talk about other engagements, and other feats of heroism he'd witnessed in that war. He was a proud man, defensively proud, given the image that the Army had endured, but listening to him talk, Pauline got a feeling for the logic of his life, and how a man could live within the confines of that world, removed from the attitudes and so-called realities of the taxpaying citizens he was ostensibly protecting.

She got a few more names from the colonel, collected some

quotes over the telephone, then returned to Sullivan to let him know that the story he'd assigned her had come up in spades. Pardee was a hero. The genuine article. And he'd never even mentioned it, which made it even better. He continued to refuse to return her calls, so she had to sit down to write it on her own, but the tale she'd discovered had her so excited that she put aside her bias against Vietnam, and tried to make pretend it was World War II.

Chapter 7

1

The story went in on Friday, August 20. Pauline was asked to expand it, which was easy, and the section was set by Sunday night. Monday morning she caught a flight on American, ate breakfast, then slept on and off until they hit the Mojave, a half hour from the Coast. Barren brown peaks soon appeared to the north, to form a bowl around L.A. in its doomsday haze, which tinged the ozone to a turquoise green.

They descended over the gridlike streets, the shallow canals and concrete riverbeds, skimming the cars on Highway One, to set down at LAX, the Los Angeles airport. Walking across the upstairs lobby, Pauline spotted a TV star, and was surprised to find him staring back at her. As she moved down the automated walkway, more and more heads started turning, until she realized that it had finally happened. She herself was a celebrity now, *Pauline Reese*, she read their lips, and stood up straighter.

Outside, waiting for a cab, she got caught up in the obsessive monotone of the public-address system:

> The White Zone is for immediate loading and unloading of passengers only. No parking.

As the message repeated, it began to take on sinister overtones:

The White Zone [no blacks, Japanese, or Mexicans need apply] is for immediate loading and unloading [she saw people as freight, stiff as boards, balanced on the skycaps' dollies] of passengers only [no luggage, no loved ones, no pets, and . . .]. No parking. *La Zona Blanca es para.* . . .

Crazed, hypnotic, the recording droned on, first in a woman's voice, then a man's, one threatening, one beseeching, three in English, one in Spanish, until she felt like screaming. At last she caught a limo that drove her north to Santa Monica, where she had taken a room, so she could do what she was doing now —strip off her business suit, the silk shirt, the stockings, etc., slip into a bathing suit, and run down to the sea. Summer was nearly over, but apart from a dip at the hotel in Texas, she had yet to get wet.

She went out the front door, crossed Ocean Avenue, and descended a hill just south of the Pier, keeping herself wrapped up in a towel, embarrassed about the way she looked. Her skin felt pasty and loathsome, as if she had just crawled out from under a rock, or some manhole cover in Manhattan.

She used to spend all her summers outdoors, getting nut-brown, with only the little private parts beneath her bikini tops and bottoms, like little *zona blancas* of her own. *No parking.* She was skinny as a rail until fifteen—the halter was superfluous—then her breasts burgeoned and threatened to tip her over. Gorgeous but gawky through seventeen, she thought that her childhood would last forever, but she was fast approaching thirty, and had let herself slide.

Pauline had been working for so long that she'd almost forgotten that that's what it was. Work. It might be fascinating, but no amount of it, no matter how satisfying, could ever make up for what she'd lost. The young girls she passed on her way to the beach now put her to shame. Skinny thighs and tight little middles—not an ounce of fat. She decided she despised them.

Not that anyone else would have noticed, but Pauline could see herself this winter, grunting and sweating in some fashionable uptown exercise class, taught by a crazed Latina with the sinews of an alley cat, who had been dancing since she was three. She could see herself fighting the losing battle for the next twenty years, with that woman spiking up and down the rows, crying, "Ready girls? One, two, three, and *push,* two, three, and hold it, *push,* go for the burn . . ." She felt dreadful, and with great relief made it across the sidewalk, away from the people and into the sand.

Dropping her towel just above the tideline, she stepped into the white water, foaming at her feet, and broke into a run, her thighs blobbling as she high-stepped through the surf. Pauline felt weak from the inside out. She ran on until she broke into a sweat and her calves began to stiffen, then jumped a series of breakers and dove into the sea.

The salt water shocked her, but it wasn't really cold, so she started to swim, out beyond the point where the waves were crashing, marveling at the fact that her very survival depended on her own ability to keep going. She'd been scouring the country in search of news, and here it was, the whole story, the big picture—the sea, the sky, the air, and her hair against her back. There was nothing else to worry about and nowhere to report. Her ears were filled with the sound of her own breath.

Sidestroking casually, then floating, Pauline watched the gulls and pelicans fly by, feeling the immense expanse of emptiness that led out to Hawaii. The water pitched and rolled in a gentle breeze, it lapped her thighs and balanced on her belly. Drifting along, kicking at intervals, she was starting to get tired when a riptide grabbed her and pulled her into a trough. She got a mouthful of seawater trying to escape—almost swam free, then a huge breaker caught her, and drove her down to the ocean floor.

She flipped and spun like a T-shirt in a washing machine. Panic was useless, so she gave in to her helplessness. The heightened reality lasted but an instant, then she planted her feet on the sandy bottom and tried to stand, as the tide pulled her backward. Sputtering, choking, and laughing like a kid, Pauline fought to regain her balance, looking for someone to share the moment; then her laughter stopped, but she felt even better, letting the air out in little sighs meant only for herself.

She caught her breath, dove back in, and rode a few more waves, on purpose this time, before one last curl carried her back to the beach. She had a smooth, fast lift for about four seconds, then the tube closed out and took her down again. Again she panicked, and again she laughed, as she struggled to her feet and the brine rushed past. She pulled back her hair and leaned against the turbulence, dizzy and alive. Her skin was goose-bumped and her heart was pounding. She wanted to make love right there and then.

2

She showered and dressed, then took a cab to Dodger Stadium, to broadcast a game won by Cincinnati in ten, but even with the extra inning, the early start for the stations back East give her plenty of time to get down to Anaheim, where she met Pardee, but found him distant. That last abortive phone call was apparently between them, but on top of that, he was beat. He had played eighteen games in nineteen days, and every muscle in his body was bruised. He didn't want to go out for a drink, wasn't into talking, and although they made love, it was just a formality, and Pauline wound up lying in the dark, frustrated.

She'd been nervous about seeing him, nervous about her story, and had fully intended to discuss it in his arms, but now she was beginning to wonder if it was worth it. All that building him up in her mind, and now this. "Maybe it's over," she thought. "Perhaps I'd do better to pull out now."

Whatever it was, this night had been a drag. She found herself thinking of other men she'd loved, and somehow that thought was transmitted to Pardee, who jerked as if he'd been hit with a small electric shock. It was uncanny. Every time her thoughts turned on him, Darryl jumped again. He was tied into her, reading her mind. She tried to think of something else.

When he climbed up to make love the next morning, it was her turn to be unresponsive. Last night's desire had turned to resentment. It had taken Pauline hours to fall asleep, and now she wanted to rest. When Pardee saw that she wasn't getting into it, he rolled off, and when she woke again, he was gone on the bus to the L.A. airport, where the Ballclub got thrown in with the Cincinnati Reds, on their way back to Ohio after sweeping their own three-game series with the Dodgers.

Nothing felt better than taking some of the glamour out of Tinseltown, so the two teams sang in one loud voice: "Hollywood . . . ya-da-da-da-da-da-da, *Hollywood* . . ." pushing and shoving down the aisles, fighting over window seats, and cheating at cards until lunchtime, when the Reds staged a riot.

It appeared that their portions were smaller than the Ballclub's, and it looked like war, with the Redlegs banging on their fold-down tabletops, until Goldhammer was hustled forward to explain over the intercom:

"You see, I always pre-order Kosher meals on flights, because the other stuff is dogmeat"—he held up the tray of a perplexed civilian—"and my teammates have started doing the same . . . so if you guys don't like it, then in keeping with our ancient dietary laws, just stick out your dicks an' I'll *circumcise* ya." Then he took off with a knife after the Reds' Ralph Pine, and the discussion broke down into a free-for-all.

Hunsicker stole the World Series Ring off the finger of a sleeping Tom Buell, and nearly got pushed through an emergency door. Leary lit up a stick of sinsemilla; Fuller, true to form, got a stewie in the head; and Hamilton, who'd been bribing people to buy him nips of booze ever since he had reached his limit, got bombed and barged into the cockpit, asking if he could steer the plane.

A security detachment met the teams at the gate and had to

be talked out of making arrests, but a group of reporters who were waiting at the ropes ignored all the fuss to make a beeline for Pardee. The *Lifetimes* story was set in type, and word had leaked over the A.P. wires.

"They said you got the DSC . . . is it true?"

"No comment."

"Come on, Pardee, don't be modest. Why the big secret? Why break it now?"

"No comment." Darryl walked quickly, his eyes fixed forward, as they trailed along, yipping at his heels. *"No comment."*

PART FOUR

Inside Ballpark

Chapter 1

1

Ballpark, Ohio, September 1. It was the First Annual Labor Day Weekend Memorial Traffic Jam and Truck Strike, and to help celebrate, they called out the National Guard. Those fast shooters, who acquitted themselves so well against Kent State, had their hands full with Independents bludgeoning Teamsters, sandbagging the underpasses, and turning Interstate 70 into a six-lane parking lot; while inside Ballpark, oblivious to it all, Fast Phil Raneer was pulling off the greatest week-long killing in the history of the American Holiday System.

People were desperate to get off the roads, many abandoned their cars and walked, so Phil tacked on a three-buck-a-head Holiday Tariff, expanded his campgrounds into the fields next door, and did a carnival business in Army cots and sleeping bags, while organizing a massive airlift—flying in batches of fresh merchandise, frozen fish, milk substitute, and 100-percent all-meat hamburger (fat content guaranteed not to exceed 33 percent) by helicopter.

The first time one of those things spun in, Pardee was asleep, thirty yards and a thin roof under its blades; and he jumped up screaming, knowing that even naked as he was, a cry like his would keep away anything but a damned fool, man or beast. He watched the chopper set down on the corner of Home Plate and Foul Tip boulevards, punched out his window screen to get some air and to make sure he really was where he was, but although the night reeked of Ohio, he was not reassured.

Darryl didn't care what kind of meat they carried; when he heard copters, he wanted out. There was, of course, nowhere for him to go right then, so he sat up most of the night, and the next. Years ago they gave up guessing what went on in his mind when he got like this. The Army doctors were carefully guarded:

March 6, 1968

Captain William Strunk
First Cavalry
Pleiku, Vietnam

Sir:

In response to your inquiry of 2/27/68: Sgt. Pardee underwent an emergency thoracotomy on 2/15/68, with an uneventful postoperative course. His mental state postoperatively appears normal; however, he has at times exhibited enhanced startle responses marked by assaultive behavior, possibly related to stress from his combat experience. Current management comprises rest and sedation. We trust that this will prove a transient phenomenon, and we anticipate eventual recovery. Thank you for your interest. Will keep you posted.

Captain S.R. Mann, M.D.
Dept. of Psychiatry
U.S. Army Hospital
Camp Zama, Japan

What that meant was that for weeks, if Darryl even imagined that someone was coming at him, he stopped it in a flash. No one ever had time to explain. He did recover, as the doctors had hoped, but up until the end, his fears could be triggered by the sound of helicopters, and Pardee had the ears of a jungle cat. Now that they were rolling in every night over Ballpark, he didn't even try to sleep. He would pick up the vibration at a distance of ten miles, and by the time they were overhead his heart would be synchronized—pulsating and beating so fast he would practically lift up off the bed.

Once again his hitting slumped, but this time Gowdy didn't say a word about being the batting coach. He didn't advise him to take extra swings, or spread his stance, or move a little closer to the plate—Gowdy left Pardee alone. He steered clear of the ballplayer radiating menace down the end of the bench, as did everyone, until the coaches brought it up during a meeting in Hart's office. In their opinion, Pardee was coming apart at the seams, like a baseball made in Hong Kong.

"Sewed up in Veetnam . . ." Lacy Stokey spit and hit the trashcan by the door. "Ever seen them scars? Gettin' mighty jumpy. Ain't worth shit." Wa-Wa Wagner mimed a bomb and blew it up in Pardee's brain.

"All right, gentlemen . . . I get the picture. Pardee!" They left the room. *"Pardeeee!"* it echoed like a siren.

"Yessir?" He stepped in.

"Sit down."

"Mind if I stand, sir?" He put his hands behind him in a stiff at-ease.

"All right, Pardee, what's got into you?"

"Sir?"

"What's botherin' you?"

"I couldn't say, sir."

"Suppose you try. It wouldn't have anything to do with that magazine business . . . ?" Pardee didn't answer, and the Kraut waited. He'd seen kids all shook up before, he'd served as a sergeant in Italy—something he never saw fit to mention when people give him flak about his crummy career. He lost four years to that war, probably his best, and even if his coaches were right about Pardee, he suspected that they didn't know the half of it. "Come on, son . . . now, what's going' on?"

"I've got this feelin' . . ."

"Yeah?"

"Like somethin' might happen . . ."

"And?"

"I guess I'm afraid of what I might do."

"Let's see . . . you're afraid a' somethin' happenin' . . . but you don't know what." Darryl nodded. "And you're worried what you'll do . . . but you don't know what."

"Yessir."

"Well, what the hell do ya know?"

"I know I'm not hittin'."

"That makes two of us. Now we're gettin' somewhere. What should I tell ya?"

"I don't know."

"All right, listen. Until you do know something, or you do start hittin' . . . I want you next to me on the bench."

"Sir?"

"Sit with me, talk to me between innings, ask me how I feel. Get your mind off yourself, Pardee. You got that?"

"Yessir."

"We're all in this together, right?"

"Yessir."

"Then don't let it get to you."

"Nosir."

"Anything else?"

"Nosir."

"All right, then. Dismissed."

Darryl walked out, and the Kraut grunted. He didn't like what he saw in those eyes. He didn't like what he *didn't* see in those eyes. Pardee had a problem. That meant Fritz had a problem—winning the pennant. After that there'd be no more problems that a few good trades and five months of rest wouldn't cure. The Kraut leaned in his chair and lit a cigar. He scowled and put it out.

2

The official story of Darryl Pardee was like the official story of the war itself: not the whole truth, and often nothing like the truth. You could peel away layer after layer of both of them and never discover what had really gone on, and both his life and that war were in a class of experiences that did not make more sense with the passage of time. For the first time since returning, however, the thoughts and memories of that period were suddenly flooding over him, like it or not. He'd be sitting in the dugout, listening to the *thwock* and *thwack* of batting practice, hearing ancient conversations and answering dead men right out loud. He knew it was no time to be doing this, but he'd been saying that for years, and it no longer worked.

Everyone had heard by now how Pardee had singlehandedly held off the enemy in an abandoned, no longer strategic hamlet, but Pauline's story left out a lot. He was patrolling over by the border of Cambodia, north of the firebase known as the Oasis, when his platoon got cut off, communications got broken, and one by one the men got killed, until he was the only one left.

Several nights passed, without food or rest, until he was delirious, unable to tell if the bullets whistling past him at random intervals were aimed at his head or in it. He was down almost to the last of his ammo, the last rounds from guns and clips stripped from the dead lying all around and starting to rot. Darryl had been crawling from hut to hut, firing at intervals, so the enemy troops would think there were guards. They had his strength estimated at ten men, which he wasn't, even on a good day.

The siege had become a war of nerves, but Pardee's were shot. He wasn't even dreaming of rescue anymore, he was fighting entirely out of bile and spite, because he didn't give a shit, and because that small part of his mind that remained to him was curious, in an idle sort of way, to see how long he could keep it up.

The first hint of help was a dull throb, sounding through the trees. Darryl heard it getting closer and closer, waited until the chopper was nearly above him, then jumped out, whistling and waving, to catch the attention of the gunner in the side door.

Before he could tell if the man even saw him, he dove through the doorway and rolled to the corner, as streams of gunfire poured through the walls. Pardee kept his head down, waiting for the occasional lull to answer with a few rounds of his own. He had no idea how long it took, deep in that lost world of his, before he heard the choppers returning, beating down the dried grass, landing to his left.

Caught in a crossfire, he flattened in the dirt, listening to the sound of people screaming through the unearthly inhuman bark and pop. There was an incredible roar as the flamethrowers moved by, then quiet. Just the sound of branches burning, like rain dripping on a roof.

3

The next few days he was wound so tight that no one could get near him. One poor medic, trying to test his reflexes, poked his knee, got kicked in the groin, and was nearly dismembered. They sedated him and shot him full of antibiotics, and when the drug-goofy private expressed willingness, even eagerness, to get back to action, instead of concluding that he'd gone a little loose, they promoted him, pinning that medal to his chest, then cast him from the shelter of their tender care, citing him as a fine example of the fighting spirit so often lacking in your modern foot soldier.

After a brief attempt at R&R spent ripping up the streets of Bangkok, Darryl was assigned to a new combat unit, which was the best that could have been done for him, because the fact was that he was fit for little else but battle over the next few months. Vietnam was a democratic war, thanks, in part, to the breakdown in authority, and Pardee was one of those people whom the men just followed if they wanted to survive. He was something of a legend, even back then, during that strange civil conflict that made brothers-in-arms of so many damned Rebels and black Yankees; and he enjoyed a reputation as a fighting man's man, a main man's man, and a feared object of respect, until late one afternoon in the middle of July, when a mortar round landed beside his platoon, and took out the lineup in a blaze of fire.

Darryl hit the deck in a reflex that saved him, and listened to the bits whistling past him for an eternity, until three slugs with his name on them in grinning oriental characters slammed into his right side, shattering his ribs and piercing his lung. Amazed, he heard the air rush out and listened to the wheeze. Two seconds after they hit there was still no pain . . . and then it hit.

There was no blood gushing—the damage was all inside—just three small holes the size of cigarette burns. He experienced no flashbacks, or sudden yearnings, his thoughts were focused mainly on his immediate surroundings; but the thing that bothered him most as he lay there close to death was that he had never made his peace with old Tom, the news of whose passing had reached him the month before. He threw his legs over a rock, so the blood would stay down around his heart and brain, and waited.

"This is stupid," he thought, as his skin grew pale and he went into shock. "Get me outta here . . . I want a cigarette. . . ." Meanwhile, off to his left, signalman Charles "Bump" Patterson was spilling out his sides, mingling with his radio in a pool of blood. Bump was a black dude, a natural, the kind who hauled a big chrome stereo around the streets of L.A. He died with his fingers on the dial.

Next to him was Roland Lee, the preacher's son, Pardee's home boy from New Orleans, stone gumbo gone, and worst of all—not alive, not dead—Martinez, the sergeant, feeling no pain as they scooped him onto a stretcher. Nobody liked Martinez, a tough prick of a spic field boss, and now his survivors were licking their lips, joking about his last ride to that big Taco

Stand in the Sky, laughing into his mute, imploring eyes, as they hooked him up for the long lift to the helicopter hovering overhead.

Pardee rode up in his own little basket into the green belly of the rescue craft, where they racked him across from Martinez, open wide and ticking away like a clock en route to its last alarm. The chopper spun off, back to base, as Martinez's men raised a salute of single fingers in a final "Fuck you"; then they picked up their gear and climbed a hill to reconnoiter the surrounding lowland, but instead of the enemy, all they saw were ARVN—our side; you can't tell the players without a program —Vietnamese regulars celebrating the end of another day of war by throwing down their weapons, stripping to helmets garlanded with underbrush, and dancing delicately under the twilight sky.

4

He was lucky. A few inches to the right and his windpipe would have been blown away. Another few minutes and his blood pressure, which was cruising down to forty systolic, might have dropped out for good. Right up until the operation, however, Pardee lost consciousness only once, when he woke to the voice of a medic, saying, "Talk to me, soldier, don't go away."

Darryl kept his eyes open after that, confident that when the time came, they would shut them for him. He lost five pints of blood through a chest tube inserted at the bottom of his ribcage, as they ran fluids and sliced him open, cutting between his ribs and prying them apart, in order to tie off his arteries. The aftermath of the operation would prove more painful than the injury, but the doctor had no choice.

When Darryl asked later if they'd removed the fragments, the doc just laughed and said, "They only do that in the movies, pal. Poking around does more harm than good. If we stumble on something, we grab it, but otherwise we just do what we have to, and get the bleeding stopped.'' He showed Darryl an X-ray of the three slugs split into a dozen pieces scattered through the film—white spots in the gray tissue—and assured him that his lungs would heal up around them.

Each time he breathed he felt debilitating pain, but although they warned him to take it easy, he was out of bed in two days, clamping his own chest tube, dragging around his IV, and demanding to be set free. His condition was remarkable, but meanwhile he was a menace, with his judgment clouded by doses of morphine.

Pardee plagued his ward in the 91st Evacuation Hospital in Pleiku, until they decided that he was stable enough to be shipped to Japan. His last morning, when no one was looking, he borrowed a uniform hanging by the door and snuck out of the screened-in tin-roofed barracks, past the guards and out of the compound, into the streets.

Hopping a trishaw, he held onto his side, wincing, as they rolled down to the market. He got off and paid the man, then did his best to protect himself as he negotiated the jostling crowd, through a nauseating swirl of fruit colors and human smells. There was too much light, a blinding sun. He felt awkward and ridiculous, a starched white Yankee giant, mocked by laughter as he stumbled on.

Young girls glided by in their *ao-dais,* all smiles, while the boys held hands; and small children staggered his path, flaunting their tiny penises and pudenda, foul from the open sewers. Giddy with the smells and dizzy from the heat, Darryl wouldn't have missed this for the world. One last look, that's all he wanted. He heard the Shirelles from a juke box in a gyp joint, and thought of that time when a lovely young whore dropped her hand on his leg—he came, right on the spot—then laughed, calling him a cheap date, and took him upstairs for his first night of love.

They could ship him out of here if they wanted, but they'd never get this place out of him—especially now that he had small bits of it lodged in his chest. They could fly him to Japan, or mail him to the States, but it wouldn't matter. Vietnam had taken the piss out of Pardee. It was the next best thing to home.

5

Darryl spent three weeks in Japan, and another month down at Fort Sam Houston, Texas, before arriving home during a week-long frost that blanketed the Gulf. He flew to New Orleans, took a bus to New Iberia, then a cab the rest of the way to Crawbanks, and the house that was just as his father had left it.

One night in his old bed and it all came back—the bad dreams, those voices—and how he found out what they were one night, when he snuck down and spotted old Tom with some woman, heading out back. Tom Pardee wasn't proud of himself, a washed-up factory guard with a burned-out shoulder, but there was nothing he could do about it. If he thought the kind of women he wound up with would have done Darryl any good, he'd have married one of them; but they wouldn't, so he didn't, and he tried to sneak them in when he thought the boy was sleeping.

Darryl was fourteen when he first wised up, and although he never said a word about it, he felt doubly betrayed—once for his mother, whom the child in him longed for, and once for himself, for being a fool. It got so bad he couldn't look his father in the eye, then Tom started drinking and it just got worse, until all they seemed to do was fight—and the whole thing climaxed with his decision to enlist. By signing up, he was saying, "Too bad, old man, 'cause I don't care . . . and I don't care if I get ruined too." And he didn't. Not until he got hurt.

They left each other on the outs and never made it up, and that was the worst feeling of all. Not that he'd been sullen and stupid as a kid, but that now, when he knew so much, it was too late. Now that he finally did understand, there was no way to set it right. Tom Pardee was a good man, he deserved a lot better.

He awoke the next morning and threw off the covers, letting light from the window paint his body, as he lay there under his collection of pennants, their felt colors faded and covered with dust. He stepped into the bathroom to take a leak, slipped into his clothes, then grabbed his bag and wandered outside.

A cat froze on the garage roof, then leaped from the drainpipe, stunning itself. It shook off after a moment and bolted for a bush, as Darryl put his stuff down alongside the asphalt and stepped in through a stumble of rakes to the far corner of the garage and the scuffed-up Spalding basketball, official size and weight. He laughed. He had never seen one that wasn't.

Down on one knee, he reached for his bicycle pump, drooled onto the little black nipple, then wiggled in the needle, releasing that familiar rubber musk. Ten pumps later he popped it out, bounced the ball, and stepped out to the foul line, where his breath turned to vapor in the unusually cold air.

He looked to his left, half expecting him to be there watching, then lined up and gave the ball a one-handed push. The orange Spalding rotated backward, bent the rim, and dropped right through, but the net was so old and shrunken from the rains that it never hit the ground, and as far as he knows, it may be hanging there still, for by that time Pardee had his satchel in his hand, and was heading down the driveway.

Chapter 2

1

September 4. The Labor Day fiasco had grown to such proportions that Pauline was sent down three days early. Raneer had hosted the Fairfield County Fair, August 27 to September 3, and so many people were packed into the place that Ballpark looked less like America's newest small town than Ohio's answer to Singapore. The gloss was off, it was littered and seedy, that highly touted air was no longer pure, and by now the din of helicopters had everyone looking up nervously. There was something ominous in that sound, whether one knew why or not.

The County Fair folded, but Raneer wasn't through. He sent out fliers to Ohio State, just up the road in Columbus, inviting the fraternities to celebrate what he called Greek Week at Ballpark, as his (paying) guests. The school year wouldn't start for another two weeks, but the Buckeyes had an early TV game, and their loyal supporters had shown up to attend it, with plenty of beer, and nothing else to do.

Discovering to their glee that security was inadequate, the Greeks went wild, drinking, puking, and rampaging through the parking lots, ripping off antennas and spraying paint. They tied each other naked to the lampposts, beat up the people who tried to protest, and capped off the night by commandeering a freezerful of dry ice, dropping it into the rest-room toilets, flushing all at once, and blowing out nearly fifty thousand dollars' worth of plumbing.

Pauline felt obligated to check it out, but on her way down the Esplanade, she bumped into Howie Needleman, heading someplace, in a hurry. "Hey, Howie . . ."

"Not now, Pauline." He changed his course and walked right over. "Do you believe this?"

She looked around. "Boys will be boys, eh?"

"Boys, my ass . . . fuckin' animals. I don't know about you," he said, "but I am scared. We might get the state police comin' in . . . do you know what *that'll* mean? Hey, I have to be out here . . . what's your excuse?"

"I love ya, Howie . . . I'm just doin' my job."

"Well, do it someplace else, Pauline. Really . . . *please,* I am not kiddin'. You've seen it all . . . so go watch from a window somewhere. If anything happens, I'll call you up. *You* call *me* up. Listen to me, will ya? It's just not safe. Don't go lookin' for trouble, OK?" She nodded, sort of sideways. "Listen, I gotta run. Don't say I didn't warn ya," and Needleman took off.

"Good old Howie," she thought, then laughed. "Always dramatic, a little bit bent . . . but in this case he's probably right . . . see one fistfight, you've seen them all."

She walked past her hotel, over to Pardee's, to let herself in with the key he'd given her, the last time she was through. Pauline sat down and started to write, losing track of time until a little before eleven, when he stepped in, saw her, and quickly turned away. "Hey, Darryl . . ." she said. "Can't you say hello?" He didn't answer, but she felt she had it coming. Pauline had been expecting repercussions from her story, and it was time to get it over with. "What's the matter?" she asked.

"Nothin'." He was so tense she could almost feel the force waves.

"Darryl, it is not nothing. Talk to me . . . please . . . I can't stand it."

He sat down on the bed. "I was walkin' home tonight, an' I saw this fight."

She turned, a bit confused. "It was nuts out there, wasn't it?"

Pardee ignored her. He was talking to the air. "This guy was screamin', 'Don't go down!' but I didn't know why, until his buddy got tripped, then they kicked him, an' curbed him."

"They what?"

"They dazed him, opened his mouth over the edge of the curb, then stomped on his head, ripped him right open."

"Oh, my God . . . couldn't you stop it?"

"I thought it was just a fight . . . just a buncha kids."

"Did they catch them?"

"Are you kidding? I had to hold him together till somebody came . . . the cop said they do it a lot. . . ." Pauline suddenly noticed the blood on his shirt. She put a hand on his shoulder, as he shook his head, saying, "I don't know why I'm tellin' you."

"I'm sorry, Darryl." She took his hand and put it to her lips.

"Sorry? Who's not sorry?" He leaned back onto the bed, staring at the spackled ceiling, until Pauline hit the light, then settled in beside him. Fireworks could still be heard, ripping up the sidewalks. Pardee was trembling. She had never felt anything like it.

"Why?" he asked, as if he had never stopped asking, "*Why?*"

2

They spent the night together and made love until dawn, kept falling asleep, waking up, and making love again, then the next day Darryl had his first good game in weeks. He went three for four with two home runs, and leaned in like a wall at third, and folks finally got a glimpse of the athlete who would earn two and a half million over the next five years. Pardee did it all. He dove into dugouts, caught foul balls falling into the stands, signed autographs, took out the garbage, and slid head, hip, and elbow first, double-clutching for the extra base.

He was larger than life, historic, the Hall of Famer in his prime, and those lucky enough to witness it had the frozen moments of that series patched into their memories like news-reels, old Pathé Ciné photo montages ending each night with Pardee trotting in from third, modestly tipping his hat. He bat-ted .640 for the rest of the home stand, and got a round of applause the last night that escalated quickly into a standing ovation. The fans knew they had just seen the very best who had ever lived. Grown men shouted, women wept, *Hart* wept —it was a joy to behold.

Raneer, meanwhile, cut his losses, and very cleverly co-opted the Greeks by handing out T-shirts emblazoned *Ballpark Brigade,* and inviting them to police themselves, which they did with a zeal bordering on the vigilante. They were good clean boys, after all, said Phil, and now that they'd had their fun, they could all sit together in a section out in right, and get to work on the visiting teams. Raneer had finally found his own hard core of fans, and if it took a few punch-outs and ten thousand feet of bathroom pipe to get them, he figured it was worth it.

He held a press conference Sunday to introduce those shirts, then shocked reporters by announcing his intention to break new ground in Major League concessioneering by serving wine. "I'm a traditionalist as much as the next guy," said Raneer, glancing at Needleman, whose credentials were suspect, "but I'm out to find us a nice crowd a' people, who can enjoy them-selves in a civilized manner. We are *tired* a' people who like to eat glass, an' crush beer cans against their heads. I mean, beer's fine . . . but wine . . . ?

"I have a vision," said Fast Phil, who also had an uncanny knack for getting quoted at length, "I hear thousands a' people cheerin', as a cork pops in the box seats. I see waiters in red jackets an' bow ties, servin' Chenin Blanc, and Beaujolais''— he pronounced them correctly—"an' ballgames where people are out to have fun, not to get all drunk an' disgustin' . . . an' wind up throwin' up over the rails.''

No longer content to tame the wild hordes, Raneer was going uptown, looking to attract a new crowd, wine drinkers, the smart set, what one writer dubbed "the *quicheoisie*.'' He was angling for the high-class trade, probably thinking of opening a casino, which would require changing the laws of the state, but Phil no doubt had worked that out too. Pauline took notes, wondering where he was headed, then afterward caught him on a side street outside, to ask if she could have a few minutes of his time.

What she really had in mind was more like a week, because although she had scored with the Pardee story, she and Sullivan both knew that she'd really tried to duck it. He was giving her credit for her work down at *Lifetimes,* and while her follow-up was actually quite good, he would raise his eyebrow every time it got mentioned, to remind Pauline that she owed him one. Frank was playing the father figure, and Pauline, his protégée, was still in the position of trying to earn his praise.

Her one current prospect was the feature on Raneer that she'd been chewing over since her trip to Fort Worth, and now she was about to suggest the idea, to see if he would let her follow him around. Her plan was to observe him in his regular routine, to stay with Raneer long enough for him to get used to her, so she could catch him in a few rare unguarded moments, and maybe even penetrate the front of this man, who thus far had presented but one face to the world. It did not figure to be easy, but she was counting on his vanity to outweigh his suspicions, and intended to dare him to take on the risk.

"Sorry,'' he said as he hurried along, "I'm busy right now. Call me next week.''

"I won't be here next week. Could you try and squeeze me in? The last time we talked, you said, '*Anytime. . . .*' '' Pauline darkened her voice, just a touch, and it worked.

"Follow me," he said. "I'm headin' to the stadium, we can talk down there." He led her to the press gate, over to an elevator, and up to the owner's room, which was secured by double doors, as in an airlock, with closed-circuit TV cameras for constant surveillance. "Open up, I'm comin' through," said Raneer, then the door buzzed and he gestured for Pauline to precede him, taking full advantage of the view.

What she found on the other side surpassed even the rumors. There was miniature golf on a velvet carpet, zebra-skin chairs on a marble floor, a pool table, hot tub, and TV consoles six feet tall, a glass wall facing the playing field, several sofas with fox-fur spreads, a dining room of baronial proportions, guns on racks, crossed swords, moose heads and stuffed sailfish—a gaudy display that ran the gamut of macho Texas icons.

Pauline was stunned. It was all she could do to keep from laughing. Raneer held out his hand and had a bourbon placed in it by a liveried black man from central casting. "Drink?" he asked.

"Why not?" she responded with a touch of Bacall, a kind of tongue-between-the-teeth dash of recklessness and innocence that made Fast Phil's eyes bulge out and his palms begin to sweat. "This'll be easier than I thought," she decided.

"Well," he said, pointing at the room, "whattya think? Don't answer that, I like it, an' that's all that counts." He took a long pull, rattled the ice, then snapped his fingers and signaled for more.

"Looks like you're set to do anything in here."

"This is just the main room. I got private quarters you would not believe." He took his refill.

"Would you believe that I'd believe it?"

Raneer smiled, turning to the window. "You wanna talk? Go ahead. You talk, I'll listen. I'm tired a' talkin', I been talkin' all day. You're a very attractive young lady, you know that? I was delighted you got that TV job."

"Why, thank you, Phil. Mind if I sit?"

" 'Course not! Be my guest." Pauline sat down and crossed

her legs, balancing her notepad on her lap, and when she looked up, Raneer looked away.

"From your press conference, Phil," she said, "I take it you're a wine drinker. I never would have guessed."

"You bet. Wine, women, and . . . a good wine holds it age, unlike a woman. On the other hand, a wine can be too young." He smiled at Pauline, who did her best to smile back.

If she weren't conspiring to rip him in print, she would never have let that wisecrack pass, but this was no time to be challenging Raneer, so she played along, asking, "What kind of wine do you prefer?"

"Well now, all good wines meet up at the top, but I'm into French . . . how about you?" That second bourbon was history, so he walked to the bar and poured himself a third. "I'll have to take ya out sometime, or have ya over here. I've got a cellar you would not . . . 'course the best is in New York— we'll have ta do it there. . . ."

"Fine, Phil, that would be nice. That's actually what I wanted to talk to you about. I've been thinking of doing a profile on you, to get at the man behind the mask."

"What mask? If this were a mask, you think I wouldn't find a better one?"

Pauline smiled. "You know what I mean. We both know there's more there than meets the eye . . . but if I'm going to find it, I'll have to get to know you, maybe follow you around for a few days, sit· in on your meetings, become part of the woodwork. What do you think?"

"Woodwork, huh? You think it *would work?* You think I'm gonna take that for a *table* leg?"

"You'll get used to it."

"I'll bet." He took another sip. "I'll bet I could. But tell me . . ." He walked over, wavering, put his drink on the table, then flopped down onto the sofa beside her. "You've been givin' me a hard time ever since I laid eyes on ya . . . I mean a *real* hard time. Now, I don't know what I did to deserve it, but one thing I wanna know is: First, why this change a' heart, an' second . . . why should I go outta *my* way to help *you?*"

"There's no real reason, Phil . . . you certainly don't have to . . . but I thought it might be interesting. Of course, if you're afraid I'll . . ."

"Yeah, uh-huh . . . boy, you are somethin' . . . you don't miss a trick, do ya? That was a mighty fine story you did on Pardee, by the way."

"Thank you."

"A genuine hero, huh? How'd you come up with it?"

"Just lucky, I guess."

Raneer leaned over. "Maybe you'd like to get lucky again." Pauline froze. "Whattya say? I know how you got that story, kid . . . I know all about it."

"All about what?" She put her notepad on the table.

"All about you an' your *ball*player friend."

She sat up quickly. "It's not what you think."

"That's a laugh. But it don't matter what *I* think, I know what *I* think, what matters is what *you* think. How about it?" He slipped his fingers into her hair, lightly encircling the back of her neck, his eyes glazed with the effects of all that booze, and the thought of one more scented auburn trophy for his wall. "You want that story? I'll set ya right up. I'll give ya some good stuff . . . some *real* good stuff."

Pauline reached back and removed his hand. "Excuse me, Phil, the interview's over."

"No it ain't." He held her back. "It ain't even started."

"Phil, you're drunk. Now, let me go."

"Come on, kid . . . *I'll do anything you want.* . . ."

Pauline knocked over the coffee table and jumped out to the center of the floor. "You touch me again, I'll sue you, Raneer."

"Go ahead . . . sue, ya goddamn tease . . . we'll call in Pardee, he can *testify.*"

"You bastard. You couldn't shine his shoes."

"Bastard, huh? Go ahead an' laugh, ya fancy smart-ass New York slut!"

"Fine, Phil."

"It's fine with me. James . . . *James!* Escort the lady out!"

"Really, Phil . . . who writes your dialogue?"

3

Figuring that there was no point in getting him involved, all she told Darryl was that Raneer had made a play for her, but his lackadaisical response of "Typical" bothered Pauline in much the same way that she was beginning to be annoyed by his basic refusal to act jealous, be suspicious, or brood about her at all. Pardee, of course, had his own way of brooding, but the way he kept it hidden was doing her no good. In the end she decided it was better off ignored, so she set about trying to forget the whole thing, especially some of the things she had said.

Monday's broadcast was in the afternoon, because it finally, and officially, was Labor Day. There was plenty of action to keep her hopping in a 7–4 Ballclub win over Detroit, but as she was signing off for Donovan and Letts, a large crowd gathered beneath the booth, shouting, "We want Pauline! We want Pauline!"

It was a joke at first, so she smiled and waved, but as more and more fans joined in, she grew more and more uneasy. They were just showing off for national TV, but while they might be nice boys if taken alone, she had already seen what they could do together, and the fact that it was *her* name they were calling was giving her a chill.

Pauline had received her share of obscene fan letters, describing what those anonymous males out there would like to do to her, and an equal number had come from covens and devil worshipers, with insane scrawlings, signed *666;* but while she wasn't quite ready to take on a secretary to screen her mail and save her such abuse, she wished she could get it all out of her mind, as she hurried down the back stairs onto the street. "We want Pauline!" the chant continued. They had yet to realize she was gone.

Darryl took even longer than usual to come back to his room, so she gave up waiting, deciding that he must have gone out for a beer; little suspecting that the reason he never arrived was that Raneer had stopped in the locker room after the game, making his usual overbearing show of himself, before drifting over to Pardee's locker and saying, loud enough for most of his teammates to hear:

"Saw your lady friend yesterday, Pardee. She is *amazin'* . . . that girl will do *anything* for a story . . . but she left this behind, so I thought I'd drop it off." Raneer took Pauline's bourbon-stained notepad, dropped it in his lap, then skipped out the door; and Darryl got so steamed up that he had to take a long walk afterward, so Pauline went out alone to the main gate, where her bags were waiting in the limousine.

The last light of day was fading from the sky. The colors were chaotic, streaming from the mirrors on the carousels. She passed by the Bullwhip and the Penny Arcade, where black lights strobed to a disco beat, down the long Walk of Fame, with its fifty bronze busts, to the entranceway, littered with stubs mixed in with the first leaves falling from the trees. Turning around to take it all in, Pauline said her goodbyes to Ballpark, then pushed through the slatted rotating gates, out into the world. A calm had finally descended on her that even the madness of Fast Phil's dreamland couldn't obscure.

Chapter 3

1

Thursday, September 9. She was down at *Lifetimes,* working on the pennant race, when Sullivan called her in, saying, "All right," as soon as she arrived, "what's going on?"

"I love these setups, Frank . . . you tell me." She sat.

"I just got a call from Raneer."

"And?"

"He wants you off his team."

"I'm not on his team."

"That's what I said. But he wasn't through. He said you got that story by sleeping with Pardee."

"What did you say?"

"I said to fuck off. That it was none a' my business *who* you slept with."

"Thanks, Frank."

"What happened out there?"

"Can we keep it in this office?"

"Of course."

"All right. I have been seeing Pardee"—Sullivan gave out a long low whistle—"and Raneer found out. He must keep tabs on his whole team. I was trying to arrange for a feature on him, to see if he'd let me follow him around . . . but he got a little drunk . . . and since he knew about Darryl, I guess he figured I'd sleep with him.''

"Now I see why you didn't want that story. Why didn't you say so?" She scowled. "So Raneer put the move on, and you told him to . . .''

"That's right. Just like you. It was kind of ugly.''

"I gathered that. I doubt you've heard the last of him.''

"What should I do?''

"Who the hell knows? He was pretty damned mad.''

"Maybe I should go after him. Something's wrong in Ballpark, Frank. He fired his front office—''

"That was a month ago.''

"There was all that violence—''

"We covered it. Listen, I don't like the guy myself, but we can't give him more space, he thrives on it. I already feel like a shill. What made you think I'd assign a feature?''

"If you'll—''

"Let it drop, Pauline. I want you down at Yankee Stadium today, to see what the fuss is all about. And how's that update coming?''

"It's due on Sunday, right?''

"Right.''

"So what are you asking me now for?''

"Touchy.''

"All right, Frank, I'm going back to work." She got up. "But thanks. I mean it. It means a lot to me.''

"Well, it rots my gut. It's nobody's business but your own. Pardee, huh?" He smiled slyly, shaking his hand, "Nothin' but the best, I always say.''

"Get outta here, Frank, I'll see you later." She walked back to her office and shut the door.

2

The House That Ruth Built was a house divided, with the new manager and free agents on one side and the established veterans on the other. Pauline did her best to track down the problem, but although she was a big shot with a mike in her hand, armed with a pen she was just a raw recruit, trying to hold her own in the media wars of New York against cutthroat pros from the *Post,* the *Times, Sports Illustrated,* the *Daily News,* and half a dozen other major magazines and papers. Players kept disappearing with the columnists of their choice, and when Pauline would stand over a shoulder, listening, she'd be met with an angry glare.

Only by running around twice as much as anyone else did she finally come up with a decent story, and then only because Phil Plank, of the *News,* was willing to open his notepad to her, knowing he'd be out tomorrow, and scoop her by a week. Returning to the office, she worked late that night, and turned in ten inches by the next morning. Sullivan was pleased, but he had no idea how inept she felt.

With that out of the way, her only current project was the update she'd been writing, but there was no way to proceed on that without the next day's scores; so, faced with a Friday with nothing to do, Pauline grabbed the phone and dialed information for the *Fort Worth Star-Telegram,* to contact one of the writers she'd met after the Rangers' broadcast.

"Sports desk."

"Jerry Davis, please."

"You got him."

"Jerry? This is Pauline Reese."

"*Hello, Pauline . . .* comin' down again?"

"Not for a while. Listen, I've got a few questions."

"Shoot."

"What do you know about Phil Raneer?"

"Not much."

"He's from Fort Worth, you must know something. What's his background? Are you busy?"

"Not too."

"What can you tell me? Anything at all would be a help."

"Well, I moved down here about five years ago, so all my

knowledge is secondhand, but the way I heard it, he was raised by his aunt—"

"Why's that?"

"Don't know."

"Keep going."

"He was one of those kids who'll do anything for a buck. Always hustling. Organizing car washes down at the high school . . . dances . . . concession stands . . . worked as a checker at a little local grocery store, wound up managing the place—this was still in high school. Said he'd be a millionaire some day. People laughed."

"I'm not surprised."

"Is this any help? I wrote it all up in a story once. It's nothing but hearsay, but I could send it along."

"That would be great, but keep on going." She was taking notes all the while.

"Well, he dodged the draft taking care of his aunt . . ."

"That's funny. I distinctly remember him talking about the Army."

"Must have seen some movie then, because I know for a fact that by the time the war was over, he was all set up with a few small businesses, among which was his very first burger stand. It didn't go anywhere for the longest time, then all of a sudden the whole thing took off, and that's the last they saw of him down here."

"Where are you from, by the way?"

"Missouri."

"How old is Raneer?"

"Fifty-three, fifty-four."

"Listen, Jerry, I need a favor. Is there anybody down there who'd look something up? I'll be happy to pay one of your research people, but I'm curious about that burger stand and how it took off. I'd like to know if there was anything behind it."

"Just an empty lot."

"I mean if . . ."

"That's a joke, Pauline. Let me guess . . . you want someone to look at the county clerk's . . . I'll do it."

"I didn't call up to get *you* involved."

"You said you wanted a favor, right? Well, I might need a favor too. I was thinking of moving up North some time . . . maybe you'll introduce me. What do you think?"

"It'll be my pleasure."

"Besides, I haven't done anything like this since college. Used to hate it. What are you looking for?"

"Just see if there's anything unusual in there. Any names you might recognize, some kind of pattern. It shouldn't take *too* long . . . and I promise I'll make it up to you."

"I'm gonna hold you to that, Pauline. I'll make you wish you never said it."

Chapter 4

Saturday the 11th. Word arrived that Bill King, Baltimore's only lefty, had just sustained a fracture on his pitching hand, which meant that (a) the Orioles were in big trouble, and (b) Pauline had to spend the day revising her copy, because Baltimore had been coming on, and she'd seen fit to tout them. She got a phone call from Davis, in Fort Worth, reporting what he'd found; then just before quitting time her phone rang again, and a voice said, "Pauline?"

"Yes?"

"It's Bob Sylvester. Are you free this evening? I'd like to talk to you."

"What about?"

"Business."

"OK, what time?"

"Seven?"

"I know this Italian place at Twenty-eighth and Lexington—shall we meet there?"

"Fine," he said. "What's it called?"

"Francisco's. Anything else?"

"No."

"See you then." She mulled it over on her way uptown, then took a bath, lay down, shut her eyes, and napped. At six-thirty she woke, and combed out her hair, but she wasn't dressed until six fifty-six, when she did up the double bolts and ran down to the street.

Seven-oh-two. "Oh, cab . . ." she called, then stepped up on the curb, to avoid getting hit.

"Where to?"

"Twenty-eighth and Lexington."

"Hop in." The driver had a portable radio on. Muted horns and Gershwin, the forties, Gene Kelly.

"Nice night," said Pauline.

"Yeah," said the cabbie, wistfully.

"What time do you get off?"

"About three." He shrugged.

"Sorry about that."

"Yeah, well, I need the dough." She sat back and put on her makeup as the cabbie checked her out in the rearview mirror. When they got caught in traffic, around Fifty-fourth, he turned and said, "Aren't you that TV actress?"

"Not exactly."

"Yes you are, I saw you . . . I watch you all the time."

"Really? Do you enjoy it?"

"Not if it's a lousy game." He grinned.

"Any suggestions?"

"Yeah, come home with me, my wife's in Connecticut."

"Look out!" she screamed.

The cabbie veered left. "Idiot! You see that guy?"

"Yeah, and it's a good thing."

"Whaddya say? You think I'm kiddin'? They all think I'm kiddin'. Hey, you like baseball? This friend a' mine's drivin' a cab in Brooklyn, gets beat up by four black guys with Louisville Sluggers. So he's lyin' around the hospital the other day, an' says, 'You shoulda seen 'em, they were .400 hitters, every last one of 'em.' "

"Oooo . . ."

"Nice, huh? You like that? At least he's laughin' . . . but that's why I asked where you was goin', 'cause I'll take Manhattan, but . . . what was that, Lexington and . . ."

"Twenty-eighth. It's right over there." Seven thirty-one. She stepped through the door. Sylvester, who'd arrived early, had been waiting forty minutes. He rose when he saw her, took both her hands, and kissed her on the cheek.

"I'm late."

"Not at all."

"I'm sorry. I was sleeping."

"You look great," he said, and she shot him a glance.

If she looked great, it was a miracle. Sylvester, however, did look great, in khaki slacks with a camel's-hair sweater. "Watch it," she thought, as he held her chair.

"Business, huh?" she said, sitting down.

"Right. We can start now, or wait till after dinner."

"Afterward, *please,*" said Pauline.

They smiled and ordered. The food was good and Sylvester was impressed. He laughed and bantered, enjoying himself (the other diners had them pegged as lovers), then later, over espresso, his mood changed, and he said, "Well, is it time?"

"If we have to."

"I got a call this afternoon."

"Let me guess. It was Phil Raneer."

"He wants you off the broadcast."

"On what grounds?"

"That you can't be objective."

"Is that so? And did he tell you why?"

"He says you're sleeping with Pardee." He paused. "Is it true?"

"I don't think it's anyone's business, Bob."

"Of course not, Pauline, excuse me for asking, but this is no joke, he's a big account. What's going on with you two? I mean, you and Raneer."

"What else did he say?"

"I asked you first."

She hesitated. "I'm only telling you so that you'll know my side."

"All right."

"This is in strict confidence."

"I understand, Pauline."

"Raneer got drunk and made a play for me, and when I turned him down, he got angry."

"Is that all? That's not so bad."

"You had to be there."

"Well, I already told him I had no reason to get rid of you, so I'm glad to hear it was nothing important."

"Like what?"

"What?"

"What would be important?" Pauline felt a flush of resentment. That was hardly the sort of rousing defense she had gotten from Sullivan. "Never mind, Bob."

"It would have to be a serious breach, but whatever you do, try to be discreet."

"I am discreet. Raneer has spies. OK? Are we through?"

"As far as I'm concerned."

Pauline sipped her coffee and tried to simmer down. She hated to be lectured about how to live her life, and was particularly irritated to have to talk about Pardee. Sylvester took a look at her and tried to bring her back.

"I'm sorry to get involved in this."

"Forget it."

"If he calls up again, I'll tell him where to go."

Pauline had a hard time trying to picture that. Sylvester wasn't the type to go telling people off. His motto was more like: Give them what they need. There was a lull. She tried to relax, to keep from building a case against him. "You know, he tried the same stunt at the magazine?"

"I'm not surprised. Are you planning to retaliate?"

"I'd like to, believe me. What do you know about real estate? I've been told that Raneer has all these multiple mortgages. The guy who looked it up said that all his titles read something like:

'This is a third deed of trust, subject to a second deed of trust, and first deed of trust of record.' "

"So?"

"Does that mean anything? Does it mean he's in hock?"

"I doubt it. A guy like Raneer starts out with a few grand, and makes a down payment on a property. When the value rises, he goes back for a second mortgage, at the increased price, and takes the extra cash and buys something else."

"And so on and so on?"

"Right. He sells his burgers to pay the rent, but makes his real money off inflation. As long as things keep going up, he keeps remortgaging, and gets all this cash for nothing. That's what they call pyramiding, Pauline, and he's built more pyramids in his day than King Tut."

"Keep going."

"This is pretty basic stuff."

"I'm just a sportswriter, Bob."

"Well, I heard that in order to get Ballpark going, he had to swing a loan from his own employees' pension fund."

"Is that legal?"

"Legal, schmegal . . . the fund's with one of his insurers, right? So he goes to them and says, 'Gimme a loan, or I'll transfer the account.' "

"How do you know all this?"

"Raneer's been looking into cable TV, and is talking about setting up a satellite network. We've been making some inquiries."

"Does he worry you?"

"Well, cables worry us, and satellites are a big threat, but I don't think Raneer'll make it. He's pretty overextended already."

"Why do people keep backing him? How does he operate?"

"Seems like you'd be the expert on that." He smiled. "He's slick, see . . . keeps a large liquid reserve on hand, about ten million."

"Then he *does* have money?"

"Just listen. By keeping all that cash around, he looks good on paper, so when he asks for a loan, what can they do? Turn him down, he'll withdraw his account, and they'll lose all his money to invest, or loan out."

"So he keeps it with them, and takes it from them. It doesn't make sense."

"That's the point. He waves that ten million in front of their faces, but meanwhile he's got operational costs—rents on properties, salaries, management fees, purchasing and publicity—he's got a nut you would not believe."

"Can I take this down?"

"Go ahead, only . . ."

"I know. Don't quote you." She took out her notepad and started to write.

"Want me to repeat anything?"

"No."

"Well, the banking term is 'operational leverage.' Cash on hand versus cash demands. Raneer's got his ten million—I made that figure up, incidentally—but if something went wrong, if the prime jumped, or a source of income dried up, or if there were some new drain on his resources—"

"Like Ballpark?"

"—or cable TV, he could run through that cash in nothing flat. It's thin, Pauline. He's managed to leverage what really is very little, given his scale, into an enormous debt, and if you see the operation as a giant wheel, then every spoke is vulnerable."

"Think he'll pull it off?"

"I think with Ballpark he's reached his limit, but the bigger you are, the easier it gets . . . and he's an incredible con artist, he knows just how to play them, so who knows? He's a powerful man. I wouldn't want to get in any feuds with him."

"I'm afraid it's too late."

"Ah, guys like that like to blow off steam. It'll die down."

Pauline didn't answer. She stared off into space. Raneer had tried to screw her—three times—but at least she had something to go on now. Sylvester had quite an authoritative air; she had almost forgotten she was several years his senior. She tried to grab the check after dinner, but he beat her to it with a credit card, then outside he hailed a cab, asking if she wanted to join him for a drink.

"Not really," she said, smiling at the look of disappointment on his face. "Would you drop me off uptown?"

She thought it over all the way home, then just before they reached her apartment, dropped a hand on his, and said, "Come on up." Sylvester looked over, unsure of what she wanted, and Pauline had a hard time understanding it herself. He was her boss, after all, he had pissed her off at dinner, and it did seem odd with what Raneer had said, but along with her partner, the night was young, and she was ready to take advantage of both of them.

PART FIVE

The Final
Weeks

"The American League office writes letters to the players: 'Don't use foul language on the fans.' When you're talking about fans, you're not talking about people who come with their families. You're talking about the idiots who pay their $2.50 to sit in the stands and throw things at you. . . . I don't see any letters going out to the fans, saying, 'Don't use abusive language on the players and don't throw stuff at them.' But we get fined if we drop a 'motherfucker' on somebody after they spend five minutes calling you an asshole."

—Sparky Lyle, former relief pitcher for the New York Yankees. From The Bronx Zoo, *by Sparky Lyle and Peter Golenbock.*

Chapter 1

1

Chicago, Tuesday, September 14. The White Sox regulars were finishing up, hopping in and out of the cage, laughing and cursing. One thing about baseball—either you can hit, or you can't. You don't have to hide your swing or come up with a complex computerized game plan; if you have a weakness, it's already known. If you have a good arm, you air it out, you give them something to think about.

Darryl loosened up on the line until the Sox were through at six-fifteen, then moved to the plate. He caught some lip when he first stepped in, but cut the banter to a long low whistle with his first three shots to left. The next two went over the fence, four went up the alleys, then he laid down a bunt and stepped out, saying, "Too bad they don't count."

They batted around until six-forty, when the grounds crew ran out to clear away the backstop. The Ballclub took ten minutes of infield practice, then went down to the locker room, where Darryl lay on a canvas-topped table, his arms folded over his chest, listening to the slap of cards from Stutz's office, where the trainer was socking it to Hamilton and Reed.

At seven-ten the call came, and Pardee was glad. He lived for that moment late in the day when the shadows of the grandstand drift across the mound, and the grass glows a perfect green, theatrically lit under an open sky. Smells and cries of "Popcorn! Peanuts!" fill the air, "Get yer programs here!" and the babble builds as the teams hit the field, then remove their hats for the silent tableau, and everyone pauses for that consecrated moment while the anthem is sung, until the first cheers rise.

2

They flew to Ohio for their last home series, and beat the Brewers and Blue Jays four out of six; but the next stop was Cleveland, where a packed house of seventy thousand fans showed up. Before the first game even began, Zarino, out in the bullpen, got a pizza dumped on his head when he objected to the beer that preceded it, and was only barely restrained from climbing the wall to find out what happened to the anchovies.

The abuse was intense, and the toll that all the previous games had taken was starting to show. Leopold, at second, had lost fifteen of his original 158 pounds, and looked like a kid under an old man's face. Alvarez had shin splints; and Martinez had scabs on his hips, four inches wide and a quarter inch thick, that tore off every time he slid; but the worst disaster of all was Bernard.

The Big Fromage needed a rest. He needed a rest home in the Laurentians and the ministrations of French Canadian nurses of no more than twelve or fourteen years. Every time he squatted, the whole bench groaned. It was a crime to keep playing him, but the backup catcher, Campbell, had been worthless ever since Radivin had taken up with Philly Mike, so Bernard told Hart to use him until he dropped, and the Kraut had no choice but to oblige.

A bruised and battered Ballclub dropped two straight to the Indians and saw the pennant flying out the window—with two little wings flapping, just like in the cartoons (Hart was attempting to convince himself that it was impossible, unreasonable—even worse than that, naive—to expect a team to win its first time out)—when starting pitcher Danny Leary got so mad at both himself and the quality of the fielding behind him that he threw the ball at Kenny Carlton.

Leary got a warning, then went right back and did it again, and when Carlton dropped his bat and approached the mound, both dugouts emptied on the run. Leary claimed in his own defense that he'd only thrown at Carlton the second time, that the first one slipped. Bernard, limping around like the late Walter Brennan, kept insisting that Leary's straight ball—he refused to call it a fastball—wouldn't hurt anyone anyway; then Carlton broke loose and took a swing at Leary, who was asking for it, and the fun began for real.

It was a typical barnyard fracas, which Pardee watched from the left field line, with people climbing over people's backs, to deliver blows while other people's hands were being held—the highlight of which, if there was one, came when Stokey blinded Carlton with a gob of gooey tobacco spit, and the shortstop had to be led from the field as in a summer stock version of *King Lear*. When calm was restored, seven men had been ejected, starting with Leary, who detoured by the Indian bench to flip them all the bird.

Tiny Tim had done his job. With Foster firing fastballs in relief, the Ballclub stormed back from a 4–1 deficit, to take this absolutely crucial game by a score of 7–5. Back in the locker room, Hart locked the doors, to watch in disgust as his team licked its wounds.

"Contrary to popular opinion," he admonished, breaking the silence, "the best team does *not* always win. The *toughest* team wins. The team that will not *lose* wins! Look at ya! You call that a fight? Try it in New York an' they'll crucify ya!

"All injuries report to Stutz. I don't want nobody hidin' nothin' . . . an' the rest a' you can think about it. Maybe if you're ready to kick some ass, we can start talkin' *pennant* around here! You can all chip in for Leary's fine, an' thank him, as pitiful as he is . . . for havin' the guts to wake you up!'' He slammed out the door.

"What the hell is he krautin' about?" said Leary. "We won the fuckin' thing."

"Right! Raw! Rooo . . ." came the chorus, as they gathered round to slap him on the back, then they threw him in the shower, where they rehashed the fight, washing all the cheap shots clean. The good people of Cleveland might know better, but the Ballclub was leaving town anyway, so fuck 'em.

Nothing could bring a team together like a brawl. Hart didn't know which of his prayers had been answered, but it was nothing short of a miracle. Even his own faith had been wavering, and that was something of a miracle itself. He grabbed a pocket calculator and figured out the standings:

	W-L	Pct.	Games Behind
New York	89–62	.589	—
Boston	88–62	.587	½
Ballpark	88–63	.584	1
Baltimore	87–64	.576	2

"Only .584," thought Hart. "Not even .600. In what other sport do you have to work so hard to win a title? In football they sometimes go undefeated. *Undefeated,* fer Chrissake. . . ." The Kraut cut it off. This was no time to get wistful. The Orioles were down in fourth place and Baltimore (he wasn't sure which was worse), just waiting for someone to waltz in dreaming. That city was tough enough to begin with, they had stoned both sides during the Civil War, and now it was the Ballclub's turn to face a citizenry whose habitual ill will was about to be stirred up even further, by the printing of a column picked up from Cleveland:

WAR HEROES AND TRUE GRIT
by Art Schneider

CLEVELAND, September 27—No one in their right mind advocates violence, but the only thing worse than violence on the playing field is fear. Fights may be the worst thing about ice hockey, but as things stand they're part of the game, and the team that won't fight can't win.

These thoughts come to mind in the wake of a brawl between the so-called Ballclub and our Cleveland Indians, during which Ballpark's shortstop Paul Hogan was left facing three men, while the so-called war hero Darryl Pardee stared off into space.

People have been wondering about Pardee, whose production this year has been erratic at best, but I have this theory: It takes guts to win a pennant. The main difference, in fact, between the guys in the Majors and a lot of the rest of us is the courage to stand up to those hundred-mile-an-hour fastballs. (If you're looking for guys who bail out—sign me up!) Certain kinds of risk go along with the game, but if you'd rather avoid them, as Pardee seemed to in a rather gritless display of what passes for team loyalty in these days of the million-dollar contract, then as a fan I can only say, I'm glad you're playing for somebody else.

At one point I'd have taken a Pardee at any price, no questions asked. There was a time when five teams were bidding for his contract, but the times they are a-changin'.

We've all read our fill about the Vietnam vet, how he went off to fight a lousy war—as if it were worse than any other wars—and came home without honor; but if Pardee's performance yesterday is any indication of the kind of war they fought—and he was supposed to be one of the best—it's no wonder they lost.

Darryl never looked at the story himself, but he heard about it from the first time he took the playing field, until the very last out of the very last game. "Hey Pardee!" They would wave it from the stands. "No guts! See that? It says so right here! Hey, Pardee . . . can you read? Read *this!*" punctuated by some sort of obscene gesture.

Darryl wound up going two for thirteen, but he was just a minor casualty of the Baltimore series. Hogan got spiked at second on a late throw from Leopold, and took eleven stitches up the left leg. Martinez fouled a ball off his foot, severely bruising his big toe; and relief pitcher Dan Radivin, who hadn't hit since the inception of the DH rule, enraged Hart and earned a five-hundred-dollar fine by jamming his thumb in the batting cage.

Bernard, meanwhile, was taken to the hospital after a game-ending collision with Garrett Haines. Oriole manager Earl Clark called it "hardnosed baseball," but the replay showed clearly that it wasn't Haines' nose lodged firmly in the Canuck's groin, but his knee. The Frenchman held the ball to preserve the win, but had to be carried from the field in a fetal posture that broadcast the nature of his injury to the great delight of the departing crowd.

Puck's pecker swelled up like a mule's, but on the whole the Kraut felt lucky. Although they were racked, they'd won two out of three, to get out of town in second place. Now it was up to the pitching, and outside of a blister on Leary's middle finger (which he delighted in showing to reporters) and Radivin's thumb—Hart didn't talk to him for days, he wanted him scared to death the next time he took the mound—all hands were intact.

Chapter 2

1

Pauline Reese and Bob Sylvester. It didn't take long. Ever since their first *soirée* they'd been enjoying New York in a way that she and Pardee never could, for any number of reasons. They took in a play, went to a concert, and were spotted in a small Portuguese place that no one had ever heard of, except the thousands of New Yorkers who make small places that no one's ever heard of an obsession. He had a few friends over when she was there, they got to know each other, and the longer it went on, the more she found that she enjoyed the kid, so she saw him when she felt like it, which was constantly, and tried to think it through.

Two men? While there was nothing inherently wrong with the notion, the deeper question wasn't whether she wanted both of them, but whether she really wanted either one. The way things were going, she was just fooling around (the last time she was serious was her senior year in college, when it was nearly terminal—the house, the kids, the doctor, the Volvo . . .), but now that she had two such formidable men in her life, her habit of staying at arms' length was worth another look.

Just for the sake of argument, she took out a pad and drew up a scorecard, to see which one she would choose if she had to:

PLUSES AND MINUSES

1. Sylvester is witty. Quite quick, actually . . .
   Pardee is taciturn.
2. Pardee's the best third baseman in the history
   of baseball . . .
   Sylvester plays a mean game of tennis.
3. <u>Get serious</u>!! [underlined twice]
4. Looks: Sylvester . . . a little too good.
   Pardee . . . [she left it blank]
5. Smile:
6. Teeth:
7. Income: Pardee . . . 500,000 a year.
   Sylvester . . . a mere 150.
8. Friends: Sylvester . . . doctors, lawyers, movie stars, politicians, musicians, dope growers from Humboldt County, writers and cameramen, athletes and professors . . . etc., etc. . . .
   Pardee . . . teammates (??) . . . me . . . *Lanette.*
9. Lovers:

"Oh, brother," she sighed, putting down the pad. Pardee made love with an ardor that consumed her, while Baby Bob was expert, as in everything he did. Problems. Problems. She wondered what was bothering her. Was Sylvester using her? Absolutely. And she was using him. And they'd go on that way, using each other, until one of them came up with a reason to stop.

2

Pauline took a week to map her strategy, trying it out on Baby Bob, then went right back to see Sullivan again. "You look chipper," he said as she walked in. "What can I do for you? Coffee?"

"I'm here about Raneer."

"I thought we discussed that."

"I've got some information."

"Look, Pauline, I can't conduct any vendettas around here. You have a personal grudge against the man? That's your business."

"Will you just listen? I had someone check out the county recorder's—"

"Jesus Christ, it's Brenda Starr."

"—and it turns out that not only does he have all these multiple mortgages—"

"So what?"

"—but he's overextended, Frank, way out on a limb. There's a story there, I know it."

"Listen, we gave thirty lines last week to the parliamentary crisis in France. Will you forget it? Some day we'll have a magazine of our own, just you and me . . . with no space problems . . . no deadlines . . . no *subscribers* . . ."

"Look what's happening to baseball, Frank. What kind of people are running it now? It's like Gresham's Law, bad money drives out the good, and it's not just Raneer, it's everywhere."

"Gresham's Law, huh?" He gave up and listened.

"What I envision is a story that by focusing on Ballpark would delve into all the problems of modern ownership—the decline of the farm system, the consequences of free agency—it's a disaster, Frank, and we haven't seen a thing. What happens when the owners get tired of spending and try to break up the Players' Association? We'll have walkouts, strikes . . . and what happens if Raneer, or *any* of these owners, goes under?"

"Someone else'll buy it. They're linin' up all over the place."

"Maybe so, but the whole thing's unsound and Raneer provides the perfect example. He's overspending, underfinanced, and if he does go down, you'll have all these gigantic salaries to deal with, deferred over God knows how many years. Who the hell's going to pick them up if he keeps on this way? Someone with more money but even less sense? Great! That's just what baseball needs."

Sullivan didn't respond, and she knew better than to push him. The longer he thought, the quieter she got, until, "The salary thing's your hook, Pauline. How much does he owe, to the players themselves?"

"Pardee's getting two point five, Fuller about the same . . . Martinez, Alvarez, Phillips, and Hunsicker . . ." She ticked off the names on her fingers. "The other teams are furious about what he's doing . . . and that's *nothing* compared to what he owes for Ballpark, Frank, which is why he's in trouble to begin with. And now he's talking about satellites, and cable TV. If he makes it, fine. But if he doesn't . . ."

He thought some more. "I can't have *you* running around on this."

"I don't want it, believe me. Business is not my forte, although I will chip in with a profile if you want."

"I'll think about it."

"It's a great story, Frank."

"Get out." She was gone.

3

That night at home, she typed up a list, composed of tidbits she'd picked up over the years, including a filler blurb she had found in the *Times,* which stated that the power bill alone for Yankee Stadium amounted to four hundred thousand dollars a year, and that maintenance was well over three hundred grand, along with other notes, specific to Ballpark, listing expenses Raneer had incurred, including:

—Buying the land, and laying in the basic services (water, gas, sewers, and electricity)
—Building the place, with plenty of overtime
—Moving the Clippers to Muncie, Indiana
—Organizing a lavish series of promotions
—Overpaying his players
—Compensating the other owners
—Starting up a minor-league system
—And sponsoring his own games on TV, which looked fine at first, until Pauline realized that he was depriving him- self of a major source of income—by paying the station

to broadcast the shows, and at the same time losing out on his fee.

Obviously the Ballclub had to be seen as a tax write-off, or a loss leader for Ballpark itself, but either way, the costs were staggering. Without a word she took her list and left it on Sullivan's desk.

There was nothing more until Friday, the 24th, when he stopped by her office after his morning meeting and said, with some resignation, "Well, it's a go. I've gotten approval to check him out. We're still not sure if the story should be on him or on baseball in general, but whatever it is, I want you to stay out. This kind of thing is difficult to research, he's a private corporation, so we can't get at his books, so until or unless we have something more to go on . . . forget it's even happening. Is that clear?"

"Fine, Frank, I promise."

"Not that I believe you . . . but if I catch you working on this on *my* time, Pauline, I'm going to be very upset."

"I think you're doing the right thing."

"I know what you think. Now, what about the Dodgers?" He pointed at her copy, then took off down the hall.

Later that day she ran into Bill Matheson, from the financial section, who told her that her notes had been a great help, that since he wasn't much of a baseball fan, there were a few things he might have overlooked. He was beginning to sound out Raneer's backers, and would be getting in touch with the Commissioner's office, to find out the procedures in case of a default; and he told Pauline that if she had any more thoughts, she should send them along.

4

Monday, September 27. Matheson told Sullivan he would need some help, then Sullivan got the go-ahead from his managing editor, Ralph Brill, to name Barbara Wilson, reporter, a special assistant on the project. When Pauline stopped by to wish her luck, Wilson looked up and said, "You too . . ." Ruefully.

"What does that mean?" thought Pauline. "Someone's been talking. Well, obviously I'm involved, but . . ." She caught herself. "Paranoid . . . great."

At two P.M. she took the Metroliner south to her broadcast in Philadelphia. The seats were first class, with plenty of legroom, and the ride had always been one of her favorites. Take Trenton, New Jersey . . . *please*. Even the sign said, "Trenton Makes, the World Takes," on the railroad bridge by the road running in. *Take it takka-tokka take it, Take it takka-tokka take it* . . . down through the hard brick back of North Philly, over the tree-lined banks of the Schuylkill, then underground, to Thirtieth Street, into a cab and down to the Vet.

She spent the night with a girl friend from Smith, in an apartment by the Penn campus; came back to New York to spend her days off with Sylvester, then returned to work on Thursday, September 30, to find that prospects for the story were not looking good. Matheson explained that Raneer's holdings were spread out so effectively that the banks and insurers were interdependent, propping each other up, and acting as guarantors. If Raneer was to fall, they'd all lose out, so basically he was under their protection. While Matheson agreed with Pauline that the figures were suspect, he told her he doubted he could bring the story in.

Friday, September 31. Pauline flew to Boston, north over the ocean, where the waves seemed not to move at all, but were textured in a blue-gray glaze that might have been laid down by a mason's trowel. At one-ten the plane descended toward the Cape Cod shanties of the Boston archipelago and came screaming in over the harbor, and the long-suffering residents of East Boston, to land at Logan airport.

She took a cab to the Hyatt Hotel, in Cambridge, where a bellhop showed her to her spacious room on the eighth floor of the spectacular pyramidal hotel, open through fifteen stories.

She tipped him, then went down to the bar and grill, to order a sandwich, a coffee, and a Coke.

Two-fifteen. The doors sighed, and sixty tired men filed in, the Compleat Entourage of the Ballpark Traveling Road Show, with majordomo Howie Needleman, shouting orders, followed in nothing like order by Jerry Lasky, the new PR and stat man; Billy Colangelo, the equipment manager, who had made the wires a week before by impounding all of Zarino's equipment, until Fireball Steve, a notorious tightwad, coughed up what was laughingly called a gratuity for the past six months of slavish service; the six-man radio and TV crew, including Billy Blatt and Marty DeVries, the voices of Ballpark baseball (a simulcast); Artie Stutz; the six-man coaching staff; twenty-five regulars shambling along, their arms dangling down like primates'; fifteen rammy rookies, otherwise known as Turds ("Turd, do this. Turd, go shag flies . . ."), brought up when the rosters were expanded to forty; and five trusty sportswriters, lugging their Telerams—thirty-pound keyboards in their technological infancy, with TV screens for editing copy, which were worth their weight in rewrites and transmission through the phone lines, but just barely.

The writers tilted toward the elevators, as the players headed directly up for lunch. Pauline spotted Pardee, sitting down with Goldhammer, and went over to join them. "Howdy, Ira. Hi, Darryl . . . have a nice flight?"

One eye looked up, then the rest of him looked up. "Some people liked it." He stared at her. "Some people like makeup."

Pauline looked at Goldhammer, who shrugged, then she slid into the booth, as the Hammer put his arm around her and said, "Hey, Pauline, I got one for you. What's the difference between parsley and pussy?"

She lifted his arm and slid underneath. "I don't know, Ira . . . I give up."

"Nobody eats parsley."

"I do," she deadpanned. "But I always wash it off in my water glass." She picked hers up and took a long seductive sip, as Pardee got up to leave. "Excuse me, Darryl, I didn't mean to *offend* you . . ."

Pardee paused, was about to answer, then thought better of it, turned, and disappeared.

Chapter 3

1

He was angry with her, that much was obvious, although she had no idea why. It could have been Sylvester, but she didn't think Darryl knew about him, and even if he did, a reaction such as she'd gotten this afternoon would not have been in character. Especially in front of Goldhammer. He'd have kept quiet and said nothing.

She puzzled it over until six-thirty, when she crossed the river, heading for the stadium, and just as it happened most of the time, the knowledge that she was about to see a ballgame brightened her mood and erased all her concerns. The process was like a return to childhood; no matter that she did it for a living now, there was still a trace of those bygone days when her father would take her brothers, dragging her along, to a twinight doubleheader, that would end with Pauline being carried upstairs, asleep but not asleep, stuffed with hot dogs and dazzled by the lights, happy as only a little girl can be whose daddy let her share in the secrets of his sex.

Her excitement began on the short drive in, when she first spotted the lights. It built as she walked by the parking lots, where the young men raced ahead of their dates, and peaked with her first glimpse of the playing field, which conveyed a sudden elegance to the night. She stood and watched from behind the stands, as the grounds crew dragged around its hemp mats, then she wandered down to the side of the dugout, where a group of young punks were badgering the players as they loosened up their arms. "I'd never miss one if our field looked like *that*," said one guy. "Hey, Hogan, you suck!" He refused to turn around. "You stink, Hogan! Hey, Hogan, whattsa matta? I'm talkin' to you."

"Ooo-ooo . . ." His buddies, meanwhile, were swinging on the railing, saying, "Hey, Leopold, have a banana," making jungle calls and ugly ape noises, before turning to Darryl, shouting, "Hey, Pardee! Ya geek! Ya get any gooks lately?" at which point Pauline took off for the press box.

Pardee wound up taking the collar (0–4) and made a careless error in the field, and the whole team seemed a little shaky that night; but when reporters suggested to Hart back in the clubhouse that he was lucky to escape by a count of 4–3, thanks to a game-saving catch by Alvarez in center, the Kraut informed them that in his book there was no such thing as luck this late in the year, only winners and losers.

2

Pauline hit the locker room after the game, but instead of plunging into the interviews, she took a place against the wall, thinking as she watched that the players seemed tense. Tonight's win only meant they had to win tomorrow, so none of them even had his heart in having fun. The Kraut had so brainwashed them that they found, to their amazement, that they were just like him, and it really pissed them off, because they knew quite well how distorted he was.

Pauline trailed Darryl out to the bus, then pulled him aside and into a cab, so they could talk; but the beat-up independent Checker she'd flagged down was driven by an intense beady-eyed guy named Ron (it said so on the side) who recognized

Pardee and launched in on the story of his life—how he'd been a grad student in philosophy at Harvard, until the war blew the positivism right out of his logic. "It was nuts around here, you wouldn't have believed it."

"I'd believe it, all right," said Pardee, "Look at it now."

When they reached the hotel, the cabbie shook his hand. "A pleasure, Darryl, but do me a favor. If you have to win here, at least go down and take the Yankees, will ya? Take it easy." He grinned, and tooled off into the night.

"Guy likes to talk," said Pauline.

"What's wrong with that? Seemed pretty decent to me. Listen, I'm beat. I'll see ya later."

"Darryl, stop." He kept on walking.

"Darryl, *please*," she said loudly, as he stepped back from the automatic doors. "Don't make a scene, I really have to talk to you. I don't know what you've got against me . . ." She waited, as several people walked by. "But you've been treating me like dirt, ever since I got here, and I wish you would stop. Now, I don't intend to have it out on the street, so if you feel like it, I'm in 815."

Pauline went into the glass-walled elevator, as Pardee watched from the downstairs lobby; then she disappeared, and he followed her up. Hugging the inside of the eighth-floor corridor, so he wouldn't be visible from below, he arrived at her room, which he found unlocked.

Pauline was sitting at her desk. She turned, as Darryl fell onto her bed. It was her place to begin. "All right, what's the story?"

"No story."

"Let's not play games, shall we? What's bothering you?"

"Nothin'."

"Here we go again."

"Listen, Pauline . . . I don't care what you do, you're a big girl, you can do what you want . . . but the one person I'd expect you'd have the sense to stay away from is Raneer."

"*Raneer?* What are you talking about?"

"The guy comes in, makes a fool outta me . . ."

"Darryl, this is crazy."

"Don't lie to me, Pauline."

"I'm not. I *told* you what happened. What are you so mad about?"

"How come he knows about you and me? Half the guys on the ballclub know."

"Look, Darryl . . . I don't know how he found out, but he thought I got that story from you, so he figured I'd be willing to do the same for him."

"And you didn't?" She looked at him. "Then why didn't you tell me that he knew?"

"I didn't want to get you involved, but I was obviously giving him too much credit. He's told you, my boss at *Lifetimes* . . ." And here she thought of Baby Bob and decided to hold her tongue. "It's not you he's after, it's me. He's been trying to get my job. Now, why would he do that, if I slept with him?" Pardee didn't answer. "Darryl, I'm talking to you. Do you believe me, or not?"

Silence, as he sat forward, his eyes fixed on his hands. "All right, I believe you."

"Then what's your problem? You won't even look at me. Can't you please come clean . . . just once?"

"All right, Pauline . . . if you really wanna know, I'm still a little ticked at that story you wrote."

"What do you mean, still? You never even mentioned it." He stared at her. "Now, wait a minute . . . you didn't want to help me? Fine. But I've got a job, just like you." Pardee got up and walked to the window. "You want to hand out guilt trips?" she said. "Stay mad at me for the rest of your life? Go ahead, you probably will." Suddenly she got furious. "What the hell is the matter with you?"

Pardee was gazing out through the glass. His voice was flat and far away. "I've had it. I mean it. I don't want to hear it anymore. I am just tryin' to play baseball . . . that's all. Isn't that enough?"

"Darryl . . ."

"Forget it."

Chapter 4

Pauline woke around one A.M., to find his body rigid, completely tense, while his eyes fluttered beneath his lids, watching the approach of something so palpably frightful that she had to look twice to make sure they were alone. "Wake up," she said, reaching for his arm, as he jumped, ripping the bedsheets from her, and let out with a howl. "Darryl . . ." she cried, trying to hold him, but his wrist swung up and caught her in the eye.

Pardee was screaming, and Pauline was afraid to go near him now, as outside someone started pounding on the door. "Open up!" they shouted.

"Darryl, wake up . . ."

"Open up!" Pauline heard voices.

"Go away! We're fine! *Darryl* . . ." He began to come to, but the pounding continued.

"Open the door!"

"Jesus," said Pardee, "what's going—"

"It's all right . . . it was just a bad dream. *Hang on, will you?*" she shouted, wrapping herself in the blanket. "You OK?"

"Yeah," said Pardee. "I'm fine . . . hold me." Pauline took his head in her arms; there was a scratching at the lock, then the door was opened by the house detective, who was trailed by a large crowd of people, peering in.

"All right, what's going on?" He flicked on the light.

"Nothing," said Pauline. She walked over, hoping to turn him around.

"Yeah, sure, nothin' . . . look at ya . . ." He pushed his way past her, into the room.

"OK, buddy, what's the idea?"

"It was a nightmare," she said.

"Nightmare, huh?"

Pauline stepped over to check in the mirror. Her eye was streaming and starting to swell. "It's the truth. I'm a reporter. It's not what you think."

"Oh, no? Whattya call this? An undercover assignment?"

"Would you please ask these people to leave?"

"All right, folks . . . go back to your rooms, it's all over." He chased them out and shut the door. "You all right? Want a doctor?" He held her still to check it out.

"I'm fine," she told him, pulling away. "Can you keep this quiet?"

"Look, lady, did *you* keep it quiet? I don't imagine you two are registered together."

"We both have rooms in the hotel, OK?"

"Fine. I'm not lookin' for trouble. Just keep your hands to yourself." He pointed at Pardee.

"Will you go now?" said Pauline. "It was really just an accident."

"Okey-doke, lady . . . try an' get some sleep. Have a glass of warm milk . . . it's good for the nerves."

The guy took off, she locked the door behind him, then killed the light and came back to Darryl's side. "What happened? What was it?"

"Nothin', Pauline."

"Once again, it's none of my business."

"I didn't say that."

"You might as well. Look, Darryl . . . if you don't tell me what's bothering you, then I hope you enjoy the next few hours, because after that, we're through. I don't *need* this aggravation."

"If that's the way you want it."

"What I want is someone who'll share things with me, but you can't seem to hack it." She got up and stalked away.

"Sure, I'll tell you, then read it in the papers."

"Bullshit, Pardee."

"It already happened."

"Not because *you* told me anything." There was silence.

"You're really somethin' . . . makin' *heroes* a' people . . ."

"I didn't make you a hero, Darryl . . . you did."

"Oh, I did, huh? I didn't do a goddamn thing, Pauline . . . I saved my own ass, all right?"

"That is not the—"

"Whatta *you* know about it?" He pulled on his shorts and walked to the window, to look across the river at the Coca-Cola sign, blinking on and off, one bright-red letter at a time.

"All right, I'll admit, I don't know a thing."

"What do *they* know about it?" He gestured outside. "Anything they get they turn on you."

"Listen, Darryl, it was a rotten war . . . people can't forget that . . . but you were fighting for your life, and nobody's going to blame you for it."

"No one has to blame me, Pauline. I know what I did . . . I know why I did it . . . I know how it happened, I know everything, y'know? I can *live* with it . . . ." his voice began to break, "but there were all these people, an' you can't bring 'em back, an' it didn't make a damned bit a' *difference,* Pauline. . . ." Suddenly she saw what she had done to him.

"Oh, Darryl," she said. And he burst into tears.

Once it started, it wouldn't stop. Pardee's grief was so bitter that he almost felt guilty about letting it out. Each little thing kept setting him off, and now that the tears were finally falling, he went through so many stages of catching himself and then letting go again that it took nearly an hour to subside. Afterward he nestled in the dampness of her hair, and they held each other, and fell asleep.

Chapter 5

1

Up early, but barely rested, Pardee took a table by the window to watch the crews stroking downriver, the coxswains beating the sides of their shells, laying down a cadence for the long arms that moved the boats like waterbugs. The sight of those collegians transported him to another time, another century, until he looked up and realized that he already was in another century, the next one, and wasn't sure he liked it. This Hyatt House's roof spun, its elevators blinked on and off—he thought, "Now, what kind a' place is that for breakfast?"

He sipped his coffee, trying to clear his head, until Pauline joined him about fifteen minutes later, wearing dark glasses to cover up her eye. The two of them ordered and ate in silence, reading the paper; while across the room, Clay Harper of the *Globe* pulled out a camera and started clicking away, going unnoticed, until Needleman walked over to exchange a few words with him, after which the newsman got up.

"Uh-oh . . ." said Pauline.

"What?"

"Don't look now, but . . ."

"Hi, Pauline."

"Hi, Clay."

"Morning, Pardee." Harper waited. "Listen, I hate to ruin your meal, but I got a call last night, concerning some kind of scrape in your hotel room."

"No comment, Clay. Could you tell me who called?"

"How about you, Pardee? They said you roughed her up."

"Nobody roughed up anybody, Clay. Who's saying these things?"

"Look, Pauline, there's all kinds of rumors . . . why not give me your side? This story's gonna break whether you like it or not."

"I'm sorry, Clay, but do me a favor and stick to the facts."

"Sure," he said, clicking his pen, "just the facts. What happened up there?"

"Nice try." She smiled, adjusting her glasses. "Now would you leave us alone?"

"OK," said Harper, taking off. "Good luck."

"Son of a bitch."

"Let's get out of here," said Pauline.

They took a cab to Harvard Square, where they window-shopped, killing time until noon, when Darryl returned to the hotel to rest. Pauline ate lunch at an outdoor cafe, then walked over to the kiosk newsstand, where she picked up the afternoon edition of the *Globe,* and found herself in a tête-à-tête on page one, Sports, frozen in a grainy snapshot with Pardee, next to a column by Harper, with his own photo, ten years younger, entitled:

MIDNIGHT AT THE HYATT
by Clay Harper

BOSTON, October 1—Private lives are meant to be private, no matter what their owners do for a living. It's all right to follow an athlete into the locker room, but not into the bedroom, unless, of course, his exploits in the latter are beginning to affect his performance on the field.

Reluctantly concluding that the relationship between Ballpark's All-Star third baseman Darryl Pardee and *Lifetimes* reporter and NBC sportscaster Pauline Reese may indeed be affecting their performances as both journalist and ballplayer, I offer the following report:

According to certain reliable sources, Ms. Reese and Mr. Pardee have been conducting an affair since the beginning of the season. That would be their business alone, were it not for the fact that Pardee has had a disappointing (for him) year, and were it not that he awakened an entire floor of the Hyatt Hotel in Cambridge last night, where he was discovered naked in Ms. Reese's room, having struck her across the eye.

Ms. Reese, it should be noted, was the author of a recent copyrighted article in *Lifetimes Magazine,* which for the first time disclosed the fact that Pardee was decorated in Vietnam. What these matters have to do with each other, if anything, is impossible to state, since neither Pardee, Ms. Reese, nor the house detective who came to her aid would make any comment.

While it hurts to blow the whistle on a fellow reporter, and goes entirely against my grain to discuss what two consenting adults do behind closed doors . . . last night the doors blew open.

With a pennant on the line, Pardee having his worst season in six years, and the very real possibility that someone might have been hurt if he hadn't been restrained, it seems appropriate to wonder just what is going on.

2

Pauline was scheduled for a broadcast that night, a special Saturday edition of Monday Night Baseball, slotted since the pennant was on the line. She went down to the ballpark, searching for Pardee, who had yet to arrive, then tracked down her producer, who was working in the moving van, parked in the street.

She pushed through the door, into the control room, set up

with monitors and state-of-the-art switching systems for the network hookup. The producer gave a few orders through his headset, then turned, looked up, and said, "Hi, Pauline . . . with
you in a minute."

She fidgeted. They were split-screening a horrendous crash
into the outfield wall last night in San Diego.

"Who was that?"

"Was is right. Rick Banning."

"How bad?"

"They don't even know. He's still in a coma." He flipped a
switch and removed his headgear. Swiveling around in his rotating chair, he reached up to peek under Pauline's sunglasses,
then said, "Well, Pauline, I'm glad you're early. I think it would
be better if you took the night off."

"What? Why? I don't have to appear on camera, Wendell,
and if I do, I can leave these on."

All he did was repeat himself. "I think it would be better for
all concerned if you didn't appear at all tonight."

"I thought you were innocent until proven guilty."

"It's not a question of guilt, Pauline . . . no one's accused
you of any crimes, have they?" Pauline didn't answer. She was
trying to stay calm. "It's a matter of image. Baseball is a family
game. I don't care what you do with your life, but there are
quite a few people out there, including our sponsors, who will.
I'm sorry, but until this blows over, we'll have to keep you out
of the booth."

"It's not fair. What have I done? Is Sylvester around? Have
you talked to him?"

"He's in New York."

"Can I use one of these phones?" He pointed to one, and she
dialed direct, but Baby Bob was out, and so was she. Pauline
was livid, but she didn't even have a contract to rely on, so
rather than alienate anyone further, she made herself scarce,
hiding among the fans in the seats behind third.

The second game of the Boston series almost never happened. A dense fog drifted upriver and seeped over the walls,

until the outfield was almost totally obscured. It lifted just enough for the game to begin, then played cat-and-mouse on little fog feet, stopping the contest twice.

Don Moran, who was starting his ace, and had been pushing the umps to get the game played, later changed his tune and said they should have called it—first when his team fell behind in the sixth, and particularly after Hunsicker hit a pop fly double that decided the game in the top of the ninth. Moran made noises like he was going to protest, but he knew the weather was a judgment call, and that the umpires would prevail.

Pauline tightened as the fans bugged Darryl about beating up his broad in the hotel room, but could picture what was waiting for her up in the press box, and for the same reason carefully avoided the clubhouse, to get back home and bar the door. Pardee called her when he got in, but they were both so drained that they spent the night apart.

Chapter 6

Sunday, October 2. She put on her game face and sat with the press, but answered all questions with a terse "No comment." Heading to the locker room with Hathaway and Frankel, after a 7–2 Ballclub romp that meant the Sox could finish no better than third, Pauline was stopped by security guards.

"Excuse me," she said, flashing her pass, "I'm a reporter."

"I'm sorry," they told her, "you're not allowed in."

"What?"

Her colleagues came over to listen. "We're sorry, Miss Reese," said the guard, "but—"

"This is my job, and I'm going in!" She put down her head, attempting to break through, but this time they tackled her and hauled her back, kicking and struggling. Two photographers caught the action, and their flashbulbs attracted more reporters to the hubbub.

"What's going on?"

"They won't let her in."

"Why?"

"Ask *them,*" she fumed.

"Why can't she go in?" said Hathaway.

"Orders."

"Whose?"

"Mr. Raneer," said the guard.

"Raneer, eh? What about it, Pauline? What's he got against you?"

Pauline was so angry she couldn't think. Nothing made her madder than being manhandled like that. Red-faced, on the verge of tears, she blurted, "He must be awfully nervous."

"About what?"

"The story we're doing on his credit . . . and salaries."

"What about his credit?"

"Is Raneer in trouble?"

"No comment."

"Pauline," they begged.

"Are you going to let me in?"

"No," said the guard.

"You all a witness to this? Good. Because I'm going to sue him for his last red cent!" She took off down the hallway and merged into the crowd, as a number of reporters went dashing for the phones.

Pauline caught a cab and got off at the hotel, where she sat in her room, waiting for Pardee. When he hadn't called her after forty-five minutes, she tried his extension, found him in, and said, "Can I come down?"

"Somethin' the matter?"

"Darryl. . . ."

"Sure, come on."

Halfway there she made up her mind that she'd had enough heartache and bullshit for one day, and rather than talk about it, all she wanted to do was take him in her arms and make passionate love. Darryl took one look at her and got the same idea. They were hopping around, grinning like fools, tearing their clothes off and laughing out loud . . . when the phone rang.

"Let it ring," said Pardee.

"It might be somebody."

"Obviously, it *is* somebody. Let it ring!"

"Really, Darryl, it might be important."

He looked at her, looked at the phone, then finally gave in and went to answer, but no sooner had he picked it up than he said, "Aw, nuts!" and went to slam it. Pauline just managed to beat him to the cradle and take it from his hand.

"Hello?" she said. "Oh, hi, Frank . . . how did you find me?"

"It didn't take a Sherlock Holmes, that's for sure. I can't believe what I just heard, Pauline."

"About the locker room?"

"No, about you! Did you actually say we were doing a story?"

"I guess I did."

"I don't fuckin' believe it. How *could* you, Pauline?"

"I'm sorry, Frank."

"I got two people on that thing, for a full week. What kind of reporter does a thing like that?"

"They threw me out. I was so damned angry I had to do something . . . but I just couldn't say what was *really* going on. . . ."

"Then you should have kept quiet."

"I *know*, Frank . . . but that story was washed up anyway. Ask Bill."

"Bill's right here."

"Then ask him."

"I don't have to, Pauline."

"But don't you see, now we *do* have a story. 'Raneer bars Writer for Financial Inquiry.' What's he going to say? That he really kept me out because he tried to seduce me? Think about that. I'd take him to the cleaners."

"You've got a lot of nerve."

"Is that a compliment?"

"You better get your ass down here. I'm holdin' this issue and we're workin' all night." He hung up. She hung up.

"That was New York."

"And?"

"I'm in trouble. I've got to get down there."

"Now?"

"On the next shuttle."

"And leave me here like this?"

"Believe me," she said, "it's the last thing I want." She came over and pressed herself against him. "I'll make it up to you. I promise."

"Fine," he said. "Great." He flopped onto the bed, but Pauline was already standing in her skirt, stepping into her shoes and checking herself in the mirror.

She reached the door and opened it, then stopped, turned, and said, "I'll see you, Darryl. I love you," and disappeared.

"Love?" he thought. "Now, that's somethin' new . . ." But he didn't want to think about it, or her, or the long night without her, so he got dressed himself and rode down on the elevator, to take off north along the river. Turning right on Western Avenue, he walked across Cambridge, all the way to Somerville, to a large hill looking out over the bay.

The moon was nearly full, but streetlamps conspired to obliterate his shadow and turn his skin a sickly green. Darryl hadn't been out of the city—hadn't seen it truly dark or heard it even close to quiet—in more than eight months. He knew that there was no such thing as quiet in nature, that there was always something stirring, and that if it did get "unearthly still," you just got nervous and held your breath—but there was a substantial difference between crickets and street noise, between dry grass rustling and the strain of semis hauling down the road, and just to think of it made his heart feel empty. The crackle of the power lines had him yearning for peace.

"Just hold on," he told himself, "a few more days, at most, a couple weeks . . ." Pardee was weary. He was sick of all the long nights in cold hotels, all the old sorrows come home to roost, and a woman who was at least as much trouble as she was worth, always running off somewhere. "Love?" He snorted. "Love, my ass."

Traffic on the coast was flowing up north, to New Hampshire and Maine. He could almost see the clean woods and taste the fresh pine air. His heart filled and his lungs expanded merely at the thought, then he forced himself to walk back to his room to try to get some rest. Lying down, he told himself to hang in once again, but the better part of him was still out on that hill. What he liked most about that view from the top was the sea. Pardee had gotten a whiff of it, enough to keep him going, and carried it down with him into his dreams.

Chapter 7

1

Everyone on the Ballclub felt good about things, their pitching, their hitting, and their prospects for the title, until they boarded the morning plane and saw the New York papers; then one by one as they started to read, they turned to talk to the players beside them, who grabbed the stories to see for themselves. The *Times,* as usual, was circumspect, reporting:

> *Lifetimes* correspondent Pauline Reese, whose magazine is conducting an investigation into the financial empire of Phil Raneer, was banned from the Ballpark locker room today, in an action that prompted her comment . . .

but some of the other papers, like the *Daily News,* trumpeted:

LONG-TERM SALARIES IN JEOPARDY

BOSTON, October 2—Sportswriter Pauline Reese, threatening to sue "for his last red cent," blew the cover off Ballpark owner Phil Raneer today, when she revealed, in response to being thrown out of his locker

room, that Raneer's financial dealings were the subject of an investigation by *Lifetimes Magazine.*

Hinting that the deferred salaries owed to his players were endangered by Raneer's business practices,
Ms. Reese, who prior to Sunday handled the play-by-
play for NBC's Monday Night Baseball, accused the
burger magnate of being "awfully nervous," and went
on to say . . .

"Gimme that!" they shouted, grabbing at the papers.

"Hey, Pardee, she mention this?"

"That why you hit 'er?"

"Lemme see it!"

"I ain't done!"

They shredded several copies of the *Times* and the *Post* before gathering around Leary, the player rep, who read each
account, in its entirety, out loud. At first there were some who
refused to believe it, but by the time he was done, they had all
been convinced. Hart tried to calm them, but even he was
scared. He had just bought into a condo in Chicago, on the
insistence of his wife's brother, and the thought that he might
fall behind on his payments, because Raneer might renege on
his, made him positively ill. Fritz never bought anything on
time. He had driven his last DeSoto for nineteen years.

Behind him, the boys were getting violent. "All right, you
guys. . . ." He waited for quiet. "We don't know if this is true
or not . . . but it doesn't really matter."

"Doesn't matter?"

"*Doesn't matter?!* What kinda—"

"What I mean," said the Kraut, "is that there's nothin' we
can do about it. First off, I doubt it's even true . . . I mean, we
all know about the papers . . . and the one thing we know is
that they're not always right. But either way, take the pennant,
then the Series, an' we each got twenty-five grand comin' in
. . . *guaranteed!*" Groans, moans.

"Twenty-five grand? I can't feed my dog on that!"

"Then I suggest you eat the dog, Goldhammer. Forget it,

boys, it's just a trick! To get your minds off baseball . . . huh? How 'bout that?''

The Kraut went looking for confirmation, as Hunsicker wandered up the aisle in a daze. "I can't believe it," he kept repeating. "I just can't believe it. How could he do it? I got a family in Houston . . . I coulda signed with Los Angeles . . . I coulda been a contender . . ."

"All right, men, snap out of it," said Fritz. "This is New York we're comin' in to . . . a pennant we're playin' for, an' I did not come here to look lousy." He looked around. "Any more about this till the season's over, an' you'll find yourself replaced. Raneer's the boss, we've all been paid on time, an' that's the last I wanna hear of it."

"Fuck you."

"Fuck him."

"Fuck you, too . . ." They argued and shouted as the plane banked in to La Guardia, then they piled into the buses to ride down to the Sheraton, at Fifty-sixth and Seventh, where temperatures soared and tempers flared under the cancerous brown atmosphere that was New York's at its worst. It was too hot to walk, too foul to breathe, too oppressive to do anything but lie in an air-conditioned hotel room and wait, which is precisely what the Ballclub did, except for Hunsicker, who took off in a cab.

Pardee got a single room away from his teammates, where he hoped no one would find him; and Pauline was napping in her uptown apartment, having worked all night; which left only a few intrepid writers to navigate the walled corridors of the city, looming in overpowering, tilting verticals that shimmered as if the whole thing were about to grow dizzy and lose its balance.

2

One P.M., Monday, October 3. Three of the men were heading down to lunch when Hunsicker passed them, in an obvious rush. "Hey, Dutch," said Hogan, "you hungry? Wanna join us?"

"Hunsicker turned back to say no, and walked smack dab into an ashtray on the wall, knocking himself sideways. His jacket came loose from beneath his arm, a paper bag fell open, and something hard hit the floor—then Hogan, looking closer, said, "Christ, it's a gun!"

"A gun?" said Zarino.

"A *gun?*" said Root.

Hunsicker groped to pick it up, then held it in two hands, pointed at them, saying, "Don't come near me."

"Lemme in!" shouted Hogan, pounding on a door, as the petrified trio flattened up against the wall. "He's got a gun!"

"Who?"

"Hunsicker, dammit! Open the door!"

"Who?" said the Kraut, appearing in his drawers.

"Sorry, Fritz, but . . ."

Hunsicker was moving down the hallway now, with the Kraut in pursuit, all bandy-legged and resolute. Backing him into a corner, he advanced slowly, holding out his hand, saying, "Give me the gun, Dutch. . . ."

"No." There was a scary look in Hunsicker's eyes. Something had snapped. "You can't have it. I want it."

"What for?"

"For Raneer."

"Put it down. . . ." said the Kraut.

"I don't wanna kill him, Fritz . . . I jus' wanna maim the son of a bitch, so every time he takes a step—he'll think a' me."

"Dutch, Dutch, it's not that bad, it's not even true, it's just the papers. . . ."

"So what?"

"So remember what they said about that little girl?"

"Fulla shit . . . I never touched her."

"Right," said Hart, "so gimme the gun."

"She said she was *eighteen*. . . ." His eyes were pleading.

"Right, Dutch, *right*. . . ." The gun hand dropped, and the

Kraut swept in to relieve him of it, throwing an arm around his shoulder in the old Father Flanagan routine. "Attaboy, Dutchie . . . there you go . . . can't have *you* doin' it, for goodness sakes . . . you wanna shoot somebody, go tell one a' the rookies . . ."

Hunsicker looked up to see if he meant it. The Kraut mussed his hair. "Attaboy . . . now, how 'bout a Coke?" He steered him toward the stairs. "Or maybe a nice iced tea . . . would you like that?" His voice trailed off.

"Hey, Fritz!" yelled Hogan, back at the room, holding them up. "You forgot your pants!"

3

The papers were having a field day. Along with the Raneer story, the locker room flap, and the gossip about the hotel room in Boston, afternoon editions contained new information that Pardee had a history of mental illness dating back to the service. Raneer had hired a private investigator who sneaked in posing as an air freight deliveryman, dug through her desk during Pauline's lunch hour, and came up with a copy of the medical report she'd received, along with the rest of the data from St. Louis.

Pauline had accepted its findings at face value—that Darryl was in a violent but transient state brought on by the shock of both the fighting and his wound—and had decided it was part of the tale she didn't have to tell; but reproduced in black and white in all the major dailies, with the code word *psychiatry* staring at the reader, next to reports of his beating up a woman (by now Pauline was battered and abused, and women's groups were vying to line her up to speak), the obvious implication was that he'd lost control.

When he took the field for the game that night, the yahoos went loco. One guy circled the park in a straitjacket stenciled "Pardee" on the back, drawing laughter and applause, until they beat what passed for his brains out, in a group effort down in left. People went into foaming fits trying to tell Pardee how nuts he was, but he ignored them to double his first time up, then homered in the seventh.

Down in the locker room after the win, the players were walking around holding up one finger, celebrating the fact that they were finally in first place after the long hard chase; and that any combination of Ballpark wins and Yankee losses totaling one (1) would wrap it up, and there were two (2) games to go.

Pauline made a symbolic attempt to storm the ramparts of the clubhouse, and was quite literally repulsed again, as the flash-bulbs exploded. Inside and half dressed, Pardee noticed and stepped out to join her, followed by Bernard, who in turn grabbed Goldhammer, who whistled to Fuller, who made an announcement, and soon twenty-five athletes were dripping in the hallway, entertaining questions in defiance of Raneer.

When the impromptu press conference, an odd inversion of her first day in Tideview, was over, Howie Needleman spotted her and said, "Hiya, Pauline."

"Whatever you say."

"What kinda greeting is that?"

"It's not."

"What'd I do?"

"You see the papers today?"

"No."

"Don't lie to me, Needleman. I don't care about myself, but I'll never forgive what you're doing to Darryl."

"Doing? Do what? What're you talking about?"

"How dare you play innocent?"

"Listen, Pauline . . . I had nothin' to do with that letter."

"Oh, no? What about Harper, up in Boston?"

"Harper? Jesus, I was just sayin' hello."

"Bullshit. And who told Raneer to begin with? Answer me, Howie . . . 'cause I'll find out."

Needleman sagged. "I was just doin' my job, Pauline . . ."

"Incredible."

"But . . ."

"I hope they write that on your grave. Get lost, Howie. Get out of my sight."

Chapter 8

1

Ten A.M., Tuesday, October 4. Raneer held a press conference of his own, to announce a lawsuit against *Lifetimes Magazine,* its senior editors, Pauline Reese, *et al.,* for slander, defamation of character, and interference in an advantageous business relationship, with libel due when the story hit the stands. The extent of his claim, although not revealed, was presumed to lie in excess of one hundred million dollars.

When pressed for a response to the allegations, he said, "Rumors . . . nothin' but rumors, it's that kinda vicious suggestion that makes it so hard to do business these days. All these people, who haven't got a dime, takin' potshots at ya, when a man's reputation's the most precious thing he has. They'll pay, all right. It's nothin' but lies."

Up at *Lifetimes,* the mood was guarded. When the truth emerged, Raneer would be on the defensive, but there was no telling what would happen if it went to court, where you could be perfectly right and still lose everything you owned. Pauline was sent down to the legal department to fill them in on the facts, and when her meeting was over, she went to see Pardee, who'd been incommunicado since the previous night's game.

"Room service," she cried, knocking on his door.

"Wrong room."

"Room service," she repeated.

"Goddammit, I said you got the—"

"Darryl, open up."

There was some mumbling on the other side, then he appeared, saying, "So. You got me," making way for her to enter. "What's new?" Before she could reply, he added, "Just kidding. I don't wanna know." The phone rang as he closed the door. "Excuse me," he said, answering. "Yeah? How'd *you* find me? It's my lawyer. Go ahead. . . . Yeah? No , of course not. What do you think I am? . . . What the hell does that mean? Don't be ridiculous. . . . OK, I won't. . . . Right. . . . Sure. . . . Thanks a lot. You do that." Pardee hung up.

"What was that all about?"

"Just a buncha legal bullshit. He's afraid I'll get sued. I don't know what *I* did. Told me to stay quiet, keep out of it."

"Good advice. I'm only—" Just then someone else knocked on the door, and Pardee opened it again, to find Lacy Stokey standing there, fidgeting awkwardly.

"Howdy, Lace . . . come on in."

"Fritz said to see how you're doin'."

"Me? I'm fine . . . everybody's goin' crazy around here, but I feel great."

"You sure?"

"Why? Don't I look it?"

Pauline interrupted, saying, "Listen, Darryl, I've got to run. If I hang around I'll just make you nervous." She went over and kissed him. "Good luck . . . and be careful."

"You be careful," he told her. "I'm always careful." She waved to Stokey and took off out the door. "Good kid," said Pardee.

"Not bad, not bad . . ."

"It's never dull, that's for sure." Darryl moved over to stand by the window, banging the heel of his hand against the heat register, pouring cold.

"Mind if I hang in?" said Stokey.

"Kraut tell you to do that too? Why not?" said Pardee. The black man pulled a deck of cards from his pocket, and dealt two hands of blackjack onto the bed. Darryl walked over, took a hit with seventeen, and wiped out. They watched the soaps and played aimlessly until two, when they called down for lunch; then afterward Pardee returned to the window, to peer out at the city. "Look at 'em," he said. "You believe that? Caged like rats. I can't understand it."

"Don't look at me."

"They *live* like that." He shook his head, then thought a moment and said, "Where you from, Lace?"

"Cleveland."

"Born there?"

"Georgia."

"Y'ever catch bats?"

"*What?*"

"Bats. Them little ugly awful things that fly around at night. Ever seen one real close?"

"No, but I bet you have."

"They fly by radar, right?"

"Sonar."

"Sonar. Anyway, you go out at dusk, an' you wait until you see one comin'—you can follow 'em around"—he traced a big circle in the sky—"then you take a rock an' throw it up, so it drops down right in front of 'em. They think it's somethin' to eat, see, so they drop down over it, hoverin' just off the ground . . . then you take your mitt, an' snatch 'em like this"—he made a long, quick, sweeping motion—"but you don't hold 'em long, they go . . ." Pardee convulsed, with a horrible snarl. "So you throw 'em back up, an' get the fuck out." They laughed.

"Can't say as I did," said Stokey, "but I'll bet you were good at it."

"Thought a' turnin' pro," said Pardee. "Couldn't catch 'em from the back, though . . . had to come on straight, snatch 'em by the head. *Ugly?*'' He shuddered, then turned around as Stokey got up.

"I'm goin' down early . . . wanna come with?''

"Go ahead, Lace . . . I'll catch the bus.'' As soon as Stokey had left the room, he removed his shoes, took the phone off the hook, and lay down on the bed for a short little nap. The problem was, it felt so good that he couldn't get up; and he lay there blissfully until four o'clock, when the light outside the window had changed, as late-afternoon moisture heaped up in the distance gathered into thunderclouds.

He hit the street, but the buses were gone, so he hopped a cab to ride out to the ballpark in silence. Uptown on the FDR, across the Willis Avenue Bridge, they rolled north on the Deegan, past the ruins of the slums. Darryl kept thinking of his home run last night. That feeling was still in his hands. Trying to relax, he focused on details, the peeling back of the seat before him, the meter's steady click, and the gusts of warm air rushing past his window, like a woman's breath.

He paid the cabbie, gave him a salute, then walked past the guards and into the clubhouse. Pardee laughed and threw a head fake in the mirror. He was hot. His stomach tightened up the way it always did, and sweat started off him in warm salty streams, as he looped his laces in a big double bow. He clacked onto the field, and was heading for third when Stokey came up and tapped him on the shoulder.

Pardee jumped. "Don't do that, Lace.''

"Bad news, son . . . you're benched.''

"What?" said Pardee. "Now, hold on, Lace, I'm a little bit late, but . . .''

"It's got nothin' to do with bein' late. Raneer sent word he didn't like that press conference a' yours, out in the hallway last night, so . . .''

"You must be nuts, we're playin' for a pennant! I'm not sittin' down, I'm—''

"Benched, Pardee. Those are my orders.'' He spat. "It's final.''

Stokey turned to walk away, but Pardee caught his arm and spun him around, saying, "*Your* orders? Where the hell is Hart? Why the hell are *you* tellin' me?"

"Fritz took off and told me what to do, and I don't like it; so I want you to leave me alone, Pardee." Stokey's eyes were soft brown pools, with catfish and plant life floating on the bottom.

"Aw, fuck," said Darryl, then he turned on his heels and went looking for Hart, who was nowhere to be seen; and the other coaches avoided his eyes as he walked back to the dugout, where he sat with his face in a towel all night, trying to figure it out.

Every inning he expected them to send him in, the way a jilted lover figures she'll be back, but they didn't, and she won't —so the man who might turn out to be the finest third baseman ever to play the game openly wept, as the New York Yankees slaughtered a demoralized Ballclub by a score of 11–2.

2

The only consolation Hart felt, as he watched it from a tavern, was that Raneer was costing himself a pennant; but Fritz wasn't cynical enough to let it go at that. He had staked his whole life on this Ballclub, and still had a chance to pull off the greatest coup in the history of the game, by winning with a team its first time out, and was not about to be outsmarted by a two-bit jerk who had bought his way into baseball, and with other people's money at that.

It took everything he had to maintain his cool when he met with Raneer in the clubhouse that afternoon. From the start it was obvious that arguments were useless, but there was no way he could preside over the travesty himself, so he ordered his coaches to carry on for him, and turned his rage to cold calculation. The more he thought about it, the more he wanted Raneer's ass. He wanted it so bad, in fact, by the eighth inning when the game was lost, he could almost taste it.

The problem was this: Pardee was out, under orders from Raneer, but without him the Ballclub didn't have a prayer. It wouldn't matter if he went 0–5, or if Adelaide played the game of his life at third, there were some things you couldn't do and still expect to win, and benching Pardee right now was one of them. Hart knew it in his gut.

Unable to solve his dilemma directly, he made up a different one and tossed it around. Fritz didn't care what questions he asked, as long as he got the right answers. "Suppose," he said, "it's the bottom of the ninth, an' I got Foster on the mound, but he's tired. They put up a lefty, Ramos, to get me to come back with a lefty, say, Radivin, so they can yank Ramos an' stick me with the guy they *really* want—Morris. Now, Morris is a lotta trouble, so what do I do?

"Simple. I ignore *them,* an' go with Lopez. Philly Mike knocks Ramos down three times runnin', then comes right back an' strikes him out. Piece a' cake. So what's the point?" He took another sip. "First, dummy, you don't play percentages with a title on the line. Percentages are for the long run, they win arguments, but ballplayers win ballgames an' managers win pennants. Let 'em guess, then go with your best. Play the men *you* want, not the man they want you to want." Hart grunted. He had his answer. "So what am I worried, fer cryin' out loud?"

The guys at the bar saw him talking to himself, and figured him for just another German-Irish drunk. The Ballclub manager drained off his Rheingold, wiped the foam from his lip, and staggered unrecognized into the night . . . but woe would have been unto any mugger who mistook him for a mark. Every beer-and-baseball-saturated cell in Fritz the Kraut's body was screaming for revenge.

Chapter 9

1

It was seven-fifteen P.M., Eastern Daylight Saving Time, and an estimated twenty million televiewers were standing by in four time zones for a contest originally slated for eight, but pushed back until nine to accommodate folks on the Coast with nothing better to do on this Wednesday, October 5, than watch the two hottest teams in baseball go for each other's throats, a divisional title, and the right to meet Kansas City in the playoffs.

Poised on the horizon, visible only from the top rows of the stands, in a notch that the clouds had forgotten to close, a yellow harvest moon was lying on its back, rolled topsy-turvy in a glycerine sky. Its face was full, almost bloated, with the look of someone who is about to pass out from that last drink, and is glad.

Fritz Hart hid in his office, waiting for the coaches to assemble his squad, then burst dramatically through the door, saying, "Gentlemen . . . I had a disagreement with the owner of this team about the status of Mr. Pardee . . . and had to leave this Ballclub last night—an action I did not take lightly—in order to preserve, if not my lineup, then my honor." He paused. "After a long evening thinking it over, and an even longer one watching you play . . . *I have returned!*"

Hosannas sounded in the Kraut's mind, and a sentimental tear trickled down Bernard's cheek, but everyone else was in a stupor. The last thing they needed was theatrics. Hart went on, "Right now, you're probably askin' yourself—"

"Jesus, Fritz, give us a break."

"What I am tryin' to say, Leary . . . if you'll let me . . . is that our lineup's the same as always"—the players buzzed—"only Adelaide'll start at third an' bat third for Pardee. Any questions?"

The men shifted uncomfortably. How could there be any questions? Hart had made his peace with Raneer and it was tough shit, Pardee. What did they care? They were only playin' the Yanks, after all . . . why not give the kid a shot?

"All right . . . dismissed!" The men laughed nervously, and clabbled up the concrete, as Fritz hollered, "*Pardee . . . meet me in my office.*"

"Yes, sir."

Hart waited until everyone was gone, then went back to his cubicle, found his player standing, and left him that way the whole time he addressed him. "Any idea why you're not startin'?"

"Raneer."

"Very good. They say that politics makes strange bedfellows, Pardee, but I don't sleep with fellas . . . I don't even sleep with Mrs. Hart anymore . . . and I don't vote. You follow?"

"Nosir."

"Good. Go out an' warm up. When it's your turn, you'll take your swings, then come back to the dugout. Say nothing to anyone, something to no one, an' keep your mouth shut. You got that?"

"Yessir."

"Whatever you do . . . don't attract attention. Just be ready when I say, and I'll see what I can do. All right?"

"Thank you, sir."

"Warm up."

"Yessir," and Pardee took the tunnel to the playing field, the floor of an ocean, as vast as the night. The time: seven thirty-eight, but dark, with storm clouds threatening. The place: as it was in the beginning, is now, and long may it wave . . . out on the edge of the South Bronx . . . Yankee Stadium.

2

This broadcast is brought to you by authority of the New York Yankees Baseball Club, and is intended solely for the private use of our audience. Any republication, retransmission, or rebroadcast of the pictures, descriptions, and accounts of tonight's game without the expressed, written consent of the Yankees, or the Commissioner of Baseball, is prohibited.

—Famous baseball proverb,
source unknown

Avoiding the crew at NBC, Pauline took her place in the crowded press box, sidestepping over to her *Lifetimes* slot, just up the line toward first. Looking down on the stands, filling slowly, she thought, "Either no one is coming to this game, or they're all getting tanked at the local bars, getting a head start on the watered-down brew that they sell around here for a buck fifty a shot. Not that that'll stop them once they get in, but . . ."

Down below, Darryl moved to third, scooped up a grounder, and fired to first, in a well-oiled motion, like a bolt sliding into a breech. Another ground ball and he did it again, in an action he'd repeated at least a hundred thousand times, as Pauline stood watching, enthralled. Some things she never got tired of.

He exchanged a word with Adelaide, grabbed a stick, and moved to the cage, where Alvarez was practicing his inside-out stroke, driving the ball to the left of first. Samba drew an admiring crowd, as did Pardee, who kept his bat moving to carve out a few feet for himself from the mass of reporters, most of whom he had never seen before.

A woolly-headed cameraman was down on one knee, on the ground before him, panning up. That would make quite an impression out there in TV land, where fans were dying for new developments in the saga of the poor mad Vietnam vet. Network programmers were readying tapes of Jimmy Piersall running the bases backward and climbing the backstop, to be followed by clips of Pardee himself, with voice-over commentary:

"Yes, ladies and gentlemen . . . it's just as we've suspected . . . you don't *have* to be crazy to play third base, known in baseball circles as 'the hot corner' . . . but it helps . . ."

Alvarez, meanwhile, was taking his time, but Pardee didn't care. Sometimes a few extra swings were all that was needed to iron things out. Finally, as the pitcher went into his stretch, Samba held his hand up and stepped out, smiling. That hit he'd been looking for was finally in his bat, and he didn't want to waste it.

A network announcer stepped in for a word, which Alvarez couldn't understand, so the newsman spun and shoved the mike at Pardee, who stuck up a finger without even thinking, and said, "Hi, Mom . . ." the way all the players did, but his little joke backfired, and a lump hit his throat as he stepped up to the plate. It took two or three throws for him to get himself together.

The first pitch slammed in and Darryl breathed deeply, then the next one caught him checking out his stance: feet spread, elbow up, hands loose, and fingers on the bat. He flexed his knees and cocked his hips, but the next pitch was a ball; then he married the fourth one with a sweet smooth rip.

The crowd pressed in. Many of them had never even seen a swing like that. "Ted Williams," someone offered, although he wasn't quite as fluid; then, "The Rajah," one old-timer whispered in awe, recalling perhaps the finest right-handed hitter ever, Rogers Hornsby.

For ten swings Pardee put on a display of pure power that would have cowed a Metternich. He jerked two out of the park to left center, two more down the line, then finished up with a drive to right that hit the top of the wall and caromed straight up, thirty feet into the air. There was nothing on earth that Darryl liked better—never had been, and never would be. Not even sex exalted him like the long ball.

Stepping from the cage, he was surrounded by reporters, led by a dark-haired shrew with her eyeglasses slung on a cord around her neck, who kept jabbing him with her notepad, demanding, "Who? What? With whom? And how often?"

"None a' yer goddamn business," he growled, then he tripped on a tangle of TV cables and fell into their arms. "Take it easy," he told himself, "they're just a buncha fools. . . ." He laughed, and everyone around began grinning along with him. If Pardee thought it was funny, it was funny. Darryl looked up into the stands, and when their eyes followed, he made his break, elbowing a UPI man in the gut. He started toward the bench, as Hart had instructed, but Fritz took one look at the swarm of reporters and waved him into the outfield, where Pardee sequestered himself among the rookies, keeping them company, shagging flies.

Chapter 10

1

The stage was set and the twilight dimmed, as the fans filed down to their appointed rows. A Marine color guard cleared the fence in center, out by the monuments to Yankee greats, as Commissioner O'Neill was convoyed in, waving like the Pope, bestowing favors on the big-game hunters, those thrice-blessed celebrities and corporate execs who came up with tickets whenever it counted.

While the muckamucks were engaged behind first, throwing out game balls for the benefit of photographers, Phil Raneer, in dark glasses and fedora, made his way through the crowd, unnoticed, to a seat set aside on the aisle by third. The Kraut, meanwhile, was right at home, listening to the ground rules he knew so well, and handing in the lineup that would serve as his script.

A dramatic rendition of the starting teams by the PA announcer brought the appropriate hisses, boos, bouquets, and cheers from the hometown fans, then Hart stood reverently for his favorite song, the National Anthem in the key of Francis Scott, sung by an ex-semipro ballplayer and cantor turned opera star, and Pardee, with his customary patriotic verve. His only superstition had to do with that song. As far back as he could remember, he'd never won a ballgame that he didn't sing it, all the way through.

A grim Barry Evans took the mound for New York, finished his throws, and watched the ball around the horn. Evans knew this city and its fans too well. They had no use for guys who finished second. He threw three balls to Martinez, as the crowd whistled, then fought back with off-speed stuff, to retire him on a slow roller to short. Alvarez dueled to two and two before flying out to left, then Adelaide shocked everyone by working for a walk; but never one to let a little wildness faze him, Evans tucked a fastball under Hunsicker's chin, then punched him out on three perfect sliders, down and away, to end the inning.

Frank Fuller took the mound, and filled it in where Evans had dug it out. They would go back and forth like that, digging it out and filling it in, all night. Hart was enjoying himself, watching the ritual, until he happened to take a look at Adelaide at third —then he hitched his pants and walked out to the sideline, saying, "C'mere." The kid trotted over. "What the hell's the matter with you?" No answer. "You're in Yankee Stadium . . . you're playin' for the title . . . you dream about this your whole life, right?" The kid stared. "Then *enjoy* it, you idiot! *God,* what an idiot . . ." and Fritz stalked off in mock exasperation. Adelaide grinned, and by the time he turned around, the ball was in his hands and Fuller was waiting. He dusted off the first man, as a warning to Evans, struck out two and set them down in order.

No one got a hit in either half of the second. Hogan doubled in the third, but died there. The sky was festering, Bronx pink and apple green, while the Yankee pinstripes burned a brilliant white, set off by the gleam of their blue-black helmets.

Nine forty-three. It rained, it poured. The umpires posed for a Norman Rockwell poster, then the skies opened up and they ran like hell. There was lightning, and thunder. Jagged lines flashed to the man-made peaks. The rage of its fury was hard to believe, then ten minutes later, the whole thing was over, and they cleared off the tarp and said, "Well, now, where were we?" No one let up or changed his mind about a thing—all that had happened was that God had played an inning. The game was His for the asking.

"Play ball!" yelled the ump, as the fans rose and cheered, then Wheelock tripled to the alley in right, but was rubbed out on the very next play when Adelaide made a sensational grab of a scorching line drive to double him up unassisted. The rookie looked in, blushing with delight, as the Kraut hit his forehead with the palm of his hand. *"What an idiot!"* he mimed, throwing up his arms, turning to smile at his regular third baseman, who did his best to smile back. So far so good. The third man struck out.

Approaching the bench at the end of the inning, Adelaide was mobbed. It was dawning on these men, who'd been numbed by all the tension, that all those ballgames stretching back into March, and all the money that could be won, and the history, yes, the history of the situation—everything, in fact, that meant anything at that moment was suddenly on the line. The dugout exploded in a caterwauling whine that sent chills up the Kraut's spine. When Alvarez singled to start things off, he decided to make his move.

Motioning to his All-Star, he ran out to the on-deck circle, threw an arm around the kid, and escorted him back. The batboy ran out to inform the ump, as number twenty-one grabbed three of his bats, and stepped out under the faintly starry dome. "Now batting in place of Adelaide . . ."

"Pardee . . ."

". . . playing third base, number twenty-one, Darryl . . ."

"Pardee . . ." the fans hollered, as soon as they saw him— they'd been waiting for this. The Kraut crossed his fingers and held his breath, as it built in volume, rising in pitch. *"Pardeeeee . . ."* The sound of *eee*'s, the sound of *eee*'s, the sound of *eee*'s . . .

Darryl dropped two bats, knocked the lead weight from the third, tapped the mud from his cleats, and stepped up to the plate; but before the umpire could signal time in, a commotion kicked up behind the Ballpark bench, and Evans stepped off the mound to watch.

People were shoving, as if a brawl was breaking out, then someone ran onto the field, screaming, "Let go a' me! Let go! This is my team, you got that? *Mine!*" Tearing off his hat and shades, shedding cops and ushers, an agitated Phil Raneer closed in on his manager, watching serenely from the dugout steps.

"I've had it, Hart, you son of a bitch . . . let go a' me, you asshole. This is my team, an' I want him out! You're fired, both a' ya. . . out . . . *Out!*"

Fritz just smiled, and said, "Fuck you . . ." so that no one but the Man himself could hear, and when the Ballpark owner came after him, he upper-decked him neatly with a good old-fashioned right. Down went Raneer. Up jumped the boys. For one brief flash they did precisely what they wished . . . it was most unseemly.

Raneer's mouth had jammed shut, just missing the tongue that would have put some protein in his knuckle sandwich. He lay sprawled out on the grass, belly down like a toad, as Hart, marveling at the reflexes that had never quite left him, blew on his fingers and called for the fuzz. "Out! Get him out!" yelled the Kraut in imitation.

"Go get 'em, skipper!"

"Attaboy, Fritz!"

"Get this nut outta here! Where's my protection?" The cops dragged Raneer through the clubhouse door, as stadium officials groveled in apology, saying that they thought it really was the Ballpark owner. "I don't give a flyin' fuck!" screamed Hart. "Nobody comes in my dugout, you got that? *Nobody!*"

The fans were yipping, yawping, and yowling. Every writer picked or coined a word beginning with *y,* but it was louder still in the Ballpark dugout—mutiny at last, and they were all aboard. The Kraut went back to his top step, not even trying to hide his smile as he pictured Raneer waking up like lunch meat in a paddy wagon; then he called, "Time out!" and motioned to Pardee. His theory was that at a time like this, you talk to a ballplayer the same way you'd talk to a skittish colt. All you want to do is whisper in his ear, to let him hear a familiar voice, then a steadying hand on the back of the neck, a reassuring pat as you sent him off, and that was it. There was nothing more you could do.

He brought his third baseman under his wing, gave him a squeeze, the perfunctory fondle, and said, "Up to you, son . . . go right out after him." Then Pardee went back, and following orders, jumped on the first pitch, a hard one high and away, which is right where it went, to the opposite field, for a two-run homer and a 2–0 lead.

Evans went crazy out on the mound, absolutely certain that Hart had set him up. Pardee never hit the first pitch. Never! His next toss caught Hunsicker on the leg, then Goldhammer, terrorized, dribbled into a double play; and when Bernard ducked two, fouled off three, and struck out to end the inning, the curtain fell and Act One, featuring Fritz the Kraut (as himself), was over.

2

The moment Pardee stroked his home run, Yankee Stadium went silent, stunned, but as he rounded second, thousands of voices rumbled, "You . . . you . . . you . . ." and just as many fingers pointed his way, to let him know who *you* was. He watched the next three outs from the safety of the dugout, and took the field without incident through the bottom of the fourth; but as he headed to the bench at the end of that inning, a cola cup from the third tier landed on his shoulder, exploding small crushed bits of ballpark ice that sparkled in his hair like festooned glitter. He kept trotting through the dugout and into the clubhouse, pursued by Artie Stutz, as Hart signaled for everyone else to mind his own business and tend to the game. Stutz could handle it. He knew his job.

Up in the press box, where you could look down on the whole thing, the reporters were uneasy, glancing at Pauline. "Stop worrying," she told herself, "it's nothing but a joke," but no one was laughing, and these guys could laugh at almost anything. "Why Pardee?" she thought. "There's no real reason, he's just It . . . and It's a game any number can play, the more the merrier. You pays yer money and you takes yer choice . . . and right now Darryl's a democratic favorite, a Yankee Doodle Darlin' of the crowd . . ."

"Pardee," they bellowed in the bottom of the fifth, in voices that Stokey had heard before—when men set out to lynch someone. They would call that way until they'd tracked him down, slipped a rope around his neck, and hauled till he was dead, his eyes out of his head, the dogs taking up the sound, baying at the stars . . .

"You . . . you . . . you. . . ."

When Darryl came up to lead off the seventh, Evans threw the fastball, and popped him on the hip. Refusing to let on how much it really stung, Pardee dropped his bat and trotted to first. Distracted, he missed the next signal (cap to left shoulder, indicator, skin), blew the hit-and-run, and got cut down at second.

"Cost you a hundred," growled Hart back on the bench. "Get yer mind on the goddamn game."

Stutz walked over and sat down beside him, grabbing Darryl's knee, saying, "I bet I know what you're thinkin'. I bet you're thinkin', 'Why me?' Right? Well, it ain't you, kid . . . it's them. What the hell did you do?"

"Plenty, Stutz."

"Ah, bullshit. Forget New York . . . they'll forget you. Just go out an' play some ball."

"I know."

"Then do it."

Pardee sat and stared at the floor. Getting hit was nothing new, but missing a sign meant he wasn't all there, and if he started drifting now, there was no telling where he'd wind up.

His mind wandered as the noise increased, and he forgot to take the field for the bottom of the seventh, until Hamilton hit him in the neck with a towel.

He drew a smattering of applause with a two-out over-the-shoulder catch along the foul line, but the boos redoubled when he tipped his hat, and Hart was furious. He had warned him not to do anything overt. He was digging his own grave. Bernard struck out to open the next inning; then Hogan bunted safely, but was stranded again, when Leopold and Collins both whiffed.

Bottom of the eighth. Fuller got up slowly. His knees were tight in the cold October night. He warmed up stiffly, walked the first batter, then pasted the next man right between the shoulder blades. The Kraut walked out, took a look in his eyes, and with no discussion made the sign of the hook. Fuller was beat. He'd hit that man by accident. "Gimme the ball," said Fritz. "You pitched damned good . . . I ain't gonna let ya lose . . ." Fuller tossed the ball and trudged off to the showers, as Foster caught the relay and began to warm up, looking nice and easy.

"Too nice. Too easy," Hart was warned by his pitching coach, Wedmar, but before the Kraut could do anything about it, Wheelock, who had tripled, took a strike and doubled to left. Just like that two runs scored, Fuller was off the hook, and Foster was dangling like a night crawler. Wheelock was on second with the winning run, and somebody's season was drawing to a close. Intimations of mortality filled the air. You could hear the clock tick.

Jake Monroe, the Yankee manager, called time to replace his batter, Brant, with the lefty, Ramos; then Hart called his own time and took it up the steps. Fritz had to laugh. It was just as he'd had it in the bar last night, only Foster was fresh.

Monroe was hoping for the lefty, Radivin, but Hart just dawdled, letting him stew, until the umpire came out to speed things up, at which point the Ballpark manager turned to the man he had primed all year for this moment, and said, "OK, Foster

. . . you get one more chance." He waved his finger in the pitcher's face. "You better not let any runs in, *boy*. . . ." Then he jabbed him, twice, grinning to himself, and strolled off the mound like a fat raccoon.

The black man's jaw dropped open wide, as Bernard shrugged and returned to the plate; then Hart winked at Wedmar, beside him on the steps, as Foster glared Wheelock back to the bag, and fired a fastball, inside, for ball one.

The next pitch was more heat for a strike, then Puck flashed the three, Foster nodded, and twisted a wicked screwball that had Ramos fooled, until the very last moment, when he dropped his bat, and rolled out a fierce line drive toward third.

It was time for some magic. The moment he saw that screwball breaking, Pardee dove. He was out almost to short, playing the lefty to pull, but when he saw the only place he could put it, if he hit it at all, Darryl took a stutter-step and jammed off his spikes. Talk about anticipation—if Ramos had missed, Pardee would have looked like a flyin' fool, but he didn't miss, and the ball left the lumber in a long white blur.

A little stop-action slo-mo here showed the folks back home that it couldn't have happened any other way. No one else in baseball would have made that catch, and even Pardee wasn't sure he had it, until he landed flat and the umpire bellowed "Owwwwww . . . !" like he'd hit his thumb with a hammer.

Darryl checked the webbing, saw the white, and threw from his back to Leopold, to double up Wheelock for the second time that night. Slowly the roar died, and with it, the Yankee threat. Foster stopped the next man on four pitches, then rushed back to the dugout, where he had to be restrained from punching Fritz out.

Top of the ninth. The score was tied at 2–2, with the top of the order coming to the plate, so the best manager in the world, which he fancied he was, couldn't do a thing but pop a Tums and wait. The din swelled and ebbed. Sound waves amplified, then canceled each other out, until everything was lost in a deafening silence, weaving through the constant roar.

Martinez worked the count to two and two, fouled off three, then tipped the third strike into the catcher's glove for out number one. Unlike Fuller, Evans was getting stronger. Alvarez took a look at two in the dirt, but the Yankee clipped the corner twice to even the count, then fooled both Alvarez *and* umpire Sardi, with a hard slider that was called a ball.

Evans bounded off the mound, snarling, as Sardi walked out, hoping he'd behave, so he wouldn't have to toss him from the game. He had missed the call. All right, so he had missed the call.

With the count full and Evans enraged, he changed up, this time fooling everyone *but* Samba, who hitched and slung a syncopated liner, right back at his head. The pitcher threw his glove hand up, and took it on the wrist, collapsing in pain; as the ball caromed over to Chambers at first, who made a backhanded pickup and shovel throw to Wheelock, covering, to nab Samba by a wish. Alvarez came charging back to protest, and indeed the replays seemed to prove him right, but was pulled away by Willie Wagner, mouthing a stream of obscenities that would have gotten him bounced from any ballpark south of Corpus Christi.

Eleven-fourteen P.M. Two out and nobody on. Pardee stepped out of the on-deck circle, and a fan jumped the rail. Security guards intercepted the guy, twisting his arm behind his back, as the skies opened up with a shower of debris, including flashlight batteries and ten-cent bolts, that the nuts in the upper deck just happened to have on hand.

Pardee and Sardi went racing for the dugouts. An announcement rang out: "Ladies and gentlemen . . . if the throwing of objects"—golf balls, coins, and a phosphorescent Frisbee—"does not cease immediately, this ballgame will be forfeited to the visiting team. The management and players of the New York Yankees ask you to please . . . *please* refrain from throwing objects onto the field of play. Thank you."

The barrage leveled off, but the catcalls continued, as the batboys came out to clear away the mess. Evans was throwing to check out his wrist, as Sardi emerged, looking up cautiously, motioning to Pardee to get ready to resume.

Anyone in the stadium with half a memory thought back to the fourth, when Darryl jumped on the first pitch after a similar delay, and drove it into the stands. The Yankee skipper called his pitcher to the sidelines, to warn him not to let it happen again. He told Evans to work around Pardee, or to put him on base on purpose if he liked, although he did not specify how. A free pass to the winning run might be poor percentage baseball, but Monroe thought like Hart: You could shove percentages at a time like this. Pardee had hit one out, and he could hit another. The Yankees would take their chances with Hunsicker.

Evans smiled as he looked in for his signal; but Pardee called time. It was the eyes—they had given it away. He dug in again, trying to relax, then just as he expected, a fastball screamed behind Pardee's ear, and he flattened in the dirt. The ump stepped forward to issue a warning, which meant Evans was gone if he tried it again, but Darryl sensed that he really didn't care. Maybe that wrist was hurting more than he'd admit.

He climbed to his feet, dusting himself off, looking down to Stokey at third; but even as he watched him running through the signals, Pardee knew that he was on his own. His insides were churning. Every player knows the feeling—it was out of his hands.

Again the nod, again those eyes, the windup, the stretch—and from the set of Evans' body Darryl knew he'd get hit, the only question was where?—which he found out midway through a corkscrew spin, when the ball caught him on the base of the neck, under the earflap, and Pardee went down . . . *hard.*

The sky went dark, then lit up around him, as fireworks exploded, arcing through the night; and Darryl scrambled, stunned and dizzy, away from the salvos landing at his feet, out toward the mound, where the pitcher came to meet him. Everything moved slowly, as in a dream. Someone said something, but no one heard; for suddenly the fans were pouring onto the field, as if the game were over and there were goalposts to tear down, or turf to tear up for souvenirs, but the only thing they wanted was a piece of Pardee.

Evans said later that he made a mistake, but when it mattered most, he threw a punch; and once again it was out of Darryl's hands—in his hands—automatic . . . as he came in straight with the front-page right:

PARDEE DISMANTLES YANKEES' EVANS
MOB QUELLED; NEW YORK FORFEITS TITLE

Hundreds of fans converging on the run heard the sound of bone on bone as the pitcher's jaw collapsed into his face. Pardee whirled to face them, but not another punch was thrown, because when Evans went down, the crowd slowed; and in that instant the Ballclub raced out, armed with bats supplied by Stutz; then the Yankees rallied and charged down the line, and the fans had time enough to calculate their odds against the eighty Major Leaguers standing together, who were barring their way—and it was no contest . . . so they stopped.

One false move and there would have been mayhem, but the people in front dug in their heels, stopping the ones behind them, who stopped the ones behind them, and everyone got reasonable all of a sudden—they didn't pay seven-fifty to get into a *fight,* not with the *Yankees*—and they actually started asking for *autographs,* as the loudspeakers crackled, "Ladies and gentlemen. Tonight's ballgame has been forfeited . . ."— there were strangely few boos—

". . . and awarded to the Ballpark Ballclub by a score of nine to nothing. You are reminded . . ."—the people in back started diving for the stands, pursued by the police—

". . . that entering the field of play is a criminal offense . . ."—who made a few token arrests—

". . . subject to fine and/or imprisonment. Please leave the stadium . . ."—the upper decks were wreathed in smoke, emptying fast—

". . . as quickly and peacefully as possible. Thank you."

Evans was moaning miserably now, but none of the Yankees made a move for Pardee—the damage was done and it was Evans' own fault—and even the cops were keeping their distance. What had happened here tonight was outside their jurisdiction. Diamonds were sacred ground.

"This guy's a mess," said one of the paramedics, who had wheeled a stretcher to the pitcher's side; then Hart walked around to where Darryl could see him, placed both his hands on his third baseman's shoulders, and said, "Forget it, son . . . you had no choice."

The two teams exchanged a few words, then headed for their dugouts, as they trundled Evans off; but Pardee stood motionless. There was no place within fifty miles half as peaceful as where he was right now, so he waited, not going anywhere, until the Kraut spotted Evans' mitt, lying where he'd dropped it, and the ball, which no one had dared to claim, and retrieved them, throwing the glove at Pardee, who turned around silently and trotted down to home.

Fritz moved up to the bottom of the mound and wound up slowly—it was tough getting his arms over his head—to uncoil what remained of a Pony League fastball, which caught the corner at Pardee's knee. He took the return throw in his bare hand, as the young man flashed two fingers for the curve, then the Kraut broke a wing off a duck and took it for a spin for strike two. The groundskeepers came out to cover the mound, but stopped, waiting, leaning on their rakes.

Darryl's body was shaking. His eyes filled with tears until he couldn't see, but he signaled for the Three and took it on the black, dropped the ball, picked it up, and fired it back, chattering in Creole, calling for the *gris-gris,* as Pauline, who had fought her own tears and the crowd all the way down from the press box, finally reached the front-row rail and stopped. It was just as he'd explained it, way back in March. "Nothin' simpler in the world . . ." he had told her, and that's the way it was as it all came down to the simple rhythm of a game of catch.

PART SIX

Conclusion

A race, around a track
In staggered heats of three
He ran, but no one knew
The secret of his speed.

All the way around he raced
All the way he dreamed
Sometime in his past
And there was no harm.

Chapter 1

1

Pauline took Pardee home with her that night, when he refused to go the hospital, and set him up with a bag of ice. By the time he awoke, however, she was gone, downtown at *Lifetimes*, where the issue was out with the story on Raneer. Sullivan had insisted that she tell the thing straight and now he'd set her up with yet another press conference, to negate the effect of Phil's public campaign; but although she was basically the aggrieved party, her colleagues did not let her off easy.

"It would seem then, Pauline, that you were lying in Boston, when you said it was your investigation that was bothering him."

"Let's just say there was more to it."

"Did Raneer actually know about your investigation?"

"Yes," she lied, "I believe he did."

"So Raneer tried to seduce you . . . are those your words?"

"He was drunk."

"Did he touch you?"

"Yes."

"And got angry when you turned him down"—she nodded—"because he claimed you got your first story by sleeping with Pardee. Is that correct?" She nodded again. "Well?"

"What?"

"*Did* you get the story by sleeping with Pardee?"

"No, that is not why I was sleeping with him."

"All right, I'll bite . . . *why* were you?"

She looked down. Her lawyers motioned to answer the question. "We're lovers," she said, quietly.

"And how does he feel about you, Miss Reese?"

She reached into her purse, then put on her shades.

"I'm sorry," she said, "you'll have to ask him."

Pauline turned to go as the light bulbs flashed, the motor drives churned, *chickungchickungchickung,* and the boys pleaded, "Come on, smile . . . over here . . . thanks . . ." until she made it out the door.

2

Darryl got up at ten, with a lump the size of a child's fist. He went down to breakfast at a Greek joint on the corner, and found a headline staring from the *New York Times:*

BALLCLUB STAR SUSPENDED

He picked up the paper to read for himself how Commissioner O'Neill wasn't "interested in any mitigating circumstances . . . if an eye and a tooth were good enough for Hammurabi," he was quoted as saying, "they're good enough for me. Evans' jaw is completely wrecked, so the least I can do is to sideline Pardee, until he makes it back."

Darryl called his lawyer, who had already tried to plead his case, and was told to appear in person at noon, then he finished his eggs, read the rest of the news, and walked down from the corner of Sixty-eighth and Third, to the office of the Commissioner of Baseball, 75 Rockefeller Plaza.

After a short spell in the plush anteroom, he was buzzed in to wait on the hard-weave carpet, until Darling Dan, a broad-beamed Irishman with a fine filigree of exploded capillaries

spread across his face, looked up from the papers he'd been
absorbed in and said, "Well, Pardee . . . you have anything to
say?"

Darryl answered in his mild Louisiana accent, "He was
throwin' at me, sir . . . what was I supposed to do?"

"You really wanna know?"

"Look, I didn't start the fight."

"You had no business going out there."

"I had no idea I *was* out there."

O'Neill grabbed a pencil, a Ticonderoga, and tapped it on the
desk, then he got up and walked to his uptown window, across
the way from Bob Sylvester's, to look out over Manhattan,
saying, "Sorry, son . . . I'll have to suspend you."

"How long?"

"We'll see when he gets back."

"Gets back?" said Pardee. "What if he quits? He's thirty-
four."

"We'll have to see."

"Excuse me, sir, it was nothin' but a fight. What's the big
deal? Because my punch landed?"

"That's exactly right."

"He swung at *me* . . . am I supposed to stand there?"

"That is not for me to answer."

"Look . . ." Pardee was about to beg, to get down on his
knees and say, "Listen . . . it's just not fair . . . gimme three
games, Clemmer got three games . . . make it *five* games.
I could even miss part of the Series that way, if we make it,
but . . ."

"Sorry."

"Let me finish."

"I'm sorry, Pardee."

"What has that got to do with it?" Darryl's voice was rising.
"I am asking you a question, sir . . . what has one thing got to
do with the other? You can change your mind, you know. This
ain't no ballgame in here."

"That's all I have to say."

"The man was comin' at me."

"We've got to set an example, Pardee. You have any idea what you almost started? Now, that's my decision . . . and there's the door."

Darryl almost made it. He *almost* made it out that door, but as he thought about it on his way across the room, he realized that he was tired of setting examples. In the past ten years he'd been an example of everything from the ideal fighting man to what went wrong with our boys over there. He'd been a hero, a coward—Pardee could pass for almost anything, but if O'Neill wanted examples, why, that was easy.

"Example?" he said. "You want examples? How's *this?*" He put his fist through an oil portrait of Secretariat, then proceeded around the room, redecorating it to his taste, in a calm but incredible rampage, the climax of which came when he picked up an old baseball autographed by the late, great Ty Cobb and heaved it at the window, shattering it into a spider's web of long fine shards.

"Jesus Christ," said O'Neill, dodging behind a chair. "Do what you want and get out."

"Fine," said Pardee, who wanted to grind him into an ashtray like the butt end he was, but decided against it, to deny him the satisfaction of an "I told you so," even from a hospital bed. He had kept that in for years, fearing what he'd do, but now that it was over and no one else got hurt, he felt so relieved he was almost giddy. "Stupid," he said, shaking his head. "We're much too old for shit like this." Then he took a look at that window again, and allowed himself a tiny smile . . . Ty Cobb would have been proud.

Chapter 2

1

O'Neill had accomplished what Raneer couldn't. He sidelined Pardee and cost the team a pennant. Hart, of course, was fired, and his coaches took off with him, so a minor league crew from Downingtown had to lead the troops against Kansas City, who defeated the Ballclub by three games to one. Darryl sat in street clothes in the stands, among the good Midwest fans of Kansas and Missouri, who were so excited to see their team come through that he almost felt good for them.

Even so, it cut him like a knife when Bernard popped up to end his career, the Royals did their victory dance out on the mound, and the Ballclub disappeared into a losers' clubhouse. He considered going in to commiserate, but he never said much in the best of times, so he bobbed with the crowd down the exit ramp, hearing his name mentioned every now and then, as in:

"Yeah, but remember . . . Pardee didn't play."

"Who gives a shit? A win's a win. We're in the Series and I don't care!" And that was the final comment on his season.

2

The Phillies blew their pennant, dropping three in a row to L.A. at the Vet; then the Royals, who'd had their own problems reaching the October Classic, swept the Dodgers in four to put a merciful end to this something less than banner year for baseball.

Frank Fuller won the Cy Young Award, as the premier pitcher in the American League; and Bobby Leopold was named Comeback Player of the Year. Artie Stutz took a winter job with the Detroit Pistons; while Howie Needleman jumped ship to Oakland, where he would be instrumental in persuading the new owners to bring the A's back to Philadelphia, to play American League baseball in a brand-new forty-thousand-seat natural-grass gem of a ballpark, with a statue of Phil Raneer out front.

What happened to Fast Phil was a shame. He'd been negotiating a new round of loans to tide him over a tight period when his startup costs were coming due, but instead of routinely extending his credit, his lenders got nervous at all the publicity and backed off, increasing the speculation in the press, which in turn made it more and more difficult for him.

His mortgages were sound, as long as he kept up his payments, but the huge cash loans he had taken out on Ballpark, lacking real property to hold as collateral, contained what the bankers call "insecurity clauses," which entitle a creditor to call in a debt at will, with a formal request for payment in full.

As Raneer ran through his cushion of cash, his day of reckoning drew closer and closer. If any of his backers had rallied to his support, they all would have, but if two or more gave up on him, he was doomed. His fate was in their hands, as it had been all along.

The banks and insurers watched the papers for weeks, communicating by private courier, then late in October called a top-level meeting, to play a little hardball of their own. They assembled on the morning of the 23rd, in the Nationwide Building, the second-tallest in Columbus, where they shut the doors on the crimson-curtained boardroom, and Nationwide's president, Harrison Brooks, Princeton, Wharton, Class of '44, discussed his fears that unless they ended this period of uncertainty, one of them would start grabbing, then they'd all join in, and whoever grabbed last would be left holding the bag.

His counterparts from Chase Manhattan, Citicorp, Mutual of Omaha, and Bank of America shifted uncomfortably at the prospect; then Brooks proposed that they could all agree to support Raneer, funneling their money into what seemed like a bottomless pit, or take their cue from the current press—he held up a copy of the *Wall Street Journal,* headlined:

RUMORS AND FEAR STRIKE BALLPARK INVESTORS

—and turn it to their advantage.

"What if word leaks out that we're really getting nervous? Little by little the pressure would build . . . then all of a sudden the dike might break . . . and Raneer would go under. Only instead of trying to screw each other, we could all act rationally —freeze his assets, and kick his ass out, because the way I see it, the guy is a loser. He fights with his Ballclub, fights with the press, but worst of all, he's too damned extravagant. He did a fair job setting it up, but the fact is, if any of us were running that show, we'd have *twice* as much profit at the end of two years."

"Wait a minute, Harrison," came the interruption he had expected. "I'm not interested in running any baseball teams."

"Neither am I, and with good reason, which brings me to my second point. Suppose we wait a decent amount of time, then walk in with a holding company made up of his creditors, whose primary goal will be to sell to someone else? That way we can write off our losses this year, take a profit on the sale, and still get rid of him, because Raneer will never pay off the way he should. The guy has a death wish. If he'd settle for doing things like any normal person, he'd be fine."

"And if we don't find this buyer?"

"Then we run it ourselves for a while, but what I'm really thinking is that the package might be even more attractive if we let the franchise go under. Maybe bring the Clippers back, or some other minor league club. That way we'd have our amusement park, second to none, with baseball on the side, and we'd save *millions* on salaries. Think about it, gentlemen—now I warn you—the price of baseball is on the rise. If you want to stake Raneer in these bidding wars, fine . . . but the papers are screaming about a 'crisis of confidence' . . . so I say, why not give them one?" He waited. "What do you think?"

"Shaky," said Citicorp.

"Very shaky, Harrison . . ." They smiled.

"No confidence whatsoever."

3

The bottom fell out on November 3, and when Fast Phil screamed conspiracy, everyone laughed and said he was crazy. Like the former President of the United States, who protested his innocence with equal vehemence, he was ultimately judged by his own spiritual downfall. As his empire deteriorated, so did he, until he left the public eye a bitter old man. Later there were rumors that he'd suffered a stroke, but a reporter who managed to speak to Raneer found him vituperative as ever, his hands possibly palsied or just shaking with rage as he vowed to make it back.

Pardee's lawyer posted a bond for damage to the Commissioner's office, then filed a grievance, and had his contract with Ballpark declared null and void. Darryl was fortunate that Raneer had tried to screw him, for he was once again a free agent in an ever-rising market, while his teammates, lacking independent courses of action, were still technically bound to a team that couldn't pay. That would change with a series of lawsuits, but the snafu was incredible, and O'Neill would have had to have been a Solomon, which he wasn't, to figure out what to do with his overpriced orphans of summer.

Lifetimes entered into a mutually binding agreement to cease all litigation against Raneer; then Pauline got nominated for a National Press Club Award for her feature on Pardee, but was fortunate enough to get passed over for the honor, and spared the discomfort of an acceptance speech.

She met once more with Baby Bob, to chew him out for not answering her phone calls, but as they were discussing her return to the booth, they were interviewing hundreds of equally attractive, even younger women down at NBC, until a light-skinned twenty-three-year-old of white, black, Asian, and American Indian ancestry walked in, smiled right, and got it. "That's it, J.B., she's perfect!" they said; then they signed her up at a hundred and fifty grand, to drag around to every sales conference, trash meet, and promo they had planned.

Pardee, meanwhile, was picking up his first bit of real estate, a compact bungalow on the Florida Keys. Pauline stayed in touch via his unlisted phone, until the second week in November, when she relayed an invitation to meet up in Cleveland, to share Thanksgiving with the Harts.

Fritz was sitting pretty these days, fending off a whole slew of offers, while waiting to hear from the Yanks. His wife, Laura Hart, was built just like him, and as she ordered people around, arranging the seating, it was clear that her husband had met his match. She'd invited Lacy Stokey and some families from the neighborhood (never having had any children of her own), to whom she served up mountains of candied yams, roast turkey, and stuffing with chestnuts. Darryl did her proud and ate himself silly, then he kicked off his shoes and traded stories with Stokey, while the Kraut looked on, beaming like a patriarch.

Chapter 3

Islamorada, Florida, December 24. Pardee's eyes were gray-green, filled with clouds. They watched, detached, as seagulls outside circled, laughed, and fell into the mist. Turning from the window into the darkness of his room, he was blinded, out again, under the lights—lost in the roar of sixty thousand fans —then silent, alone, listening to the waves . . . until a voice floated in, saying:

"Darryl? Hello?" She stuck in her head, and Pardee jumped.

"Don't do that!" he said. "You scared me to death."

"Didn't you hear my car?"

"I'm so used to bein' alone down here that—"

"Well, you'd better get unused to it, buster." She kissed him. "Guess what?"

"I give up."

"The owners met this morning and overruled O'Neill. They said you were justified."

"Too late."

"And that's not all. Right after they overruled him, they fired him."

"Oh, yeah?"

"There's reason to believe that he was paid off by Raneer

. . . and that that's why Phil could sign all those free agents, which might explain why O'Neill was so rough on you.''

"It might.''

"At any rate, he's history . . . and they're hoping to impose a little order on the game.''

"Too late again. It'll never go back.''

"Well, that's the news . . . are you ready for the sports?'' She jumped on his back and rode him to the sofa. "I've only got a week down here, so let's get started.''

They made love, took a nap, cooked a meal, and made love again. They took a long walk along the beach that night, sipped brandy and made love by the fire, then when Pauline had softened him up, after two or three days at this killing pace—and for the first time ever, they didn't have to split apart—there was nothing left for Pardee to do but lean back, stroke her hair, close his eyes, and talk.

Eventually the whole story emerged, and Pauline discovered that like most good riddles, he was tough to figure out, but fairly obvious once she knew the answer. Darryl's past was sad, in many respects tragic, but she helped him accept what he'd always tried to tell himself—that it was, indeed, at last behind him. He dredged up a considerable amount of emotion going through it, which she did her best to absorb, so it wouldn't get lost or come back at him; and at the end of eight days they were as close as they had ever been.

January 1. Her vacation was over. Her bags were packed and waiting in the car. She went shopping in the morning, then unloaded his groceries and was sweeping up when Pardee pulled in to dock the boat that was the only reason he had bought this house in the first place.

Darryl looked like he belonged out there, framed against the sky, instead of in some doubleknit uniform in some man-made cavern of a ballpark. He had taken to fishing every day, braving bad weather and staying out longer than anyone should unless blessed with his instincts. Pardee could take the perils of nature. They didn't get on his nerves the way people did.

Pauline watched while he tied his lines, then walked over and took his arm, saying, "Before I go . . . I've been meaning to ask you . . ." He was looking past her, as if he were still out at sea, as if she were too close to focus on. "I'm down here," she said. "Would you like to have a child?"

"Well, uh . . ."

"Take your time. My plane leaves in two hours, and it's a ninety-minute drive. Where the hell were you?"

"Are you serious?"

"Yes."

"Then I wish you'd stop bein' so goddamn smart."

"I am not being smart. I'm thirty years old. I have to know how you feel."

"You know how I feel."

"Not about this." She waited. "What's the matter? Afraid you'll miss the hunt?"

"The *hunt?*" He laughed.

"What about your friend?" said Pauline. "In Chicago."

"What about her? You wanna get married now, too?"

"I really don't know. I go back and forth. I don't even know what it would mean in our case . . . you can't stand the city, and I have to work there, but . . ." She shook her head. "I need an answer."

"Oh, you do, huh? Tell me somethin' . . . you're not . . ."

"What? *Pregnant?*" She made a face. "I doubt it."

"Good." He grinned, then picked her up, and shouldered through the screen door into his room.

"But my plane!" she protested.

"You'll have to catch the next one." He dropped her softly onto the bed, and jumped in next to her, rattling the springs. "I love you, babe . . ." His eyes were laughing; then suddenly they filled, and they both began to cry.

Later, he lit a cigarette, took a puff, and put it out, trying not to think about where he was headed. Not that he cared what city he played for, Big League towns were all pretty much the same, but there was still the matter of that World Series Ring, and he knew, like Pauline, that he wasn't getting younger.

He got up, put on his pants, picked up his glove, and started to saddle-soap it, waxing the laces, slapping the clean fragrant leather. He did the same thing every year about now, but something had changed. Pardee would never be just another ball-player, but for the first time he was looking forward to a season, and that's all it was—just another season. He had finally broken in.